PRAISE FOR ROBERT RODI

For *What They Did to Princess Paragon*

"Hilarious . . . the quips fly in all directions . . . memorably raucous moments . . . fiercely humanistic and wildly funny."
—*Lambda Book Report*

"A rowdy and witty comedy . . . with crisp, naughty dialogue and colorful supporting characters." —*Library Journal*

"Rodi's best so far . . . fast-paced and ingenious." —*Genre*

For *Closet Case*

"A joyride of a book . . . infectious . . . hard to put down."
—*Boston Phoenix*

"Uproarious . . . in the grand tradition of British bedroom farce . . . a winner on all levels. Along with Paul Rudnick, Robert Rodi will doubtless become one of the premier gay humorists." —*Bay Windows*

"Irresistibly funny." —Quentin Crisp

For *Fag Hag*

"Absorbing and powerful . . . a one-two punch of outrageous humor and sobering pathos . . . Succeeds admirably as satire and as flat-out entertainment." —*New York Native*

"Scathing satire . . . a side-splitting commentary on the bond between gay men and straight women." —*Genre*

ROBERT RODI is the author of *Fag Hag*, a comic novel about obsession; *Closet Case*, a comic novel about paranoia; *What They Did to Princess Paragon*, a comic novel about fanaticism; and *Kept Boy*, which has a healthy dose of all three disorders. He lives in Chicago with his partner, Jeffrey Smith.

ALSO BY ROBERT RODI

Fag Hag
Closet Case
What They Did to Princess Paragon

Drag Queen

robert rodi

Ⓟ A PLUME BOOK

PLUME
Published by the Penguin Group
Penguin Books USA Inc., 375 Hudson Street, New York, New York 10014, U.S.A.
Penguin Books Ltd, 27 Wrights Lane, London W8 5TZ, England
Penguin Books Australia Ltd, Ringwood, Victoria, Australia
Penguin Books Canada Ltd, 10 Alcorn Avenue, Toronto, Ontario, Canada M4V 3B2
Penguin Books (N.Z.) Ltd, 182–190 Wairau Road, Auckland 10, New Zealand

Penguin Books Ltd, Registered Offices: Harmondsworth, Middlesex, England

Published by Plume, an imprint of Dutton Signet,
a division of Penguin Books USA Inc.
Previously published in a Dutton edition.

First Plume Printing, November, 1996
10 9 8 7 6 5 4 3 2

"Put on a Happy Face," by Lee Adams and Charles Strouse © 1960
(renewed 1988) Lee Adams and Charles Strouse. All rights reserved.
Used by permission of Warner Bros. Publications, Inc., Miami, FL 33014.

 REGISTERED TRADEMARK—MARCA REGISTRADA

The Library of Congress has catalogued the Dutton edition as follows:
Rodi, Robert.
Drag queen / Robert Rodi.
p.   cm.
ISBN 0-525-93925-3 (hc.)
ISBN 0-452-27344-7 (pbk.)
1. Gay men—Fiction.   I. Title.
PS3568/O34854D7   1995
813'.54—dc20   95–21785
CIP

Printed in the United States of America
Designed by Steven N. Stathakis

PUBLISHER'S NOTE
This is a work of fiction. Names, characters, places, and incidents either are the
product of the author's imagination or are used fictitiously, and any resemblance
to actual persons, living or dead, events, or locales is entirely coincidental.

BOOKS ARE AVAILABLE AT QUANTITY DISCOUNTS WHEN USED TO PROMOTE PRODUCTS
OR SERVICES. FOR INFORMATION PLEASE WRITE TO PREMIUM MARKETING DIVISION,
PENGUIN BOOKS USA INC., 375 HUDSON STREET, NEW YORK, NEW YORK 10014.

For le divine *Jeffrey;*

with thanks to Christopher Schelling,
Robert Drake, Peter Borland, Christian McLaughlin,
Jim Hoffman, and Mary Herczog. You go, girls!

Drag
Queen

chapter

1

A place for everything, thought Mitchell Sayer as he set his briefcase on the credenza and slipped off his suit coat. A place for everything, and everything in its—

Wait a minute.

Where was his letter opener?

It was supposed to be right there, on the credenza, next to the Wedgwood clock. Here he was, the day's mail in hand, and no letter opener. Who the hell had moved the damn letter opener?

Well, it was no good letting his anger take that route. He lived alone. There was no one else to blame.

He placed the mail on the credenza and folded his suit coat over his briefcase. Then he dropped into a crouch and scanned the floor for the letter opener, which must have fallen somewhere close by. Shouldn't be hard to spot. It was lapis lazuli, inlaid with gold. A gift from his grandfather on his graduation from law school.

He got a noseful of something floral and sweet. Turning

his head, he saw that the foolish postman had delivered to him his neighbor's copy of *Glamour*. The magazine was sticking out of his pile of mail, seeping the various scents of its scratch-and-sniff enclosures. He pushed it aside in disdain, then continued his search.

His knee accidentally grazed the floor, and he examined it at once for dirt. Of course there wasn't any; he had his cleaning lady damp mop this slate foyer once a month. Twice in winter.

No sign of the letter opener here. He arched his back and let his eyes scour the adjoining rooms in his pristine Wrigleyville townhouse. Nothing. Not a trace.

He took another look at his pile of mail. Felt a barely controllable urge to curl up on the couch and flip through *Glamour*.

But no, no time for such silliness. He had things to do. A letter opener to find. And now, on his knees, he noticed that his antique Chinese rug—a threadbare treasure he'd purchased at the estate sale of a board-games magnate felled by AIDS—had been placed on the sitting room floor crookedly; it veered at a very slight angle from the teak floor panels.

Well, he'd soon put that right. He got to his feet and trotted into the sitting room, where he flipped his Hermès tie over his shoulder and began tugging at the marble coffee table that sat like a stone upon the skewed rug.

The table was astonishingly heavy, especially for someone of Mitchell's slender, boyish build. At first he thought he might not be able to move it at all; then he grew angry, snorted, and gave it a tremendous yank, nearly barking as he did so. It gave some ground; three, four inches at most.

"For heaven's sake, at least loosen your tie," said someone from behind him.

He recognized the voice and gave up the effort. Massaging the small of his back, he turned to greet his mother.

"Well," he said, his face still flushed and his voice slightly breathy. "Pleasant surprise."

Bettina Varney, trim as ever (if not downright gaunt), was meticulously attired in a simple black Escada suit, her blond hair lacquered over her head in the manner of a papal skullcap.

She smiled as she stepped into the house. "Sorry not to ring, but the door was hanging open," she said, and she turned her head to allow Mitchell to kiss her cheek. "Glad you're replacing that dreadful thing. Always hated it. How are things at the firm?"

"Fine," he said, flipping his tie back onto his chest and smoothing it there. He gave the table a kick. "I'm not replacing it, I'm moving it so I can realign the rug. Why do you hate it?"

"Nothing wrong with the rug's alignment," she said, studying it with one eyebrow arched. She plopped her purse onto the dislodged coffee table. "No juicy new cases with which to regale me?"

"In real estate law? Hardly." He pointed to the floorboards. "Look, it's not in line with the teak. Sit down. Why do you hate the coffee table?"

Bettina gracefully lowered herself onto his orchid-pattern sofa. "It's not in line with the floorboards, but it *is* in line with the walls. You can't expect mathematical uniformity when you buy vintage, Mitchell. Something's going to be askew. And the coffee table's vulgar. Sit down, I need to talk to you."

He hovered over a chair, looking at the floorboards. "I'd rather have it in line with the teak. Get you a drink?"

"No, thank you, dear, not this early."

He plopped into the chair facing her. "This is a perfectly attractive coffee table," he said, patting it.

"It's hideous and Scandinavian. Listen," she said, leaning forward and clasping her hands. "I have something to say to you. I've come to a decision about my life and I must let you know of it."

Mitchell froze. "Don't you have a therapist for that?"

"I have two. *Had.*" She gave her head a little shake as she corrected herself. "That's part of the change."

Mitchell looked at his fingernails. "Um—"

"Mitchell, look at me."

"Mother, I—"

"I said, *look at me.*"

He raised his head and tried to meet her eyes with a weary,

I'm-patronizing-you air, but his face was ashen, spoiling the effect. "All right," he said, "I am now officially looking at you."

She grinned. "Thank you. I know you hate this type of thing, so I'll try to be brief. But I want you to listen carefully to *everything* I have to say before you interrupt. And I mean that. Because I have certain things to tell you that will affect you materially, but I mustn't be sidetracked by your objections or questions or we'll be here all night, and I have an engagement for later."

"When don't you?"

"Quiet." She cleared her throat. "All right. I've mourned your stepfather for six months, and I've decided that's more than sufficient. So as of tomorrow, I'm out of mourning. And into something quite different. You see, I've come to the conclusion that three husbands is enough for any lifetime, and that I should do something different with what time I have left. I'm sixty years old and I don't want to turn into one of those ridiculous women who keep chasing millionaires into their dotage, racking up facelift after facelift until they look like astronauts under tons of g-force. So I've decided to sell the apartment and all my possessions and move to Wisconsin, where I'll be joining a Tibetan convent as a *chela*, or student. If I like it, I may even become a Buddhist nun."

This was really too much for Mitchell to endure; he broke in with, "Now, just a min—"

"Mitchell, I asked you one favor, didn't I? Was it really such a great one?"

He sat back in the chair, his lips pursed.

"Now. I've noticed a lack of spiritual grounding in my life, and this seems to be the time to attain some. And since your grandmother's devout Christianity did nothing but turn her into a bitter, judgmental, hate-soaked old termagant, I've decided to look elsewhere. So I'm going to go into retirement to study the teachings of the Dalai Lama. With any luck, I'll achieve peace and bliss and harmony with the universe, just like Richard Gere. You may now offer an opinion."

Taken by surprise, he found that scorn and derision had

stopped up his throat. "I can't," he said, after a few glottal sputterings. "You appear to have left me speechless."

She sat back and crossed one of her legs over the other. "Very well, then. On to part two."

"Part—two?" he stammered.

"Yes. You see, in order to begin my new life in accord with *dharma*—which you'd understand, I suppose, as having a clear conscience, though it's more than that—I have to confess to something I've kept from you your entire life." She balled her fists and took a deep breath. "Mitchell, I am not your natural mother."

The room reeled. The antique Chinese rug and the hideous marble coffee table spun up to the ceiling above Mitchell's head, then dipped back into place.

"Your father and I weren't able to conceive. Or I should say *he* wasn't—after he died and I married Chester, I had no trouble at all producing your two sisters. But back then I thought I'd be with your father forever, so in order to have any children I had to adopt."

"I'm adopted," Mitchell said in a shockingly calm voice that he only barely recognized as his own.

"Yes, I'm afraid you are."

"May I speak now?"

"Not yet. There's one last bit of business. The hardest yet."

He clapped a hand over his forehead and shut his eyes. "Oh, God. What? I'm really from Krypton?"

"Dear, I honestly think you should loosen your necktie before I go on. You're allowed. Extenuating circumstances. I promise to tell no one."

Angrily, he yanked at the tie until it came undone, then sat glaring at her.

"Well," she said, observing him, "maybe you could unbutton your top button, too."

His fingers very nearly didn't work, but he forced them to do his bidding. He didn't want her—this *stranger*—coming over and helping him.

"Now, then," she said when he'd finally liberated his Adam's apple. "Mitchell, this is going to require some forgiveness on your part."

"Some *more* forgiveness," he corrected her.

A stricken look crossed her face for a second, then was gone. She reached over, plucked her purse from off the coffee table, and began to fondle its clasp. It was an uncharacteristically insecure gesture from a woman not known for her lack of confidence. Mitchell began to feel real dread.

"The thing is, Mitchell, you have an identical twin." Her voice actually cracked on the crucial word. "Your father and I—well—I don't know what to say to make you understand. We didn't have much money. Not in those days. We couldn't afford two children. We didn't *want* two children. But the adoption agency didn't have any other suitable infants at that particular time, just you and your brother—"

"My brother." The rug and the coffee table were once more whirling around the room, like figurines on a nursery mobile. Mitchell gripped the arms of his chair lest he be swept into orbit with them.

"—so we took only you. I presume your brother was adopted by someone else not long after. You were just the kind of orphans people wanted back then: newborn, male, whi—"

" 'Orphans'? I'm an *orphan*?"

"Yes, I'm sorry, didn't I mention? Apparently both your natural parents died in a freak badminton accident."

"A freak *what*?"

"Don't ask for details, I only know what I was told." She opened her purse and took out a slip of paper. "I understand that you may want to attempt to locate your brother, so I've written out the adoption agency's name and address for you. If you're serious about this, my advice is, hire a detective and let him track your brother for you."

He shook his head. "My *brother*." It still sounded unreal.

Bettina stood, a little unsteadily, then tucked her purse under her arm, strode over to him, and kissed him on the forehead. "I'm sorry for never telling you, but you were such an emotional boy, always given to theatrical displays of—well, never mind, you grew out of that. But I always feared you were on the verge of running away."

"That was just because I was afraid of how you'd react to my sexu—"

"Oh, yes, yes," she interrupted with a grimace, "it always comes back to that, I know. And I'm such an ogress."

"That's not quite fair."

"I know. Forgive me." She turned and headed for the door but stopped after only a few feet and retrieved the letter opener from the floor. "Bet you've been looking for this," she said.

"Actually, yes."

"And I saw it right away, didn't I? As soon as I made my confession!" She beamed at him. "*Dharma*, Mitchell. No other explanation."

She placed it on the credenza; then appeared to catch her eye on something.

She slipped the copy of *Glamour* from the pile of mail and held it aloft. "I didn't know you subscribed, dear. May I have it once you're through?"

"It's *not mine*," he snarled. "I *don't read* women's magazines!"

She raised an eyebrow at this sudden vehemence; then dropped the magazine with a shrug. "Oh, well," she said. "I probably shouldn't either, anymore." A brilliant smile. "Ta, darling!" And she sailed through the door.

Mitchell sat for almost ten minutes more, waiting for the furniture to swoop back into place.

First things first, he decided. He had to sort this mess into a kind of crisis hierarchy. Decide which disaster should take top priority.

He accordingly dismissed his mother's new fixation on Buddhism. It was doubtless no different than her previous flings with veganism, Esperanto, and aromatherapy. She was one of those women with enough money and free time to spend developing these smart little obsessions. They never lasted more than a season or so. The aspect of this one that most upset him was her intention to sell her apartment and possessions, but he'd put in a call to her attorney, Max Chafner, tomorrow; Max was an old family friend, and would talk some sense into her.

But this other business! Mitchell couldn't handle that as easily.

A *brother.*

A *twin* brother.

All this time—all these years—he'd felt so alone, and now he'd discovered there was no need. All during his youth, with a cold, remote father (not even his own, he now knew!) and an ambitious, exhausting mother (not his own, either!), and he'd never guessed that he had a connection with someone else on this earth far stronger than his tie to his parents. Stronger even than his ties to his sisters (not really his sisters!), whom he loved but who were so unreachably young.

And of course, there was the matter of his being gay.

If he'd been lonely in the family before his adolescence, that loneliness had doubled and redoubled as he passed through puberty and found himself feeling inexplicable things —things he knew better than to mention to his parents. Romantic crushes on school chums. A strong desire to be near, to touch, to smell his Uncle David. (Even now it was a kind of thrill to realize the man wasn't *really* his Uncle David.) A vacuum of loneliness pierced only by suspicions (*Why aren't you dating, Mitchell? Is there something you're not telling us, Mitchell?*) before he found the courage to "come out," as the vulgar parlance would have it, and disclose to his parents what they, in turn, disclosed they already knew. Not understood, not countenanced—but knew. "Just don't get in the papers," they'd said.

And now Mitchell had learned that all along there had been someone else—someone exactly like him. Hadn't he seen a segment of some so-called news magazine show in which it was reported that identical twins—even long-separated identical twins—almost always possessed identical character traits?

The light in the room was fading. How long had he been sitting here? And the twilight now was making him feel—well, less rational. He was forced to admit to himself that there was an incestuous element to this speculation. (Relieved of guilt over Uncle David, now he risked suffering it over someone infinitely nearer.) It was a mortifying admission, but he knew better than to hide it and let it fester. Funny, his gay friends who had brothers turned up their noses in disgust at the very idea of any interfraternal kinkiness, but gay men like Mitchell, who had no brothers, found it a powerful fantasy.

But this was appalling, really appalling. Admitting the fantasy was one thing; savoring it was another.

Still, he couldn't help idealizing this newly discovered brother. Mitchell imagined him as a stronger, better version of himself. Less cowardly. More comfortable in the world. Bolder. More successful.

Well, there was only one way to find out, wasn't there?

He pulled the cord of the floorlamp to his left. White light flooded him like a bucket of cold water. Jolted into action, he opened the drawer of the end table next to the chair and, with a grunt, hauled out the Yellow Pages, which he kept there with the White Pages and his own personal telephone directory. A place for everything, and everything in its place.

And it was time to find a place for this new brother, this twin.

He flipped through the unwieldy ocher volume until he came to the heading DETECTIVES—PRIVATE.

chapter 2

Mitchell stopped by his secretary's desk and said, "Morning, Bereneesha. Anything on the front burner?"

Bereneesha, who had just painted her nails a color Mitchell thought could only be called Oxidized Green, flailed about in panic for a moment, then managed to open her appointment book with just her elbows. "Nothin' till ten," she said, waggling her fingers by her ears.

"Good. I've asked a representative of the Deene Detective Agency to come in first thing." He checked his wristwatch. "Should be here any second. Show him in, will you?"

"Okay," she said as he strode toward his office, "if you an' Mr. Trilby are finished by then."

He stopped, then turned to face her. "Finished with what? Where is he?"

She arched her eyebrows and nodded her head toward his office door.

He sighed. He had a hunch about what the firm's senior partner wanted to discuss with him. Yesterday he'd bungled a routine condominium closing for the daughter of one of the firm's biggest industrial clients. The title search uncovered a lien against the seller's building dating from 1976, and the spoiled rich-kid daughter had had to sit fuming for three hours while Mitchell and the title company worked out some kind of agreement with the sellers to absolve her of any future inconvenience caused by the lien. Afterward she'd stormed out vowing to have Mitchell fired.

Mitchell gulped, then swung open the door to his office. Cyrus Trilby, trim, curly-haired, freckle-faced, and absolutely fearsome in spite of it all, turned to greet him. He'd been fingering Mitchell's collection of Russian nesting dolls, which Mitchell had purchased for mere pennies during a college-sponsored jaunt to Moscow.

"Interesting pieces," Trilby said, sealing the little babushkaed grannies back into place, one by one. "Any mystical significance to them? Some kind of womb analogy or something?"

Mitchell put his briefcase on his desk and shrugged. "Not that I know of."

"Be interesting to find out." He shoved the single remaining doll back on the wrong shelf and turned to Mitchell. "Anyway, good morning."

Mitchell made a mental note to put the doll back in its proper place after Trilby left. "Morning," he said with attempted brightness. He hesitated at his chair, then decided not to sit while Trilby was standing. Anxious and upset, he blurted, "Listen, I'm sorry about the whole Diana Wheeler mess. My fault entirely. I didn't discover that lien, I didn't go back far enou—"

"Oh, bosh," said Trilby with a wave of his hand. "Anyone could've made that mistake. People *have* made that mistake. Been dozens of closings in that building over the last ten years, some using this firm, and not one of them disrupted by that lien. No, your misfortune was that Frank Wheeler chose an unusually scrupulous title company for the job."

"Well, hardly a misfortune," said Mitchell, dizzy with relief at Trilby's offhanded manner. "In the long run, I mean. If the lien hadn't turned up now, it might have later—to Diana Wheeler's detriment. And our—*my* job was to protect her against that.''

Trilby crossed his arms and sighed. ''Mitchell, you've got to learn to lighten up.''

He felt stung for a moment. ''But, Cyrus—it was *my fault*. And she—Diana Wheeler, I mean—she said she was going to raise a stink with her father. Have me fired.''

Trilby chuckled. ''Diana Wheeler has tried to have *me* fired on two separate occasions, so I think there's little to worry you there. Frank Wheeler is a friend, and just between us—'' Here he pulled his right hand from his pocket and put his forefinger to his lips. ''—he knows she can be a real shrew.''

Mitchell looked at his shoes. He couldn't possibly comment on this; it'd be unseemly.

''Good thing I stopped in,'' Trilby continued. ''I have just the thing to brighten your day.''

Mitchell's heart sank. He knew what was coming.

Trilby reached into his breast pocket and removed a cassette tape, which he gently waved in Mitchell's face. ''A bootleg of Blossom's gig at Mister Kelly's in sixty-six. Don't ask how I got it. And for God's sake don't ask what I *paid*.'' He looked around Mitchell's office. ''Where's your tape player? We'll give it a listen. It's about twelfth-generation, but the genius comes through.''

Mitchell felt a shiver of dread. He actually would have preferred to be yelled at. This was the sole drawback to being so completely accepted as a gay man by the firm's partners and associates. None of them had blinked an eye when he'd revealed his homosexuality. As a group, they hadn't altered their behavior toward him in any respect at all. Except for this. Cyrus Trilby was the proud possessor of the country's (and maybe the world's) largest collection of Blossom Dearie memorabilia, and when he learned Mitchell was gay, he instantly assumed that Mitchell must be profoundly interested in it. After all, weren't all gay men in thrall to aging cabaret divas? So, while Mitchell's musical tastes tended toward nothing more contemporary than

Bach (he even found Beethoven haphazard and fulsome), he pretended to take keen interest in Trilby's endless stream of display cards and eight-by-ten glossies and sheet music and reel-to-reel master tapes and concert programs and even actual microphones used by the immortal Miss Dearie.

"I think Bereneesha may have misplaced it," Mitchell said, a plan formulating in his head. "Just hold on a second." He pressed his intercom button. "Bereneesha, what've you done with my tape player?"

"It's in your closet, last I looked," she said, and even over the tinny transceiver he could tell she was put out by the accusation. "An' listen, that detective is here now."

He felt a little leap of joy. He'd bet himself that if he accused Bereneesha over the intercom, she'd try to get back at him by reminding him of his appointment—to put him in a tight spot with Trilby, not knowing that such a tight spot was exactly what he wanted.

"Thank you, Bereneesha," he said. "Send him in, please."

"You have someone waiting?" Trilby asked, still clutching the cassette.

Mitchell shrugged. "Alas, yes. Can I take a rain check?"

Trilby winked. "Plenty of time. I'll check in with you later." As Mitchell showed him to the door, he said, "A detective, eh? What's this about?"

"Personal emergency," he confessed. "No costs to the firm."

"Say no more," said the senior partner, and as he exited, a large, sandy-haired, middle-aged woman in a kelly green jumpsuit squeezed past him and into Mitchell's office.

Mitchell regarded her in some confusion, then looked out to see if anyone else was within view. There was only Cyrus Trilby, retreating, and Bereneesha at her desk, trying to answer the phone with her elbow and chin.

"Mr. Sayer? I'm Cora Deene," said the woman. She shifted her enormous purse onto her shoulder and extended her hand.

Mitchell extended his own and they shook. "As in Deene

Detective Agency?" he said, his disappointment perhaps too naked on his face. "You're—you're—"

"It's a one-woman agency," she said with a little laugh.
"And I'm the one woman!"

He shook his head. "I didn't realize that."

"Well, now you know." She eyed the chair before his desk.
"Do you mind if I . . . ?"

"Oh—no. Sorry." He trotted around to his own chair and
sat. "Forgot my manners." He rolled up as far as the chair
would go, and stared at Cora Deene.

"All right, now," she said, taking a pad of paper and a pen
from her voluminous purse. "The message you left said you
want to track down your long-lost twin brother, from whom you
were separated at only a few weeks of age. You were, and correct
me if I'm wrong, placed with your adoptive parents by a certain
DeMarillac Agency. Do you happen to know if you were living
at an orphanage at that time?"

"No, I don't," he said. Then he shook his head and said,
"Listen, I'm sorry, but—don't take this personally or anything,
but—are you—I don't know what the proper word is. Accred-
ited? Certified?"

She put the pad down with a breathy little sigh. "The word
is licensed. And yes, I am."

"I—uh—" He began nervously pushing back his cuticles.
How could he tell her that he was expecting someone who
looked more like Peter Falk?

She once again clipped open her watermelon-size purse. "I
have my license in here somewhere, if you'd like to check it
out."

"No, no," he insisted, waving his hands at her. "I believe
you. It's just—the nature of the work I need you to do—I have
to wonder if—"

"Look," she said, crossing her arms, and as she did so
Mitchell noticed that her wristwatch bore a smiley face. "Just
because I'm a thirty-eight-year-old housewife who drives a Jeep
Cherokee doesn't mean I can't find your brother, Mr. Sayer.
It's not like you're asking me to track down and apprehend a

serial killer or something. The truth is, yes, I did get my license after taking a mail-order course while I was pregnant with my Joey. But it's still a legitimate license. And all anyone needs to be a private investigator these days is a computer and a modem, and my Timmy is a hacker, so I almost never even have to leave the house. Two years ago I got the goods on a gang of drivers'-license forgers in Arlington Heights and I never missed cooking dinner during the entire case. Even the tough stuff, like Cornish hens and strudel. I have the newspaper clipping on that in my purse, too, if you think I'm lying. Now, will you please decide if you'd like my services or not? Because I left my Tina out in the Jeep expecting to be dropped at her scuba camp in twenty minutes, and God help me if I make her late."

And she glared at Mitchell with such a potent brew of indignation and pride that he thought, *What the hell.* And to his surprise, he heard himself saying those very words.

"Well," replied Cora Deene, picking up the pad and pen again, "I hope your enthusiasm will be a little more convincing after I've found your brother. Now, to continue." She poised her pen over the paper and looked up at him. "Oh, by the way, I charge a hundred dollars a day, plus expenses."

Mitchell didn't know if that was cheap or expensive, but since she brought it up without his asking, he didn't think it could be so unreasonable. "Fine," he said. And he settled back in his chair and answered her questions.

chapter 3

The weekend passed uneventfully. On Monday night, when Mitchell got home from the office, the message light on his answering machine was blinking. He rewound and played the tape, which said, "Mr. Sayer, this is Cora Deene of the Deene Detective Agency. I've found your brother. Actually, my Timmy found him, when he was playing with his laptop while waiting for his oboe lesson. Your brother is living on the north side of Chicago under the name Donald Sweet. *Joey, put that litter box down! Put it down this instant!*—Sorry. Where was I? Oh, yes. His name is Donald Sweet. He lists his occupation as 'hand model,' and his phone number is 555-0482. Call me if you have any questions. Otherwise, I'll be sending you a bill for a hundred and seven dollars. You have a good night, now!"

Mitchell rewound the tape and listened to it again. Then he rewound it once more and stared at the phone connected to it for several minutes. The clock on the machine read 6:47.

"This is silly," he said, rebuking himself. "Just call him."

He nodded in affirmation of this sage advice, then went into the kitchen and ate a pear. As he sliced perfectly identical sections from it and chewed them, one by one, into a fine pulp, he stared at the phone on the opposite wall.

"There's nothing to be afraid of," he told himself. He deposited the core of the pear into the wastebasket, the knife and plate into the dishwasher, and folded his arms. "Just pick up the phone and call." His wristwatch read 7:02.

At 8:00 he fixed linguine al pesto for dinner, with steamed broccoflower, and he ate it all with a glass of Brunello. And as he ate, he counted up all the good reasons for forging right ahead and making that call without delay.

At 8:30 he spent a few minutes practicing picking up the receiver and putting it back again. Proud of himself, he sat down and read the new issue of *Harper's*.

At twenty to ten, having exhausted all other avenues of procrastination, he made the call. His heart was banging around his chest like a rat caught in a coffee tin. On the third ring, he remembered that he hadn't yet brushed his teeth, and was about to hang up and do that when a man at the other end of the line picked up and said, "Hello?"

"Oh! Uh—is this Donald Sweet?"

A short pause. "Who exactly wants to know?"

Startled by this response, Mitchell blurted out, "His twin brother. Mitchell Sayer. He doesn't know me. I mean—"

"This is Donald Sweet."

A longer pause.

"Oh," said Mitchell, unsure of what to say next. "It is?"

"In the legal sense," said Donald. "In every other, there's room for debate. So you're my twin brother?"

Donald sounded amazingly unruffled. Mitchell, however, found himself sweating heavily. "Yes, I am," he said, loosening the sash on his burgundy silk bathrobe and opening the collar a little. "My name is Mitchell Sayer."

"So you said. Well, how do you do, Mitchell?"

"You—you don't seem surprised."

"By what?"

Mitchell held the receiver away from his head and looked at it for a moment, then put it back to his ear and said, "By *me*, of course."

Another pause. "Well, I suppose I'm waiting to hear what you want."

Mitchell rubbed his forehead. "I want to get to know you! What else?"

"Why all of a sudden?"

Mitchell found Donald's behavior inexplicable, until he realized something he should have considered before. "Because I just found out about you," he said. "Do you mean to say you've always known about me?"

"Oh, I knew I had a twin, honey. 'Course I did. You really *just* found out?"

"Two days ago. My mother—my *adoptive* mother—told me."

"Touch late in the day, wasn't it? Deathbed confession or something?" Then, a beat later, "Oh, I'm sorry, that wasn't funny."

"It's okay, she's not dying," Mitchell said with a little laugh. "She just—well, you have to know her—"

"Plays her cards close to her brassiere, does she?"

Odd turn of phrase; Mitchell ignored it. He also decided that this was quite enough about his mother. "Listen," he said, "if you knew about me all these years, why didn't *you*—I mean, it wouldn't have been so hard to find me. I found *you* in one day, and—"

"Oh, hell," Donald said with a sigh. "So that's what you want. To inflict a little guilt. Should've known. That's what families are for."

"No, no, that's not what I—"

"It's okay, doll; as it happens, there's a decided *lack* of guilt in my life these days. I could actually use some. Help me in my work. But anyway, to answer your question, yes, I've known about you since I was, oh, thirteen or so. My parents told me. But I was a shy kid, gawky and not very, you know, grace-ful—"

"Same here!" Mitchell exclaimed, sitting up and placing a hand on his chest. "Me, too!"

"Well, then, you can imagine. Last thing I wanted was some twin brother showing up. What if you turned out to be this macho version of me who was good at baseball and football and all those other balls? And who liked the Rolling Stones and Bruce Springsteen and, you know, all that crap? And who knew all about car engines? I was terrified of you. Thought you'd make me feel completely inadequate. Even now, I picture you as some megajock type with a house in Lake Forest and a wife and nine kids and a thriving dental practice."

"Wrong on all counts," said Mitchell happily. "Listen, I think we may have more in common than you think."

"Oh, I'd be *very* surprised by that," said Donald with the kind of laugh that implied he'd just made a private joke.

Mitchell flushed scarlet but soldiered on. "Well, maybe you *will* be surprised. Can't we meet? I've never had a brother."

"Lucky you! I've got three."

"No kidding!" He leaned back into the cushion and whistled. "All adopted?"

"Every last one. All older, of course. After me, Mom and Pops lost their mania for adopting. Wonder why?" Another private cackle.

Mitchell was feeling unaccountably jealous. "So, do you see them often? Your brothers, I mean."

"Little as possible. Tommy lives up in Michigan, Ernie followed his wife out west, and Ronny—well, Ronny and I don't see eye-to-eye, now, do we?"

"But you and Mitchy might! After all, we're identical twins. I saw a television show that said—"

"Listen, love, I hate to interrupt, but I'm on my way to work right now. Running late as it is. Not that I'm ever on time, but—well, anyway, yes, I'd love to meet you. Be a kick."

"Great! When can we do it?"

"When would you like?"

"Soon as possible! Tomorrow, if it's okay. But we should

go by your schedule, since I'm nine to five. I had no idea hand models worked such odd hours."

"How'd you know I'm a hand model? What are you, a private dick or something?" He accentuated the word "dick."

Mitchell snorted a laugh. "No, but I hired one to find you, and got a little information on the side. I'm an attorney, myself." He lazily scratched his chest in self-satisfaction.

"Well, fiddle-dee-dee! A shark in the family! Anyway, for the record, honey, hand models don't usually work odd hours. I'm on my way to my *second* job. I'm a nightclub singer."

Mitchell raised his eyebrows. "No kidding!"

"Yep. Every night, tennish, up at the Tam-Tam Club. Heard of it?"

Mitchell was loath to appear unsophisticated. "Oh, sure," he lied. "Sure. Never been, though. Otherwise, who knows? I might've caught your act."

"Well, why not catch it tonight? Where are you calling from?"

"North side. Wrigleyville." He started to panic.

"Hell, you're practically there! A five-minute cab ride. Come on over!"

"No—uh—listen. I can't tonight. How about tomorrow?"

"Fine. Like I said, I'm on every night 'round ten."

"Okay, then. It's a date."

"Glorious!"

"Just one thing, Donald."

"What's that?"

He snickered. "How will I know you?"

Complete silence.

"That's a joke," he explained. "You know, because we're identical twins?"

"Oh," said Donald mirthlessly. "I get it." He attempted a polite chuckle. Then, "Mitchell, listen; we may be identical . . ." He seemed to trail off.

Mitchell waited a few beats. "Yes?"

"Nothing. See you tomorrow night. I'm glad you found me."

"Makes two of us."

Mitchell hung up. He was no longer sweating, but his robe felt crusty, as silk will when sweat dries on it. He got up and went into the bedroom to change into a new one. As he did so, he reflected with pleasure on the conversation—on Donald's lilting tone, peppered with "honeys" and "dolls." There was no doubt about it: Donald was gay. Plus, he was a nightclub singer! Mitchell envisioned him as being a witty, worldly Noel Coward type in a smoking jacket and bow tie, singing patter songs and French ballads, debonair and irresistible.

Then, a stab of anxiety. Mightn't Donald find him dull and colorless? He was, after all, just a typical, cut-from-the-mold guppie, an ambitious careerist lacking any kind of personal life. An eighties leftover—a sad anomaly.

He sat on his bed, naked, the new robe (magenta) crumpled in his lap. He almost wished, now, that he'd agreed to see Donald perform tonight, just to kill the suspense. But that kind of spontaneity was beyond him. He needed time to think over the entire conversation—to "process it," as he liked to say. He couldn't just walk into a situation like this without first having gone over all the possible angles. And of course he'd also have to share the information with his best friend, Simon; nothing in his life seemed quite real until he'd run it past Simon.

He dialed Simon's number and got a busy signal. At this time of night, that usually meant Simon was having phone sex with one of his nationwide network of long-distance lovers. In which case, his line would be tied up for the foreseeable future.

Restless and frustrated, yet giddy with expectation, Mitchell folded up the unworn robe and placed it on the nightstand, then got under the covers, curled up, and went to sleep.

At a quarter to two, he awoke with a start, having made a distressing realization.

Wasting no time, he dashed into his bathroom and at long last brushed his teeth.

chapter
4

Mitchell and Simon, fast friends, had in fact been lovers once. It was during the brief period between Mitchell's graduation from law school and his joining Ingersoll, Ebersole & Trilby. It was this professional leap that doomed the relationship; Simon was a clerk in a veterinary clinic, a lowly wage earner who felt pangs of inadequacy when Mitchell came home with his big new title and even bigger paycheck. Likewise, Mitchell felt that a boyfriend who was a former International Mr. Leather finalist, who wore big black boots and a leather cap even with cutoffs in July, was scarcely the kind of spousal equivalent he'd like to have on his arm at his prestigious new firm's social events. So they parted amicably and remained friends, with only an occasional squall of jealousy.

Mitchell was now feeling the first cloudburst of one such squall. He'd been leaving messages on Simon's machine all day, and not one had been returned. This could only mean Simon had a new man. He was usually unfailingly polite, to an almost comical degree (Mitchell well remembered him, the day after his twenty-seventh birthday bash, sitting at his desk in a leather jock strap and harness, dutifully scribbling out dainty thank-you notes to the friends who had given him dildoes, tit clamps, and edible underwear). But when he was in the throes of love or lust, Simon left etiquette behind him like a scarf lost to the wind. Mitchell could predict the excuse he'd get for today's neglect: "How could I run to the phone with my legs stuck in the air?"

Mitchell was jealous not because of any lingering feeling for Simon; it was purely a matter of Simon having a love life, and Mitchell having none. The last time Mitchell had his legs in the air was during his ill-fated attempt at rollerblading. (He was still seeing his chiropractor over *that* fiasco.) So each time he dialed Simon's number and got his unendurable message, which was clever in the worst sense ("Hello, this is Simon. Hello? Anyone there? . . . Oh, wait, I forgot, I can't hear you! I'm a recording!"), he grew more angrily certain that Simon was off doing God knows what with God knows whom, while Mitchell was in greater need of his ear than ever.

Eventually, just as the workday was about to end, Bereneesha buzzed him with the news that Simon was on the line. But by now Mitchell was so furious with him that he decided to punish him with a good old-fashioned cold front.

"*Mitchell,*" Simon exclaimed, "what on *earth* is the matter? You must've left a dozen messages!"

"Oh really?" he replied frostily. "I didn't count them."

"Well, what is it? What's so urgent?"

"Oh, nothing. I'm sure I didn't mean to tear you away from your full, rich life."

"Don't be exasperating! I met someone, that's all."

"Of course you did." He leaned back and checked his cuticles, which still didn't look satisfactory.

"Name's Ryan. You'll have to meet him. Gorgeous. *Built.* Wild man in the sack."

"Mm-hmm."

"You want to tell me what's going on?"

"Gee, I'd love to, Simon, but it's five o'clock, and I've got to run."

"*You,* leave the office at *five?* What, is it on fire?"

That was hurtful; Mitchell turned crimson. "No, it's just that I'm meeting someone tonight."

"A date? *A date?* Mitchell Sayer has a *date?* Oh, my God! Hallelujah, hallelujah! Thank you, Baby Jesus!"

Mitchell's eyes narrowed. Someday, somewhere, Simon would pay for this call, and pay dearly.

"Well, tell me who it's with," Simon trilled excitedly.

"As it happens, it's not *that* kind of date. I'm meeting my identical twin."

"What, you met a lookalike somewhere? Someone else with the same goofball haircut?"

Someday *soon*, Mitchell thought. "I'm not speaking metaphorically, Simon. I'm going to meet my actual, long-lost twin brother."

A cavernous silence. Then, "Whoa. Mitch. Let me wrap my brain around this for a second. Since when do you have a—"

"Gee, gotta run. Sorry, Simon. Tell you all about it tomorrow."

"But, Mitch, y—"

Mitchell hung up.

There. Serve the bastard right for being such a sarcastic pig.

In truth, it *was* early for Mitchell to be leaving the office; associates usually stayed until six-thirty or seven, poring over books like medieval monks. Even the partners took no notice of the timeclock. Mitchell found himself waiting for the elevator with almost the entire secretarial staff. Bereneesha looked at him oddly, as though he might be ill or something, then turned to her companion and resumed telling her about a talk show she'd seen during her lunch hour on the topic of "Husbands with Flatulent Wives."

Mitchell turned and regarded the firm's glass doors. IN-GERSOLL, EBERSOLE & TRILBY AND ASSOCIATES, ATTORNEYS AT LAW was etched there in distinguished gravure. His chest swelled with pride. Sometimes, in the heat of the workday, he allowed it to slip his mind, but this really *was* one of the most prestigious small firms in Chicago. And who knew? Someday, the door might read INGERSOLL, EBERSOLE, TRILBY & SAYER. He grew light-headed at the thought. No, he had no reason to fear Donald's scorn.

He'd decided to leave the office at five to give himself plenty of time to run his errands and dine before appearing at the Tam-Tam Club for Donald's show. But, predictably, he'd found that five hours was more than enough time to work out at his health club, pick up his dry cleaning, head home, change into a blazer and khakis, whip up a plate of couscous and sun-dried tomatoes for dinner, and wash all the dishes. He'd even had time to tackle a long-intended project, alphabetizing his CD collection by conductor or ensemble instead of by composer. At a quarter to nine he found himself sitting in front of the television set, watching a sitcom family trade sarcastic quips to the unceasing hysteria of the studio audience, but not hearing a single word of it. He was too busy playing out different scenarios in his head. What if Donald's singing wasn't any good? What if Donald introduced him from the stage? What if Donald had a lover who took a dislike to Mitchell?

Finally, at nine-thirty, he could stand waiting no longer, and he left the house. He strolled down Halsted Street, looking for just the right cab to hail—not an off-brand, please, but a Yellow or a Checker, and with a driver who looked incapable of murder. It took some time to find one that met all his criteria, and even so, he wound up at the Tam-Tam Club twelve minutes early. Well, that would give him time to have a drink and calm his nerves.

The Tam-Tam was squeezed between a Chinese restaurant and a used bookstore on Clark Street, and inside it was dark and smelled of cigarettes and cheap perfume. Smoked mirrors lined all the walls. It was fairly crowded, and the place was humming. Mitchell was so excited he could barely see straight. He made his way to the bar, where he found a stool open next to a very hefty, tall woman who wouldn't stop staring at him. He was far too distracted to bother with her, though. He ordered a vodka martini and sipped it slowly. The heavy woman occasionally grazed his thigh with her own, and Mitchell had a hunch this was on purpose, but he refused to look at her. He stared at the stage as though he could will Donald to appear there sooner.

At six minutes after ten, a bearded, rather emaciated man in a silver lamé jacket appeared to a smattering of applause. Mitchell's heart lurched; at first he thought it must be Donald, but no, this man looked nothing like him, and was around fifty besides. After tapping the microphone, he said, "Ladies and gentlemen—and I use the terms loosely," and here there was some scattered laughter, "the Tam-Tam Club is proud to give you the Doyenne of Despair, Miss Kitten Kaboodle!"

The audience erupted into hoots and howls of approval, and the club went black except for a brilliant spotlight pinpointing the microphone. Then a very thin woman in a beaded ball gown with an astonishing, Big Bird–yellow bouffant parted the curtains behind her like Samson toppling the temple pillars, revealing both herself and an obese pianist just behind her. She smiled brilliantly, and Mitchell was forced to look beyond his annoyance and admit to himself, *She's beautiful. A little manufactured, but beautiful.* She grabbed the microphone with one gloved hand and nodded to the pianist, who fell onto the keys with tinkling gusto. Then she placed her bright red upper lip smack on the microphone and began crooning "Cry Me a River" in a throaty, almost masculine growl.

Mitchell let himself be annoyed again. Donald had said to be here around ten. And here it was, several minutes after, and some woman with eyelashes like paintbrushes was only just beginning *her* set, which meant that Donald probably wouldn't go on for another forty minutes or more. He sighed in exasperation, and when his eyes adjusted to the darkness he decided to pass the time by looking over the club's other patrons.

About half were men, half women. Well, that was to be expected. But there was something funny about them. Something not quite—*relaxed.* And what was it about the women? A kind of—well, a kind of brazenness? So much makeup, such big hair, so many stiletto heels. Like a club full of Chers.

Wait a minute, he thought.

His heart pounding, he turned to the heavy woman to his left and for the first time took a good, hard look at her.

Through a mountain of Maybelline, she smiled at him and said, "Buy a girl a drink?" in a voice a hair lighter than Orson Welles's.

At that moment, Kitten Kaboodle finished her song and, over the flurry of applause, said, "Thank you all so much! This is a very special night for me, as I have an extra-special guest in the audience: my very own long-lost twin brother, Mr. Mitchell Sayer." She extended her arms and waved up the lights. "Mitchell, honey, stand your bad old self up so Sis can have a look at you!"

Mitchell's blood went still. He couldn't seem to move. The vodka martini was evaporating beneath the heat of his hand.

Kitten Kaboodle called for him a few more times, and everyone in the club—even the heavy woman next to him—was looking around for the mysterious twin brother. As long as he remained unobtrusive, he knew he'd be safe. No one had any way of knowing he was the one being sought.

Finally, Kitten shrugged and said, "Oh, hell, looks like the bitch has been stood up again. By *family*, fer Gawd's sake. Well, never mind, we've got *much* more depressing things to concentrate on." She waved down the lights, swept a strand of hair from her face and nodded again to the pianist, who launched into "Stormy Weather."

After a few minutes, Mitchell slipped off the barstool and fled.

Walking up Clark Street in the midst of the bustling Friday-night crowds, he achieved the anonymity he needed so desperately at this moment. He kept walking and walking, until the crowds began to thin and he found himself by the cemetery on the corner of Irving Park. There, he caught a cab and told the driver to simply head south.

In the cab, he tried to sort out his feelings. He'd fought so hard to be accepted as a gay man by his family and peers; how, then, could he snub his own brother for being different? And yet, Donald was so *very* different! Mitchell would never recover from the shock of suddenly realizing that the beautiful blonde chanteuse at the Tam-Tam was in fact his identical twin.

He rested his chin on his hand and looked out the taxi window without seeing. He'd devoted his life to proving to straight people that gays were no different from them, that they were just as serious, just as hardworking—just as, in a word, dull. And now he was confronted with a brother who was the living embodiment of every cliché straights had about faggots. How *could* Mitchell accept him? And yet, how could he *not*?

Maybe, he thought, he'd been sent here for a purpose; maybe he was meant to straighten out Donald (so to speak). Get him off this drag thing and into a real, respectable lifestyle.

The only thing he was absolutely certain of was that he needed more time to think all this over. He couldn't return to the bar. No, no. Not a chance.

He leaned forward and gave the driver his home address.

chapter

5

Increasingly often, Kitten Kaboodle had been getting disturbing intimations that her life was entering a new and rather elegiac phase, but tonight was the first time two such intimations had come so closely together. The first was, of course, the sudden flight of her equally suddenly reappeared twin brother. Now, as she waited outside the Tam-Tam for the Number 36 bus, wearing an enormous greatcoat and slouch hat, and chewing a chunk of Bubble Yum, she was met by the second such Cassandra: a young manwoman dressed something like Bjork (or maybe the intended effect was Wednesday Addams) who approached Kitten in tentative steps, clutching her throat and grinning hideously.

"Miss Kaboodle?" she asked tremulously.

Kitten blew a bubble, popped it, and said, "Depends who's askin'."

The fan giggled nervously and inched closer. "I just wanted to say what an inspiration you've been to me."

Kitten smiled and did a little half curtsy. "Why, thank you."

"No, you don't know," she continued, shaking her head. "When I was a kid—I mean—" She fondled a black rosary she wore like a necklace; in Christ's place on the cross she'd nailed a Joan Walsh Anglund doll. "—I don't even know if I can describe it."

"I don't even know if you have to." Kitten took a sidelong glance; no bus in sight.

"I suppose not." The fan extended her hand. "My name's Barbarella Fitzgerald."

They shook. *"Enchanté,"* said Kitten.

The fan hugged herself. "This is so fabulous, being here talking to you!"

Kitten acknowledged this compliment with droopy-lidded grace; it was nothing to which she was not accustomed. "Yes, isn't it."

"I mean, when I was in my teens"—the girl looked no older than twenty—"I used to sneak out of the house and take the train an hour from Barrington, just to see you—just to see what I could be, that I didn't have to stunt myself or—you know—compromise. I could *be* myself. Like you! You were my idol!"

Kitten started to say, "You make me sound such a dowager," but while she was saying it, someone came around the corner walking a pair of harlequin Great Danes, each of which decided to pass on a different side of Kitten, then changed its mind and tried to double back on the opposite side. This involved Kitten, dogs, and dog owner in an intricate and lengthy gavotte, timed to a rhythm of apologies and pardons, before they were capable of going their separate ways.

Kitten readjusted her hat and tried to regain her composure before Barbarella Fitzgerald's ceaseless scrutiny. She cocked her head in the direction of the retreating Great Danes and said, "Surely one is sufficient for any household."

Barbarella furrowed her brow, as if not understanding this reference; then she put it aside. "I'd like to go on the stage too, you know," she said with great intensity. "I dream of someday performing at the Tam-Tam, just like you."

Dear, sweet child, thought Kitten. "You sing, do you?"

She craned her neck sideways and grimaced. "Well, no, but I do a mean lip-synch to old Ann-Margret records." She struck a saucy pose, left arm extended above the head, right heel at butt height. A car full of Latino boys drove by and started hooting.

Kitten felt a jab of annoyance. "Well, lip-synching is hardly performing like *me*, dear."

Apparently sensing that she'd put a foot awry, Barbarella began some serious backpedaling. "Oh, but if only I *could* sing like you, that would be my dream! But I don't have your talent. I can really only just pretend, like most girls you see these days."

"Yesss," Kitten hissed, her eyes narrowed.

"It's the best I can do." She pouted. "Now you probably think I'm just a big nothing."

Kitten shook her head. "Not at all. I just think you should be original, that's all. In whatever you do. You have, thus far— why start pretending now?" She took her gum from her mouth and tried to toss it into a trash can three yards up the street; she missed by a good eight inches. "You just think about it. Think over what I've said."

"I *will*," said Barbarella, as if this were the most potent inspirational speech she'd ever heard. "Thanks so much for listening to me and for giving me advice and everything! I really mean it!" She skipped up the street, pausing only for a moment to turn back and shout, "I still think you're sensational, no matter what anyone says!" Then she waved wildly and bolted.

Kitten's stomach fell through the sidewalk.

Who the fuck was "anyone"? And what exactly was "anyone" saying?

And what, she now wondered, had made Barbarella think that after years of worship from afar, her idol was now approachable?

Tarnished luster never hurt a real queen; in fact, a patina often gave her greater allure. But at times like these, Kitten had a fleeting feeling that something more insidious was at work. It wasn't a tarnished reputation she had to worry about; it was a diminishing one.

She scoffed, put it all out of her mind, and cursed the bus for not having appeared yet.

It was ironic, in a way. The manager of the Tam-Tam Club insisted that each of his girls take on a show-biz sobriquet. Kitten, ravished by the slow degeneration of such tragic figures as Edith Piaf and Billie Holiday, had chosen to style herself the Doyenne of Despair. But when a hint of real despair poked through her theatrical pose, she couldn't—wouldn't—face it.

Not yet, at any rate.

chapter 6

"**M**itchell? *Mitchell*?" Cyrus Trilby waved a mortgage rider in his associate's face. "You in there?"

Mitchell went rash-red, dropped his pen, and said, "Sorry, Cyrus. Let my mind wander a sec." Some of the other associates giggled.

"I asked about your caseload," Trilby said with just a hint of exasperation.

Mitchell slid his chair up to the conference table and placed his hands on his Coach binder. "Lightening up," he said, glancing down the top page of the notebook. "Gwynn Development closing is scheduled for tomorrow, and that's been my biggie."

"Strip mall, isn't that?" said Zoe Briggs, the fiercely ambitious associate all the others had dubbed a "partner hag." She tapped her pen against the table. "Glad to know we're all upholding the firm's upscale image." She grinned evilly from beneath her razor-sharp, Dorothy-Hamill-from-hell hairdo. One of her hindmost molars was ringed in gold; it showed whenever she bestowed her least sincere smile.

"With last quarter's billings, I don't think any of us can afford to be too picky," replied Trilby as he checked his watch. Zoe let a look of morbid defeat cross her face, then recovered in an instant. "No criticism meant, Cyrus," she said musically. "Just a joke to make hard times easier." The gold molar sparkled.

Trilby smiled at her dismissively and said, "All right. That's it, people." He stood up. "Till next week."

On Mitchell's way out of the conference room, Zoe shouldered up to him and said, "Gosh, Mitch, you really zoned out for a moment there."

Mitchell almost admired her for the luxuriant falseness of her concern. Every lawyer has to be a good actor; Zoe's problem was that she never turned it off. "No big deal," he said airily.

"If I didn't know better, I'd say something was bothering you," she added as she scurried to keep up with his loping stride. (She was only five foot two, which, combined with her ruthless ambition, had caused much behind-her-back analysis of the validity of the so-called Napoleon complex.)

"Nothing's wrong, Zoe," Mitchell said as he turned a corner, losing her for a heartbeat.

She rounded the corner leaning at a forty-five-degree angle. "No, seriously," she called after him (he was now a good three yards ahead of her), "if you ever need to confide in someone, I'm here."

"Thanks," he called back without turning his head. He strode into his office and shut the door.

Damn, damn, damn, he thought, leaning against the wall and taking a breath. One tiny incident upsets me, and Zoe Briggs sniffs it out like a bloodhound.

He decided he'd better bite the bullet then, and call Donald. Kitten. Whatever—whoever she was. *He* was. *Damn!*

He dropped into his chair and swiveled toward his phone. After a deep breath, he opened his Filofax, located Donald's number, and dialed.

Nine interminable rings later: "Hello?" Donald's flutey, unmistakable voice.

"Hello," said Mitchell. Then his voice dried up. A pause the size of a planet rolled into the conversation.

Finally, "Mitchell, is that you?"

"Uh-huh." What was that? A grunt? Was he speaking in grunts now? What had his mother taught him about language, about diction? "Yes, this is Mitchell," he began anew. "Listen, I called to apologize. I was there last night—at the Tam-Tam. I couldn't handle it. I walked."

"Honey, *I'm* the one should be down on her knees," said Donald, adding a moment later, sotto voce, "So to speak."

"Why should *you* apologize?" asked Mitchell.

"For not warning you. What else?" A small, nervous laugh. "The drama queen in me. Instead of preparing you, I thought I'd spring it all at once. Like shock therapy." Another pause. "How much did you catch? What did you think?"

"What—what did I—what did I—" He ground to a halt, completely dumbfounded.

"I just mean the singing. Not me, per se. Just, you know— the material, my delivery."

"Well—that—that—was very nice."

" 'Nice'? Mitchell, no performer likes to hear the results of her blood, sweat and tears described as 'nice'! Tell me you loved me! Tell me you hated me! Tell me I was derivative, or embarrassing, or offensive, or outdated, but don't tell me I was '*nice*'!"

Mitchell's mouth hung open. He couldn't begin to form a response.

He heard a defeated sigh. Then, in a low voice, Donald said, "Well, do you still want to meet? I mean, I'd understand if—"

"No, no," Mitchell said, "I think we have to. More than that, I'd still *like* to. I can get over this. Donald, I haven't got any real siblings. A couple of half sisters from my mom's second marriage. Not *even* half-sisters, when I think about it. So, this is like a dream come true for me. I can't just go through life not knowing you. Whatever—I mean *whoever* you are, you're my brother, my *twin*, for God's sake. Can't we start over?"

"Sweetie, I start over every morning. Build myself up from scratch. You think I can't start over with you? Give a girl some credit."

Maybe I won't get over this, thought Mitchell. But he forged ahead. "What about lunch, then? A nice, neutral, one-hour lunch. Take this in easy steps. Less strain on both of us, for now."

"Wonderful. I can be there in an hour. Where do you work?"

"No, no, not today," said Mitchell hurriedly. Such spontaneity was still fearsome to him. Even a nice, neutral, one-hour lunch needed a full day of mental preparation. "Tomorrow," he said. "Say, twelve-fifteen. And, listen: normal clothes, okay?"

"Anything you say," said Donald. "Just tell me where to drag my poor old self."

Mitchell flinched at the word "drag," then recited the firm's address, and as he did so he felt a kind of resigned dread, as if he were willingly committing a deadly and irreversible mistake.

chapter 7

"**H**e's ashamed of you," said Rondell Davis as he applied a subtle outline of peach to his dark rose lips. "He just doesn't know it yet. But *you* should." He took away the brush and pursed his lips in the vanity mirror. "You should be able to hear it in his voice."

Donald was donning a brand new pair of pantyhose. He hadn't shaved in a while, and he could feel his stubble snag on the nylon. *It's not pretty when a drag queen gets careless,* he thought, but it was too late to do anything about it tonight. He hitched the waistband up around his stomach and turned to Rondell. "I don't hear *shame* in his voice," he said. "I hear a sad kind of—I don't know—*longing.*" He pulled a silken slip over his shoulders and let it tumble down around his torso and legs.

"You watch out," said Rondell, now applying lotion to his elbows. "He'll hurt you, if you let him. Men are like that. They lash out. They destroy what threatens them. And *everything* threatens them. That's a F-A-C-T, girl."

"Nah," said Donald as he donned a vintage black crepe

gown with a fur-trimmed collar. "Not Mitchell. He's not like that."

"You don't know."

"I do, hon. Listen, he doesn't know it, but I *saw* him sitting in the audience last night, when the lights went up. How could I miss him? Like looking in a goddamn mirror!" He slipped his arms into the sleeves and straightened the bodice. "When I started calling out his name, and he realized who I was, you should've seen him. Like he had a goalpost up his ass. Right then and there, I knew God sent him to me for a little loosening up. And believe me, I'm just the girl to do it!"

Rondell pulled on a wig, a mass of black ringlets, and suddenly Rondell was gone, and Regina Upright, the Idol of Millions, was sitting at the vanity.

A moment later, Donald took his long blond wig, bent over, and affixed it to his scalp. But it wasn't Donald who stood up and tossed the silken tresses into place; it was Kitten Kaboodle, the Doyenne of Despair.

"How do I look?" she asked Regina.

"Like a tired old thing from H-E-double-L."

Kitten crossed the crowded room by slithering between the bed and the walls, till she reached the mirror over the dresser. She held back her hair and had a look. Her eyes were baggy, it was true, too true. "Damn it to Schenectady," she said through clenched teeth. "What's a girl have to *do?* I practically *mainline* Oil of Olay."

"Can't fight Father Time, child," said Regina, who was fully a dozen years younger than Kitten, and liked to flaunt it. She stood up and shimmied into an orange leather miniskirt.

"I can fight anyone I want," Kitten retorted as she pulled at the skin of her face from various strategic points. "I've got some moolah put aside for a rainy day. Maybe now's the time I ought to go for it. A little anesthetic, a little nip-and-tuck, next thing I know I look twenty-two again."

"Ain't no doctor that good," said Regina as she tried to pull on her white vinyl hip boots. "Twenty-eight, *maybe.* And that's if he's a genius." She grunted with effort, then said, "Give me a hand, okay?"

Kitten turned and applauded, and Regina dropped her leg and folded her arms. "Ha fucking ha," she said flatly.

Kitten turned back to the mirror and pulled her face taut again, and Regina went back to struggling with her boots. "Seriously, Gina," Kitten continued, "why *shouldn't* I get a facelift? I was a knockout ten years ago. Hell, I still am. But I'm losing it. Feel like I'm holding on by my fingernails."

"Which are F-A-K-E," Regina said as, with one herculean yank, she got her last hip boot past her hip. She stood up and swiveled around, showing her tiny, aerobicized butt to Kitten. "Zip me up?"

Kitten crawled across the bed on her knees, waggling her fingers at Regina. "You know very well that each and every one of these beauties is the genuine article," she said. "I am, after all, a professional!" She made a little feint at Regina's face with her bright red talons, as though intending to scratch her eyes out. Regina shrieked and jumped back; Kitten blurted out a laugh, then grabbed her friend's zipper and flicked it up to her nape.

"How do *I* look?" Regina asked chirpily, smoothing her silk blouse and turning coyly to regard Kitten over one shoulder.

"Like a waif," said Kitten. "Like a child of no experience. Like a schoolgirl."

Regina smirked. "You're a D-O-double-L." She grabbed her rather tattered mink jacket. "Ready?"

Kitten had one more deflating look in the mirror. "As I'll ever be," she sighed. They left the tiny, cluttered studio apartment, and as Kitten stood in the hallway and locked the door (an operation made rather more difficult than it could've been by those lethal fingernails), she said, "Cab it or walk?"

"Let's walk. There's a M-double-O-N."

They headed down the stairs, side by side, generating enough bump-and-grind to register on the Richter scale. They were best girlfriends out for a night of showing off and showing each other up. Life could hold no greater joy. Ever since Kitten had met Regina, eight months earlier, they'd been inseparable, connecting on levels Kitten had never dreamed possible with her other friends. No one was as sharp, as vibrant, as energetic as Regina. No one else boasted her glorious, triumphant bitchery. The times they'd had! The calamities they'd caused! And, if Kitten were honest, she'd have to admit that there was an element of flattery in it—a girl of Regina's age hitching her star to a matron like herself. But it wasn't as though Regina got nothing out of it. After all, Kitten had got her her gig at the Tam-Tam.

There was indeed a full moon tonight; it sputtered through the streetlamps and six-flats, covering the New Town district with milky splotches of light, as though God had taken up action painting. Despite this, Kitten and Regina stuck to the shadows.

"So, why you coming in so early, anyway?" asked Regina. "This is still your naptime, ain't it?"

"Gordy asked me to," Kitten said with a yawn. "Dunno why."

"I've got to know where you found this dress, child," Regina said, switching topics as easily as a channel-surfer switched stations. She fingered the collar of Kitten's gown. "What kind of fur you call this?"

"It's *monkey*," said Kitten exultantly, as though she'd been waiting for Regina to break down and ask. "Genuine monkey!"

Regina scowled. " 'Scuse me, I got to go make a call to Greenpeace."

Kitten snorted, clearly enjoying Regina's pique. "It's not like that, hon. I'm not supporting monkey killers. This dress is vintage. Forty years if it's a day. Got it at a shop in Oak Park run by this glorious proprietress who saves terrific vintage stuff for me all the time."

"Fancy Miss Kitt in Oak Park," said Regina. They turned a corner onto Belmont, where they immediately spotted three teenage boys in baggy calf-length shorts and baseball caps worn backwards, standing tensely outside a juice bar as though coiled for some kind of action. Both Kitten and Regina quickened their pace and moved to the outside of the sidewalk.

"I go anywhere I choose," said Kitten. "No one looks

twice, not even in Oak Park. Or if they do, it's in admiration."

"I've looked in admiration on many a gorilla at the Z-double-O," said Regina.

"Hey," said one of the teenagers. "Hey, 'ladies.' " He stretched out the word musically; his friends laughed.

Kitten and Regina passed him without looking. "You're just jealous," Kitten said to Regina. "Another example of the negative energy you're always giving off. You ought to see a shrink or something, help you get over that. It'll age you before your time."

"Could be I'll catch up to you, then."

"Hey, 'ladies,' " the boy called after them. "I'm *talkin'* to you."

"That's exactly the kind of comment I'm referring to," said Kitten, poking Regina in the ribs. "That negative stuff. It does you no credit. You really ought to see a shrink."

"That's right," said Regina merrily. "I walk into a shrink's office dressed like this, first thing he's gonna want to talk about is my negative energy."

They laughed girlishly.

The teenagers started following them. A second boy started calling out to them now: " *'Ladies'—oh, 'ladies'! Coupl'a guys here could sure use a blow job!'*"

A heavyset older couple steamrolled toward Kitten and Regina, forcing them to move aside and thus walk smack into the path of a massive streetlamp. They paused for a second, then scooted around either side of it and rejoined each other a few steps later, taking care not to walk any faster than they had before.

"You ever seen a shrink?" Regina asked.

"Come on, 'ladies'! We're askin' nice!" called the second teenager.

Kitten shrugged. "Once, when I was seventeen. Guy was gonna straighten me out in four sessions; *four.* Told my Mom, guaranteed."

All three boys were now following them, trilling in an exaggerated falsetto. *"Ladies—ladies—ladies—oh, ladies . . ."*

"What happened?" Regina asked.

"Oh, hell," Kitten said, rolling her eyes. "By the third session, I was madly in love with him."

They laughed again, and heartily too, because they didn't have to turn around to know that the danger had passed. They could hear the falsetto dropping away, could feel the lessening of the heat against the backs of their necks. The teenagers, they knew, had retreated. They gradually assumed a more reasonable pace, and continued their stream of chatter. But they never made mention of the teenage boys, any more than they made mention of the cars that barreled through the intersections in front of them, or the dog crap that dotted the sidewalks, or any of the other commonplaces they had learned to beware as a matter of course, each and every day of their lives.

chapter 8

Kitten and Regina arrived at Tam-Tam's just as the first flow of after-work drinkers was departing. Some of the men—middle-aged suit-and-tie sorts, as a rule—patted their fannies and pinched them as they passed. One guy, whose hairpiece made him look as though an alien life form had landed on his head and taken root, gave the wolf whistle to Kitten. She winked in return, then leaned into Regina and said, "God help me, I actually found that *flattering*. Time was, I wouldn't have given a guy like that the time of day!"

"We're all getting older, child," said Regina. "Better catch as catch C-A-N."

Kitten jangled her bracelets at her and sneered.

At that moment, a young LaSalle-street banker type, who smelled unmistakably of fine Scotch, squeezed past them to the door and said, in Regina's face, "Shame I have to leave now. This is the biggest thrill I've had all day, beautiful." And he cupped his hand over Regina's crotch.

Even before he was out of earshot, Kitten was snarling, "You're loathsome and I hate your guts."

"I just can't turn it off," said Regina airily. "It's beyond my control, hon." She readjusted her silk blouse over her shoulders.

They were just about to belly up to the bar when the owner, Gordy Tranh, appeared from out of nowhere, like a zany magic uncle in a sixties sitcom. Gordy, a Vietnamese refugee who had realized the American dream when he opened Tam-Tam's in the early eighties, was handsome, graying, pot-bellied, and addicted to nasal inhalers. He popped one open now and had a couple of good, strong snorts.

"Kitten, Gina, you almost late," he said frantically, taking them by the arms and hustling them down a hallway beyond the stage.

"Don't get your Jockeys in a twist, Gordy," said Regina crossly. "I don't go on for fifteen minutes. Get off my B-A-C-K."

"*Not* going on in fifteen minutes," said Gordy as he shoved them inside the dressing room and shut the door behind him. Then he turned to face them and said, "Made some changes last night. Thought about it for a long time. No arguments, either. Gordy has decreed."

"Changes?" said Regina, and there was a tremor of fear in her voice.

"Don't worry," said Gordy, uncapping his inhaler and taking another antiseptic hit. "Just moving you to later. Switching you with Kitten. Kitten, *you* go on in fifteen minutes. Better get ready. Gordy has decreed!"

Kitten put her hand on her breast. "M-me? *I* go on now? What do you mean? I've been doing the ten-to-midnight set for a hundred years! You can't just pull me off it!"

"Can, and have." He stuffed the inhaler in his shirt pocket. "So, come on! Put pedal to the metal, please!" He clapped twice, then pointed at her.

Regina placed a hand on Kitten's shoulder and said, "There's no arguing with him when he's like this, hon. Best just to accept the little tyrant's W-H-I-M."

"Oh, sure, *you'd* say that," blurted Kitten. "You're getting my spot! My star spot, the prime spot of the night! You want *me*," she continued, whirling on Gordy, "to take over the dinner-hour spot? You've got to be kidding! That's when the club's the most dead!"

"Take or leave it," Gordy said. "How come you still not getting ready?"

"But *why?*" Kitten asked, in so plaintive a voice that Gordy actually sat down, had another hit, and explained.

"Okay, I try to make it all clear. Hey, you getting older. Sorry, but no surprise to you. Voice getting deeper. Plus, material too depressing! These are nineties! Happy days for everyone. Democratic president! Many cable channels! Fat-free ice cream! But no, you insist, you must be Doyenne of Despair. Sing those torchy songs so everybody get feeling crummy. Four customers took hike last night when you came on. Four! We lose any more business, I lose *you*. Meantime, I just move you."

Kitten rose to her full height and swept her hair behind her shoulders. "That's *grossly* unfair. This little tramp here," she said, jerking her thumb at Regina, who pressed her hand to her throat in affronted surprise, "she doesn't even *sing*. She *lip-synchs*, for God's sake. Gordy, *I'm* the real thing—an artist as well as an entertainer! I have to sing what I feel, and what I feel is pure Piaf." She stood, arms folded, and looked down her nose at him.

Gordy got to his feet as well. "Fine," he said. "Then sing in French. That way nobody know you singing about death and suicide and lonely stuff." Suddenly he appraised her gown. "Very nice. Very nice trim. Monkey, huh? Had underwear like this in Saigon. Before shit hit fan, of course. Okay, I go now. Get ready. Ten minutes, you on. Gordy has decreed!"

Abruptly, he exited, popping open his inhaler as he went.

And so Kitten Kaboodle, the Doyenne of Despair, found herself facing the dregs of the after-work crowd—*seven* in all, middle-aged to a man, ties askew, comb-overs uncombed, smiles as dopey as Dopey's. When she sashayed onstage, one of them drunkenly shouted out, *"Whomma taig sharla finshay!"* and several of the others laughed sloppily. It was that sort of

audience—the sort that left English behind for a kind of com-
munal, alcoholic Sanskrit. Donald's mother often spoke of her
Charismatic church group, whose members would on occasion
ascend to the ecstasy of tongues; Donald would coo with the
requisite astonishment, but Kitten—Kitten knew better what
that was all about.

"Thank you, Wesley," she said to the sequin-jacketed host
who had introduced her. "And thank *you*, gentlemen, for coming to see me at my newly appointed hour. I'm *very* excited to
be joining you so much earlier in the evening, and I just *know*
we're going to become the very *best* of friends."

"Blyona try muh freshgate?" someone yelled, to a smattering
of hilarity.

Kitten allowed herself a delighted giggle, as though she had
found witty what she had not even found comprehensible; then
she turned, nodded to her pianist, the heroically obese Pierre,
and launched immediately into "Gloomy Sunday." A feeling of
perverse rebellion against the thrice-damned Gordy welled
within her breast, and she deliberately deepened her voice to
its velvety depths, while standing stock-still at the microphone,
as if handcuffed to it. Within ten bars of the song, most of her
audience had lost their grins; within another ten, two had stumbled out into the still-strident moonlight.

The song came to its dolorous conclusion, and Kitten took
the kind of bow Bernhardt must have taken after "Hamlet."
She then turned to Pierre and mouthed, " 'The Man That Got
Away'."

Pierre winced. "Are you sure?" he whispered. "That's not
the order we rehearsed."

"Darling, I'm quite determined."

"They don't seem to be *liking* it," he hissed.

She cast him a half haughty, half piteous glance, and mur-
mured, "Have you never wanted to smash everything?" It was
a line she remembered from Sartre's *Kean*, which she'd read in
college in 1978. Kitten had a gift for finding camp in the un-
likeliest places.

She was halfway through the number that had been the

divine Judy's apotheosis—the song that had actually threatened to replace "Over the Rainbow" as her talismanic anthem—and had wrung every heartrending shade of desperation and grief from its plangent, tolling lyrics, when, her upper lip dewy with sweat and her knees weak with emotion, she was interrupted, her spell broken by the taunting cry of a blasphemer.

"*Suck my dick!*"

Pierre fumbled a chord and lost a beat and a half to confusion, then sallied bravely forth. Kitten followed his lead, and ventured even more boldly into the murky realm of Utter Anguish.

"*Hey—homo! I said, suck my DICK!*"

Kitten had reached the end of a phrase, and stood with her hand on the mike, head bowed in awe of her own desolation, while Pierre ran through a brilliantly morbid bridge.

"*You know you fuckin' want it! Come on! YOU WANT IT! No, I WON'T sit down! Get your hands off me, you fuckin' dyke!*"

At this, Kitten knew that Carlotta, the Amazonian bouncer, had placed her sinewy hands on the heckler's shoulders, and it was thus safe to look up; no one yet had escaped Carlotta's rootlike grip. (Among the staff, she was known as "the Vulcaness"—one of the few television references that Kitten didn't get.) She tossed back her hair and took a peek at the commotion; Carlotta had her meaty arms looped around a blush-cheeked frat boy's armpits, and was in the process of dragging him out the door as though he were the carcass of a deer. His expensive gym shoes were untied, as per the incomprehensible fashion of the day, and were trailing through spilled beer, the sight of which rendered Kitten inexplicably merry. It was, she thought, as though Carlotta were dispensing not only with this horrible boy, but with the other three Kitten and Regina had earlier encountered. Christ! Two verbal assaults *and* a demotion, all in the space of an hour! One for the record books. But this was the kind of adversity over which any diva worth her salt must prevail. She spread her arms wide, hit her highest, strongest note, and held it.

"*You fuckin' pussy-slurpin' goddamn bull dyke—*"

She held on to that note; she'd override her abuser by vocal tenacity alone.

"I oughtta break your fuckin' butch-steroid neck, you—"

A thud shook the building, and there followed an uncanny silence; and after another jangled chord, Pierre and Kitten brought the song home. Carlotta reappeared in the doorway, wiping her hands against each other. Poor frat boy; he couldn't know how much his assailant hated being mistaken for a bull dyke. In her mirror, Carlotta—born Fernando Francisco Aguilar—saw reflected nothing less willowy and gamine than the youthful Audrey Hepburn.

chapter 9

Mitchell was drowning his anxiety over the prospect of meeting Donald with a steady flow of gin and tonics. It wasn't his drink of choice, but it was the only one being served at this rooftop party Simon was throwing to celebrate the birthday of Queen Elizabeth the Queen Mother. (Apparently, the old girl had a thing for G&Ts.) The drinks weren't having the desired effect; perhaps the numbing qualities of the alcohol were offset by the surreality of sharing a moonlit apartment-house roof with sixteen House of Windsor fanatics in full biker regalia. What was it about British royalty and leather that made them twin obsessions for so many gay men?

Mitchell, in his khakis and canvas shoes, had been trying in vain to mingle with a gaggle of leathermen who were discussing the latest Buckingham Palace gossip with an ever-escalating punctuation of gasps and shrieks, as though suffering from progressive oxygen deprivation. But Mitchell, who couldn't tell a duke from an earl or a viscount from a marquis, was hopelessly confused by the spray of giddy venom. Aside from that, he found himself having to break company with the gossipers after no more than fifteen minutes; it was a warm night, and the odor of all that sweat-soaked leather was beginning to make his nose hairs curl and turn his mind to vegetarianism.

He went to the far side of the roof, found a shadow, and slipped into it, then sat on the edge and dangled his feet. Emboldened by the liquor, he allowed himself to look between his ankles at the six-storey drop; immediately he felt a vertiginous rush, and his scrotum shriveled like a pair of plums turning prune in time-lapse. He leaned back, sucked in a breath, and fell into deep thought.

He hadn't yet told anyone at the firm about his long-lost twin, and was hoping he wouldn't have to do so tomorrow, either. If he could bolt as soon as the receptionist announced Donald's arrival, he could usher him straight out the door before any of the partners and associates had a chance to notice him. After all, Donald might not be in drag tomorrow, but he might very well *act* like he was. Too late, Mitchell realized that he could've avoided all this by just arranging to meet him at a restaurant.

A deeper shadow muddied the one into which he'd taken refuge; he looked up and saw Simon looming over him— Simon, in a black leather vest, black leather shorts, black leather boots, and a Union Jack pin piercing his left nipple.

"Never get a husband if you keep playing Garbo," Simon announced with mock sternness.

Mitchell squinted at him. "If I wanted a leatherman, I'd have stuck with you."

Simon grinned and sat down beside him. "Sweet talkin' thang," he cooed. "Let me guess what's bugging you."

"What else? I've got a lunch date with him tomorrow." He'd broken down and told Simon all about Donald—including the fact of his blonde-bombshell alter-ego.

Simon hiked his own hairy legs over the side of his building, and shook his head. "Just can't leave well enough alone, can you?"

"No. He's my brother. I have to do this."

"You'll be sorry."

"Too late. I started it, I have to follow through."

Simon rolled his eyes. "Still blows me away that this guy says he sings at the fucking Tam-Tam, and you don't know what that means."

"How should I know that's a drag club? What, am I supposed to be some kind of expert on every gay dive in town?"

"Maybe if you got out more. Say, once or twice an eon."

Mitchell slid his hands under his knees. "You know how my job is."

"No, I know how *you* are. Mister Fixation. You find one thing in life, and you go whole-hog at it. Used to be me, once—back in the centuries before Christ. Smothered me like a rag doll. Now, it's this fucking Ingersoll-Lysol-Whatever place. Nothing else exists for you. Think you've got a good thing going, but you're like a juggler with one ball. Pathetic."

Only Simon could speak to him like this, but even Simon could go too far. "That's quite enough. I know my faults."

"For all the good it does you." He began casually tweaking his unpierced nipple.

Mitchell, trying not to be aroused by the sight, asked, "Well, what about Donald, then? I'm concentrating on *him*. He's got nothing to do with the firm."

Simon scowled. "Guy's a drag queen, Mitch."

"I know that."

"Well, there you are. You can't trust him." Tweak. Tweak. Tweak.

Mitchell sneered. It was his turn to shake his head. "Just because he dresses like a woman, I can't trust him?"

"It's not about dressing like a woman. Dressing like a woman doesn't make you a drag queen. Don't you know anything? Drag queens *walk the walk*, Mitch." Tweak. Tweak. "They take on a complete female persona. Or what they *perceive* as a female persona, except it's got more to do with culture than gender, dig? So they end up being neither-nor. Pillars of anarchy, Mitch. That's what they are. They're not a third sex, they're a second species. Something vital is missing, something—something *human*. So time distorts around them, and ordinary phys-

ics don't apply. Trust me on this, bud. I've been around. Your
brother will cause you no end of grief, just because he can."

They sat in a little whirlpool of tension for a moment, eyes
boring into each other, Simon yanking on his nipple, Mitchell
clutching his knees, until a tall, handsome blond man in chaps
and a harness interrupted them. "Simon? Isn't it time for the
cake? I think it *must* be time for the cake."

Simon turned and winked at him. "In a minute."

"Oh, good!" He traipsed off, calling out, "In a minute!
Simon says in a minute!"

"Simon says, Simon says," the others chanted happily; it was
an old joke of which they never tired.

Simon himself seemed less than amused by it tonight. He
released his distended nipple, pulled himself up into a crouch,
and said, "Mark my words, Mitch, the only good queen is one
who's been anointed with full ceremony in Westminster
Abbey."

"What about *you*? You're a leather queen!"

"Leather*man*, please. Now excuse me." He hopped up and
returned to his guests. Mitchell sat and stewed a while longer;
behind him, the assembled guests sang a rousing chorus of
"Happy Birthday," followed by an equally rousing chorus of
"God Save the Queen," followed by a rather tentative run
through "Rule Britannia," and concluding, inexplicably, with a
complete rendition of "Sadie, Sadie, Married Lady" from *Funny
Girl.* (But Simon wasn't a queen; oh, *no.*) Then the blond man
reappeared at Mitchell's side, and introduced himself as Gary.
He presented Mitchell with a slice of cake bearing a multicol-
ored blob of frosting that he explained was part of the crest of
the Bowes-Lyon family from which the Queen Mum had sprung,
and what a shame Mitchell hadn't seen the entire cake, and
would Mitchell like to spend the night with him?

Mitchell blanched, then politely inquired whether Simon
had put him up to this, and though Gary assured him otherwise,
Mitchell chose to decline. He knew Gary was lying. How stupid
of Simon to think Mitchell could be distracted from his flesh
and blood by a substitute involvement of flesh alone!

chapter 10

Mitchell handled the Gwynn Development closing the next morning, shook his grateful client's hand, shook the hands of his grateful client's chief investors, and sailed out of the title company's imposing marble-faced building feeling happier than he had in weeks. This had been a butt-biter of a job—a weeks-long marathon of unforeseen snags and late-night phone calls. But in the end, it represented some pretty hefty billing for the firm. Cyrus would be more willing to hand him plum cases now.

This prediction was borne out as soon as Mitchell stepped off the elevator outside the Ingersoll, Ebersole & Trilby offices. Cyrus Trilby was waiting to take the same elevator down, accompanied by a thin, middle-aged man in a straight-legged, narrow-lapel suit that looked as though it had been bought in 1965 and that its owner was proud it still fit.

"Oh, Mitchell, hello," said Trilby genially as he stuck his hand in the elevator to prevent its closing. "Went well?"

"Without a hitch," said Mitchell, and he tossed his briefcase from one hand to the next. He immediately regretted having allowed them to witness such a moment of giddy self-congratulation.

Trilby nodded at his companion. "Allow me to introduce Benjamin Wrolen, a new client. Ben, this is Mitchell Sayer, one of our most promising young associates." The elevator door tried to shut; Trilby whacked it back open.

Mitchell extended his hand. "How do you do, Mr. Wrolen?"

Wrolen shook Mitchell's hand and nodded curtly; he didn't say a word. He wore an expression on his face that was searingly sober; he made Oliver Cromwell look like Alfred E. Newman.

The elevator door started sliding shut again, and again Trilby knocked it back. This time, it responded with a shrill whine.

"I'd like to have you look over Ben's file," Trilby shouted above the noise. He stepped onto the elevator, and Wrolen followed. *"Then maybe you can join Ben and me for lunch, say, next week?"*

"Certainly," Mitchell shouted back. *"Pleasure meeting you, Mr. Wrolen."*

The door slid shut, and as it did so, Mitchell saw Trilby lean into their new client, gesture toward Mitchell, and begin to speak. Beyond any doubt, he was telling Wrolen what a bright, capable attorney Mitchell was.

Mitchell let his eyes fall shut, and said, "Thank you, God."

He entered the offices and was on his way down the corridor when he crossed paths with Zoe Briggs, who today had her hair moussed up and off her face and wore a tight black suit, sheer black stockings, and black flats. She looked like a cross between a hobbit and a ninja.

"Hello, Zoe," he said in his most pitying tone, a tone that said I Am A Chosen One And You Are Not.

She grinned at him, exposing her gold-rimmed tooth. "Mitchell!" she said, not breaking her stride. "Heard the news? You and me! Wrolen Properties! *Such* fun." And then she whisked past him.

Which was just as well; it prevented her from seeing how his face had clouded over. He was to *share* Wrolen Properties with the firm's most shameless backstabber—and, worse, she was already a step ahead of him! He didn't even know what Wrolen Properties was *about*, for God's sake. Doubtless her speedy step just now was due to her ambition to check out the file Trilby had mentioned. No use him trying to beat her to it—he didn't even know where it was. In addition to which, Trilby hadn't said "I'd like you to look at the file"; he'd said, "I'd like to *have you* look at the file," which implied that he'd bring it to Mitchell himself. Mitchell was the sort of man who was helpless in the face of such a semantic fine line.

He sighed, and his shoulders slumped. His briefcase, so lately tossed into the air, now felt as though it weighed several hundred pounds.

He made his way to his office. Before entering it, he noticed that Bereneesha was away from her desk. He checked his watch; it was only 11:25. She must be off doing photocopying for one of the other associates with whom Mitchell shared her. He sighed again, and retrieved his pink message slips from the weighted spear on which she'd impaled them. At the thought of working with Zoe Briggs, he felt like impaling himself on it, as well.

He entered his office and placed his briefcase on his desk, exactly square with the desk's corners, and was going through his messages when he heard Bereneesha's voice coming from down the hall, chattering madly and laughing with great gusto. Nothing unusual about that; she'd probably just snuck a break with one of the other secretaries. But as her voice grew louder, he could discern that of her partner in conversation as well. It was unsettlingly familiar, that voice—deeper than hers, richer and huskier, albeit elegantly musical . . .

He dropped the sheaf of message notes; they fluttered to his feet like rose petals.

My God, he thought. *Donald!*

"So that's the tour," Bereneesha said in a voice exhausted

by merriment. "Let's see if that brother o' yours has made it back in yet."

He checked his watch again. No, he'd made no mistake; it was only 11:28. But Donald wasn't due here till noon!

Bereneesha buzzed him. "Mitchell? You in there?"

He depressed the button on his intercom. "Yes. I'm here."

"Well, your lunch date is out here waitin' on you."

"Thank you. Thank you, Bereneesha. I'll be right out."

"No hurry. I've just been showing her the office."

Mitchell froze, his hand still poised over the intercom.

Showing . . . HER?

Feeling unsteady on his feet, as though he were walking across a rope bridge, he made his way over to the door and looked out at Bereneesha's work station.

And there, seated on the edge of the secretary's desk, rasping out a clearly ribald story, with earrings jangling, blouse flouncing, baby-blue bell-bottoms riding up her legs, and one stiletto-heeled shoe half-hanging from her foot, was Kitten Kaboodle. The Doyenne of Despair. The star attraction at the notorious Tam-Tam Club. Except that she wasn't a blonde today. Oh, no. Today, Kitten was sporting a magenta beehive about the size of an infant car seat.

Mitchell's mouth fell open.

". . . So I told her, honey," Kitten growled, as Bereneesha held her mouth and quaked with barely suppressed laughter, "that yes, a suppository *is* supposed to be taken internally, but that doesn't mean *swallow* it!"

"She *didn't!*" Bereneesha howled.

"Twice a day for four days," Kitten shrieked, and she and Bereneesha doubled over and howled. Bereneesha had actually started hacking, and had to get up and make a dash to the water cooler in the kitchen. She saw Mitchell as she did so, and, tears streaming from her eyes, she stopped long enough to rasp, "Your sister's some riot!"

When Bereneesha had rounded the corner, Kitten raised her eyebrows, licked her lips, and said, "Well! We meet at last. Should I hug you now, or would that be unseemly?"

Mitchell felt the room spin. "You—you—we agreed—that—"

Kitten placed a hand delicately over her mouth. "Oh, dear," she said ingenuously; "am I *earrly?*"

"You know damn well you're early," he sputtered.

She shrugged and batted her eyes at him. "I *do* apologize. I just couldn't wait to meet you, and that's the God's-honest truth. Curiosity killed the cat, so you have to expect it to at least *prod* the Kitten. And I must say, my curiosity was well repaid! You're *so* much handsomer than I ever was."

This compliment made Mitchell's resolve wobble a little. But he felt he really must be firm with Donald, right at the outset, to forestall any further occurrences of this sort.

"That's no excuse," he said, his teeth clenched. "This is a place of business. We agreed to meet at noon. I had you *scheduled* for noon. Do you understand?"

"Perfectly. You're a busy man." She dropped into Bereneesha's chair, and with a great, balletic kick, swept one leg over the other. The stiletto-heeled shoe again dangled from her toe. "Just wait here for you, shall I?"

"You most certainly will not," he said, feeling sweat start to dampen his collar. "We're leaving right now." He stormed over to her, grabbed her elbow, and started pulling her down the hallway. In her impossible shoes, she nearly tripped trying to keep up with him.

"And by the way," he snarled, "I told you to dress like a man."

She shook her head. "No, your exact words were, 'Wear normal clothes.'" She extended her free arm to display her ensemble. "Well, believe it or not, for me, this *is* n—" Suddenly, she became aware that both her arms were empty. "Oh, *merde,*" she said, digging in her heels and bringing herself—and Mitchell—to a halt. "Forgot my purse. Hold on a sec." And she ran back to Bereneesha's office, swinging her tush like Marilyn Monroe.

Before he could object, Mitchell heard someone call him from the other direction. "Oh, Mitch! Mitch!"

He whirled. It was Zoe, waving a file at him as though it were a trophy she had clutched from his grasp. No, no. She couldn't possibly want to see him about it now. She could *not.*

But she did. She scampered up to him and said, "Listen, I just got the Wrolen file from Cyrus's desk, and I was going to make a photocopy for you, but I don't have time—I've got a lunch meeting in five minutes all the way up in River North, and after that I've got a doctor's appointment so I'll be out all afternoon and tomorrow as well. You don't mind not seeing these till Monday, do you? So sweet! Thanks!" And she started to skitter away.

How transparently preemptive could she get? Yet Mitchell so badly wanted her out of his hair that he found himself saying, "Of course, of course—go right ahead. I can wait."

But that was a wrong move; for it was so plainly the opposite of what Zoe had expected, that she had to pause and look back at Mitchell in surprise—only for the barest second, of course, but that second was all it took for Kitten to reappear at his side, slinging her purse over her shoulder and warbling, "Ready, doll! So, where are you taking me? Someplace *glorious,* I hope!"

Zoe couldn't help but prolong her stare. And Kitten couldn't help but notice it. She stuck her arm out. "Hi! I'm Kitten. Mitchell's sister."

Zoe was forgetting to close her mouth. "Zoe Briggs," she said, shaking Kitten's hand. "I thought I'd met both your sisters, Mitch." And though she was speaking to Mitchell, she couldn't seem to take her eyes off Kitten's hair.

"I'm of the *long-lost* variety," explained Kitten in a conspiratorial tone.

"And that means we have a lot of catching up to do," said Mitchell, his voice riddled with nervous laughter, "so let's get a move on, okay? Afternoon, Zoe!"

"Right," said Zoe, with just the slightest touch of incredulity. "Uh—bye. Pleasure meeting you."

Kitten turned and waved grandly. "I'm sure we'll be seeing lots and lots of each other!"

At that, Mitchell gave her arm a yank, and she disappeared from Zoe's view.

chapter

11

I t seemed as though the elevator would never come, but eventually it did, and Mitchell nearly shoved Kitten onto it. He was thankful beyond measure that no one from the firm joined them for the ride to the lobby.

When he had her outside (where the sunlight reflected off her wig and rendered it even more majestically unnatural), he whirled on her and snapped, "This is not exactly the best of first impressions."

She patted his shoulder. "Don't worry, I'm sure I'll find you much nicer once you've relaxed a bit."

He pressed the bridge of his nose between his thumb and forefinger and shut his eyes for a moment. Then he reached into his breast pocket and pulled out his sunglasses, hoping these were enough to keep him incognito should he come across anyone he knew. "Now," he said disconsolately, "where the hell can I take someone like *you* to lunch?"

"Oh, you dear thing, don't go to any extra trouble," she said, grabbing his arm and giving it a squeeze. "Any old place will do. You don't have to try to impress me."

He looked at her as though she'd just said something complicated in Swedish.

It was her turn to pull *him* into motion. She led him down the street, her arm gripping his like a trailer hitch. "Listen, Mitchell," she said, "long as we're a little ahead of schedule, would you mind if we stopped by my agent's office?"

"I didn't know drag performers *had* agents," he said with a sneer. He was nervously checking out everyone who passed; amazingly, even here on conservative LaSalle Street, no one seemed much interested in scrutinizing the Doyenne of Despair or her unwilling companion. But then, didn't Mitchell himself avoid eye contact with anyone out of the ordinary when he was on his daily rounds?

"I'm talking about my hand-modeling agent," Kitten said. "Her office is just up at the Mart, and she's got a check for me from my last job. Told her I'd pick it up in person, long as I was going to be in the neighborhood."

They reached a corner and came to a halt to accommodate a traffic light. A large woman in a chinchilla jacket stood in front of them. Kitten reached out and fingered the fur in admiration. The woman half turned, got an eyeful of Kitten's hair, then turned back. In a moment, the light changed, and they set out walking again.

Mitchell sighed in annoyance. "Look, I thought this was just going to be a quiet, intimate lunch with the two of us getting to know each other. You've already managed to turn it into a three-ring circus."

She squeezed his arm again and smiled at him brilliantly, and when he looked into her face he could see his own features reflected there, despite the mascara and blush and highlighter and plucked eyebrows. And her smile was—well, it was dazzling. Again, he forced himself to admit it: Donald made a beautiful woman. Was that what bothered him? That Donald, who looked so much like him, could look so much like Sigourney Weaver as well?

"It *will* be an intimate lunch," Kitten promised him, "just as soon as I pick up my check. Mitchell, we've just found each other after *three decades* apart. Those decades are lost, it's true, but we still have decades and decades ahead of us!'' She winked at him. ''Now, I'm not about to chase you away. But neither am I about to let *you* get skittish and bolt. This is me, this is the way I am. I could pretend to be something I'm not for you, but I wouldn't ask *you* to do that for *me*. So, come on—fair's fair.''

He managed to smile at her, but even though he couldn't see it, he knew his smile was a sickly, unconvincing thing. When the light changed to green, they continued their walk, arm-in-arm. ''So, I guess we should get to know each other,'' he said. ''Uh, let's see—you grew up exactly where?''

She snorted. ''Wilmette! Wilmette, where men are men and women are housefrau.''

''Huh,'' he said, impressed. ''I've got friends in Wilmette. Must've been a pretty respectable upbringing.''

''We were on the *poor* side of town, sweets. Side of town where you don't need to pack a lunch to cross the front lawn.''

As she said this, a mother passed them, leading a child by the hand. She didn't as much as glance at Kitten, but the child regarded her with a kind of astonished awe, and lagged behind his mother the better to stare lingeringly at her, until he got yanked to attention. *There it is!* Mitchell thought. Children didn't lie. Everybody *was* aware of Kitten. Of *course* they were aware.

''How 'bout you?'' Kitten said genially. ''Where'd you grow up?''

''*Oh,*'' he said nervously, suddenly newly fearful for his reputation, ''right here in town. Gold Coast, actually. Mom—my adoptive mother—married a millionaire. Couple of them, in fact. One right after the other, soon as they died. Kind of like the way normal people replace Labradors.''

''She spoil you?''

''Oh, hell, no. Mom's pretty self-absorbed. Barely saw her when I was growing up. One charitable cause after another during the day, one smart function after another in the evening. Mind you, she was always civil.''

Kitten looked at him pityingly. ''That is the single saddest thing I've ever heard someone say about his mother. 'Mind you, she was always civil.' Christ! I may start bawling.''

His face boiled with embarrassment. "Now, don't get the wrong idea. We have a *great* relationship now, we're the best of fr—"

"Oh, please! Mitchell!" She bumped him a little to punish him, and he brushed up against a jogger who gave him a dirty look. "Don't kid a kidder!"

"I'm not kiddi—"

"Not that you asked," she said, interrupting him and tossing back her hair, "but I'll tell you about *my* Mom and Pops." They came to a stop at another Don't Walk light.

"Repint or dah!" screamed a wild-looking man a few paces from them. He had a microphone attached to a boom box, and his delivery was eardrum-shattering. *"Lore Jesus is returnuh for Armageddah!"*

Kitten cleared her throat and spoke louder herself; it made her sound more masculine. "My *father*, okay, he's an insurance salesman, got a little office in Lincolnwood, a secretary and an accountant who've been with him since the burning of Atlanta. Theresa and Gil. Of course he remembers *their* birthdays."

"Only Christyuhs kin ennuh th' kingdum uv hevvuh," howled the wild-looking man.

Kitten shushed him, flapped a hand at him, and continued. "Now, *Mom* was a different story. Pampered me. Bought me anything I wanted, didn't she? Dolls, stuffed animals, costumes, you name it. By the time I was six, I had every queer-toddler accessory ever manufactured. A Barbie Beach House, for Christ's sake! A year's supply of wax lips! See, my older brothers, once they were old enough to walk, they were out of the house and into all kinds of shit. Me, I was fascinated by Mom—everything about her—her cooking, her jewelry, her clothes. I idolized her. So of *course* I was her favorite. She'd do anything I asked."

The wild man took a few steps forward and pointed at the small knot of people waiting for the light to change. *"You muss repint or suffuh the fires of eternuh damnashuh!"*

"So, guess what," Kitten said, louder yet, "I come out of the closet, and just guess. Pops—Pops who never looked at me twice without his mind wandering—*he's* okay about it. Hugs me, and says, 'Whatever makes you happy.' But Mom! I mean, you'd've thought she *wanted* me to turn out gay, the way she practically raised me to be a Carol Channing understudy! But, no, *she's* the one who flips out, leaps on top of a Bible, and starts humpin' away like she's makin' up for lost time."

"The Lore will punish us lahk he punish Soddum an' Gomorruh!"

"And speaking of which . . ." Her voice trailed off and she slipped away from Mitchell.

"Donald?" he said, as he watched her head over to the wild man. "Donald, wait! Don't!"

But she was not to be deterred. She stormed forward with all the fury of hell itself, and grabbed the microphone from her would-be savior.

"You gonna be save', sistuh?" he asked her, a bit quailed.

She wiggled her eyebrows, then turned to face Mitchell and the rest of the people on the sidewalk, who had slowed down to see what was happening.

She raised the microphone to her lips and said, in her breathiest voice, "In the spirit of this wonderful, life-changing encounter we're all sharing today, I'd like to sing for you my absolute *favorite* hymn."

Mitchell covered his face with his hands.

Then she took the scarf from around her neck, draped it over her head, and assumed a prayerful look; after a moment, she raised the microphone to her lips and trumpeted, *"How do you solve a prob-lem like Ma-ri-a . . . ?"*

And so on, through the entire treacly number, until she had reached a nearly orgasmic pinnacle of wonder at how one might hold a moonbeam in one's hand; then she finished on a high note and fell into a bow, losing the scarf as she did so. She snatched it quickly from the sidewalk, then solemnly crossed herself, turned off the boom box, and traipsed back to the appalled and horrified Mitchell.

A couple of teenage girls in plaid shirts and black boots applauded her. Kitten blew them a kiss and reknotted the scarf around her neck. Behind her, the wild-looking man scrambled to turn his boom box back on.

Kitten took Mitchell's arm again and led him around another corner, onto Wells Street.

"I suppose you're going to tell me that was absolutely necessary," he said, his voice ragged with shame and anger.

She cackled. "Imagine going through life only doing what's absolutely necessary!" She shook her head. "Oh, Mitchell, you've got such a *lot* to learn."

He whirled. "Right, you know everything, is that it? I'm a high-five-figures attorney at Chicago's most prestigious small law firm, and you sing in a nightclub dressed like Ivana Trump's stunt-double, but *I'm* the one who has a lot to learn."

They were now in the massive shadow of the Merchandise Mart; it loomed over them like some lesser god's attempt at a mountain. "My agent's on the tenth floor," she said, nodding her head in its direction. "Come on up and I'll show you a check that'll make your high-five-figures look not so fucking glorious. Especially since all I had to do for it was spend two-and-a-half hours holding a Chia Pet."

As they crossed the Wells Street bridge, Mitchell decided to humor her; after all, if he alienated Kitten, he could never save Donald. He swallowed his pride and his anger and said, "You know, I have to ask you—no offense or anything—but, how do you get clients to hire you? I mean, it's hard to imagine that—uh—"

She looked a little offended. "They come *looking* for me, dear," she said. "I *turn down* work."

"But—your nails. They're real, aren't they?"

She held them up for display. "Sweet of you to notice! Yes, they are. But what's that got to do with—" She stopped short, gasped, and looked at him with bemused enlightenment. "Mitchell! You don't really think I model these beauties as *men's* hands!"

The abashed look on his face was all the answer she needed. She laughed all the way across the remainder of the bridge; settled into giggles in the Merchandise Mart elevator; and was wiping the last of her mirth from her eyes as she led Mitchell into the offices of the Jennifer Jerrold Talent Agency.

chapter 12

The receptionist announced them, and moments later they were approached by a fiftysomething woman with a long, braided ponytail, dressed all in black. She looked uncannily like a cross between Beatrice Arthur and Zorro.

"Kitten, darling!" she exclaimed. "A delight, as ever! You look *radiant*. That wig—it's like nothing I've seen since the thirty-nine World's Fair."

"You were *not* old enough to see the thirty-nine World's Fair," Kitten said as she submitted to being kissed on the cheek.

"But I *was*," the woman insisted. "Lost my virginity there, as a matter of fact!"

Even Kitten looked shocked. "But you can't have been more than a child!"

"Well, yes," she said. "Didn't say I lost it to a *man*, did I?" She turned to Mitchell and said, in a stage-whisper, "Goddamn saddle on that carousel!"

Mitchell went white as pristine ivory.

Kitten punched him lightly on the shoulder. "Mitch, don't

let Jennifer shock you, it only encourages her. Jennifer, this is my long-lost twin brother, Mitchell. Mitchell, this is Jennifer Jerrold, Chicago's premier talent agent."

Jennifer extended a taloned hand to enclose one of Mitchell's. As she shook it, she regarded him with a raised eyebrow. "Long-lost twin, eh? Well, there's definitely a resemblance."

"Oh, come on, Jen, we're *identical*," protested Kitten.

Mitchell tugged his hand from her grasp and said, "You— you don't seem very surprised about me."

Jennifer Jerrold rubbed his shoulder consolingly. "*This* one," she said, nodding in Kitten's direction, "has lost the capacity to surprise me. She could show up with six ex-husbands and I wouldn't bat an eye."

"Bet *they* would," said Mitchell, and he was a little startled when both Kitten and Jennifer let out hoots of appreciative laughter.

"Anyway," said Jennifer a moment later, as she led them farther into the office, "come on in and make yourselves comfortable. I'll go fetch that journalist gal; been waiting a good ten minutes." She turned to a robust-looking woman at a nearby desk and said, "Natalie, the conference room free?"

"You know it is, Jennifer."

"*What* 'journalist gal'?" Mitchell whispered to Kitten.

Jennifer turned and waved them through a door to their right. "Go ahead and wait in there. I'll get Little Miss Atmosphere or whatever her name is."

"What's going on here?" Mitchell demanded as Kitten dragged him into a standard-issue, white-walled conference room, with an oak table, a three-quarter-inch VCR, a monitor, a reel-to-reel tape deck, and a fairly impressive view of the river. From here, it looked as though there was a body floating in the water.

Kitten threw her purse on the table and shrugged her shoulders. "I forgot all about it. When I said I'd be coming in for my check, Jennifer asked if I'd mind also talking to a reporter for a couple of minutes. You don't mind, do you?"

"Sit here for an *interview*?" Mitchell hissed, not wanting to be heard losing his temper. "This was supposed to be a *private lunch*, for God's sake, not a goddamn *talk* show."

"What can I say?" she replied, taking out her compact and checking her lipstick. "So sue me for wanting a little publicity. So have me put to death for trying to make a living."

"You know very well that's not the issue," raged Mitchell. "And who the hell is 'Little Miss Atmosphere,' anyway?"

Just then, a tall woman strode into the conference room and announced, "I'm Skye Armitage, *OUTlandish Monthly*. You must be the Doyenne of Despair!" She thrust her hand at Kitten, who shook it with equal vigor. Skye had very short, bleach-blond hair, and was wearing an astonishing orange outfit that looked like one of the spacesuits from *2001*.

Kitten said, "This is my brother, my *identical twin* brother, Mitchell Sayer. You don't mind if he sits in, do you?"

Mitchell felt a flurry of alarm as Little Miss Atmosphere gave him the once-over. "Not at all," Skye said. "Love it, actually. Add a whole new angle to the story." She sat down, flipped open her notebook, and started digging through her pockets for a pen.

"Listen," said Mitchell, "I don't really want to be part of thi—"

"Oh, good," boomed the voice of Jennifer Jerrold; Mitchell turned and saw her framed in the doorway. "You've all met, then? Everything's all right?"

"Fine, Miz Jerrold," said Skye Armitage. "And listen, thanks for okaying this interview. Some agents, you know, might get nervous about their biggest-billing female hand model being revealed as a male."

Jennifer scoffed. "The only bad publicity is *no* publicity," she said. "You can write that she's a Himalayan yak, for all I care. Just spell her name right." And then she ducked out.

"Okay," said Skye chirpily. "Ready to get started?"

Mitchell got up. "Listen, I really think I'd be better off waiting outsi—"

"Is that a body in the river?" blurted Kitten, interrupting him.

Skye leapt to her feet. "Where?"

They gathered at the window. "Right down there," said Kitten. "By that piling. The one second-closest to Orleans Street."

"Oh, my God," said Skye. "It is. It's a *body*."

"Look, there are people on the bridge now." Kitten pointed to a cluster of pedestrians on the Orleans Street bridge. They were craning their necks over the place where the bloated remains of what appeared to be an elderly man bobbed peacefully in the murky green.

Suddenly Skye turned to Mitchell and said, "So, how does it feel to be the identical twin of a knockout drag queen?"

Mitchell was taken completely off guard; he would gladly have traded places with the corpse in the river. "Uh—fine," he said.

She scribbled a note. "Ever tried drag yourself?"

He felt the room go quite out of focus for a moment.

"Mitchell and I are *long-lost* twins," said Kitten, coming to his rescue. "We had very different upbringings. It's a tragic story, really. The whole orphaned-as-infants thing, each adopted by a different family. We've only just reconnected."

A Chicago Police boat appeared on the river and started circling the body. The crowd on the bridge had gotten bigger.

Skye Armitage jotted something else in her notebook, but made no move to leave the window. "That's fascinating," she said. "Tell me more."

Kitten took out a cigarette and lit it, then leaned dramatically against the window jamb and let loose a stream of smoke. "Well, it's a story filled with irony, Skye. Our parents were Dutch Reform missionaries, you see—Mitchell, hon, you'll be a love and jump in if I start getting any of this wrong, won't you?—and they actually met when they were on duty in central Africa. They were deeply religious people, but passion overcame them, and dear Mum got preggers in short order. So they were both drummed out of the missionary corps, although it was late in her pregnancy that they were discovered, because Mom had taken to wearing the traditional blanket-dresses of the Kalahari tribe to disguise her condition. Got away with it for seven and a half months, till Dad let the cat out of the bag one night when he was in his cups; asked if the chieftain of the tribe would mind being a namesake to his son-to-be."

"Your father wanted to give you an African name?" Skye asked, scribbling madly.

"Well, no," Kitten continued, stubbing out the cigarette on the chrome windowsill. "The chieftain's name was Douglas. He was a convert, after all."

"Ah," said Skye, making a note of this.

Mitchell had heard just about enough. "I really can't let this pass," he said, "it's a total fabrication, a complete—"

"Oh, that's *right*," said Kitten, snapping her fingers. "*Dennis*, not Douglas. Thank you, Mitchell, dove. Anyway, Mum and Popsy were found out, and sent packing. And the stress of it must've got to Mum, because she went into labor right on the dock, and as it turns out Mitchell and I were both born aboard ship, not one mile off the Madagascar coast. Fortunately, the ship's captain had married them twenty minutes earlier, saving Mitchell and me from the taint of bastardy."

"Fascinating," said Skye, although it wasn't clear whether she meant Kitten's story, or the crane the police boat was now positioning above the floating corpse.

"So, you see," said Kitten, sitting on the sill now and drawing her legs up under her arms, "Mitchell and I weren't even American citizens until we were adopted. Which wasn't long after we arrived in the States, because during the voyage both our parents died—Popsy of cholera, Mum of scarlet fever."

Skye shook her head at the sadness of this as she scribbled away. "Didn't the ship have a doctor?" she asked.

"Yes, but *he'd* died of diphtheria a week before that."

Mitchell couldn't believe this orange woman was actually buying Kitten's story. He made a move to protest anew, but Kitten cut him off with, "Of course, we were too young to remember all this, but I have it on the very best authority."

"I'm sure you do," said Skye, wrapping up a note and smiling.

The crane had hooked onto the corpse; the police were trying to haul it out of the water without much luck. Mitchell saw the boat actually tilt under its weight.

"So then we two infants were sent to Chicago, where my father had a sister, Eugenie, our last living relative. But wouldn't you know, by the time we got here, *she* was dead, too—killed by an insanely jealous female lover named Smitty. That's how Mitchell and I ended up in an orphanage. From there, Mitchell was adopted by a very high-toned couple—a KLM Airlines executive and an ex-princess of Greece. He grew up surrounded by riches and lovely things. Waterford crystal. Henry Moore sculptures. German pool boys."

"Now, wait jus—"

"I, on the other hand, was adopted by a stevedore named Slim and his wife Polly, a woman devoted to soap-operas and hypochondria. My mother had more phantom pregnancies than Doris Osmond had real ones. I grew up surrounded by despair, squalor, and defeat. I had to *invent* the beauty in my life, Skye; and to keep it, I had to *become* it."

Skye was nodding appreciatively as she jotted this down. The police crane had managed to get the corpse out of the water, and was busy maneuvering it onto the boat. The Orleans Street bridge was now so burdened with onlookers that Mitchell thought it might give way.

"So tell me, then," Skye said, as she took a pause from writing to crack her knuckles and survey the operations on the river, "what led you to become such an *out* drag queen? Because that's what's really going to interest our readers—that instead of staying hidden in the ghetto, you're actually out there making a success of yourself in the mainstream world, without compromising your drag identity one bit. There's something quite heroic about that."

Kitten put a hand on her breast. "Why, thank you—how sweet! I'm very flattered. Well, there's a story there, too."

"I bet there is," said Mitchell under his breath. The corpse was safely aboard the police boat now, so he went to the far end of the conference table and sat down.

Kitten looked wistfully into the distance and said, "I was invited to perform at an AIDS benefit party, and afterwards, when I was backstage, I was visited by a very famous actress who became my benefactor."

"And who might that be?" asked Skye, scribbling.

"Alas, it would embarrass her if I were to tell you; let's just say, two Oscars, violet eyes, Montgomery Clift, and leave it at that."

"*Ah,*" said Skye knowingly.

"She complimented me on my act; then we got down to a little girl talk and became fast friends. And when she noticed my hands, she said they were the most beautiful she'd ever seen." Here Kitten held up the objects under discussion for Skye to admire. "She said, 'You could make a fortune with those hands.' And then she paused and added, 'In fact, I think you should.' So she helped me find my first few jobs; after which I met dear Jennifer, and the rest is history."

Skye put down her pen and looked in admiration at Kitten. "Wow," she said in a low voice.

"Yes, wow is, I think, an applicable word."

"So, you don't run into any, you know, homophobia or anything?" She took a glance out the window, where the retreating police boat was leaving a foamy wake. The crowd of onlookers was dispersing.

"Of *course* I run into homophobia. But I get the job done, Skye. In the end, people respect that." She shrugged and shook her wig a little. "And, of course, Jennifer is usually upfront with people who call and ask for me. So the real hatemongers have a chance to take a pass."

Skye nodded sagely, then picked up her pen and wrote this down. Then she smiled, cracked her knuckles, and said, "Okay. I'm happy. Anything you care to add?"

"Honey, you don't have *time* for everything *I'd* care to add."

Skye laughed, then stuck her pen behind her ear and popped the cap off her Nikon. "Okay if I take a shot to go along with the article?"

Kitten sat up again, suddenly alert, and said, "I think that would be perfectly glorious. Just give me a sec." She snatched her compact from her purse, flicked it open, and gave herself the once-over in its tiny mirror.

Skye was on her feet now, looking through her camera lens at Kitten. "Actually," she said, "if I could ask you to move away from the window—get the light on you instead of behind you —that'd be great."

"You're the *artiste*," said Kitten with a wink. She slipped off the window sill, scooted around the conference table, and posed against the wall about a foot from where Mitchell was seated.

Skye fiddled with her f-stop for a moment. "Okay," she said. "Ready when you are."

Kitten got a positively wicked glint in her eyes. "Just one more second," she said; and then, without warning, she leapt into Mitchell's lap. He spat out a lungful of air, and hadn't quite recovered his breath when Kitten flung one leg and both arms into the air and cried, *"Shoot!"*

Skye shot.

chapter 13

In the elevator, Kitten stuffed her check from Jennifer Jerrold into her purse while Mitchell called her cheap, petty, mean-spirited, and pathetic.

As they crossed the Merchandise Mart lobby, he called her a grandstander, a menace, a liar, and a fake.

While Kitten hailed a cab at the east end of the Mart, he called her vain, silly, dangerous, and pathetic.

"You already said pathetic, dear," she noted, just as a cab pulled up to admit them.

"It bears repeating," he said, opening the door for her. "Doesn't it bother you, to lie like that? To just out-and-out *lie?*"

"Not at all," she cooed as she slid in and fastened her seatbelt. "It feels wonderfully *theatrical*, Mitchell. Nothing's quite so dull as the truth. Aside from which, Skye wasn't even interested in the truth. She wanted the image. She probably didn't believe a word I said, but that wasn't the point, and she knew it."

"You're crazy," he declared as he got in and slammed shut the door. "A lie is a lie."

She cocked her head at him. "Now, go on and tell me you never make things up."

"Never. When I came out ten years ago, I swore I'd always tell the truth, from then on. No exceptions. No matter what."

They glared at each other for a few pounding heartbeats; then Mitchell, realizing that the cab wasn't moving, whirled and snapped, "Move on, driver!"

"Sure, sure," said the laconic, yellow-bearded man, from beneath a baseball cap bearing the Cocoa Puffs logo. "You wanna give me an address or somethin'?"

"*Darn* it," muttered Mitchell. "Is your meter running?" Seeing that it was, he turned to Kitten. "I just don't know where to take you. I can't be *seen* with you, that's plain. Listen, why don't we just postpone this, do it another d—"

"Excuse me!" cried someone through the open window. "I'm desperate—do you mind sharing this cab?"

Mitchell whirled, an angry retort ready on his lips, then found himself face to face with a handsome, sandy-haired man in a business suit—a man, moreover, who had under his right eye a large birthmark almost exactly the shape of Oklahoma.

"Hey," Mitchell said, the birthmark jogging his memory. "You're—aren't you—"

"Mitch?" the man blurted. "Mitchell Sayer?"

Recollection washed over Mitchell. "Zack Crespin? It can't be Zack Crespin!"

"Hell if it ain't, brother Mu!" Zack Crespin stuck his hand through the window and gave Mitchell's a good shake. "How you been doin'?"

"Great—great! You?"

"Fantastic." An awkward pause ensued while Zack retrieved his arm through the window. "Listen, buddy, you don't mind sharing a cab with an old frat brother, do you?"

"Course not!" said Mitchell giddily. Then, glimpsing the grinning Kitten from the corner of his eye, he said, "I mean—uh—I can't actually afford the time, and uh—"

"Don't be silly, Mitchell," Kitten said. "Give the guy a break!"

"Thanks," said Zack, and without further ado he flung open the door and slid in, squeezing Mitchell between him and Kitten. He then leaned over to the driver and said, "Chestnut and St. Claire, please." The cabbie nodded, shifted into drive, and was off.

Zack mopped his forehead with a handkerchief from his front pocket; Oklahoma was glowing bright purple, as Mitchell now remembered it did in times of stress. Zack said, "You're a lifesaver, Mitch. Hope I'm not taking you out of your way. I'm twelve minutes late for a goddamn lunch meeting. Couldn't tear myself away from the river. You see the corpse? Looked like a Macy's Thanksgiving balloon. Nearly tipped over the police boat when they tried to pick it up! Must've been in the water for *days*. I love shit like that. Heard it's a mob-related killing, but that's not confirmed." He seemed suddenly to notice Kitten. He smiled, nudged Mitchell, and said, "So who's the little lady?"

Mitchell turned to Kitten, as if seeing her for the first time himself. "Who, her? Oh. Uh. Well. That's easy. She's—she's my secretary. Gloria. Kitten, I mean. My secretary, Kitten." He laughed a shrill, lunatic laugh, and was immediately mortified by his behavior.

Zack leaned across Mitchell's lap and extended his hand. "Pleased to make your acquaintance, Kitten. Zack Crespin. Thanks for letting me share your cab."

"Don't be silly, Mr. Crespin," said Kitten coquettishly. "It's our pleasure, isn't it, Mitchell?"

"You really don't mind?" Zack asked Mitchell.

He cackled nervously and said, " 'Course not."

Kitten leaned across Mitchell's left leg and said, "Believe him, Mr. Crespin. Mitchell always tells the truth. No exceptions. No matter what."

Mitchell broke into a sudden and profuse sweat.

"Call me Zack, I insist. And I hope I'm permitted to call you Kitten." Zack grinned again, then turned to Mitchell and said, "So, Mitch! What're you up to these days, pal?" He slapped Mitchell's thigh amiably. "As I recall, you were majoring in animal husbandry."

"Ani—*animal husbandry?*" Kitten shrieked. She gave Mitchell a look of delighted amazement, doubling the rate of his sweat flow.

"Yeah," Zack said. "Expected to hear old Mitch was off somewhere developing new methods to birth calves or something, not cruising around the Loop in an Armani suit."

"Hugo Boss," muttered Mitchell. Then he turned to Kitten and said meekly, "It was a reaction to my parents, that's all. They wanted me to be a lawyer, so I went as far in the opposite direction as I could. Just to get their goat. I was a little melodramatic in college."

"Funny, so was I," said Kitten gaily.

In an agony of embarrassment and anxiety, Mitchell turned back to Zack and said, "Actually, I went on to law school and got my J.D. I'm an associate at Ingersoll, Ebersole and Trilby. Maybe you've heard of us."

"Nah. Sorry." Zack was staring right past Mitchell, at Kitten.

Mitchell hated to speculate on what Zack must be thinking; he found it impossible to read his old friend's face. "So, how about you?" he said, his voice colorless.

"Banking," said Zack. "Brand manager for a cash-transfer product." He was still staring intently at Kitten, who, Mitchell noticed, was pretending to be oblivious to this; but by the way she balanced her chin on her delicately curved hand and prettily surveyed the sights as they whizzed past, Mitchell knew— call it a twin's intuition—that she was posing for the benefit of Zack Crespin.

"Sounds interesting," Mitchell lied.

The cabbie quarter-turned his head and said, "Which corner?"

Zack seemed to snap out of a trance. He ducked his head and peered through the windshield at the approaching intersection. "Up at the light is fine," he said, fumbling with his wallet. He yanked a ten from its fold and said, "Here, Mitch, this ought to cover my end."

"*More* than cover it," said Mitchell, refusing to take the bill. "We've only driven eight blocks."

"I know, I know," said Zack, and he stuffed the bill in Mitchell's breast pocket. "But you let me shanghai your cab and your secretary, so I insist." By this time, the cab had rolled to the curb and stopped. "In fact, I'd like to continue repaying you with a couple of drinks tonight, if you're free. You know, rehash the old frat-house life. Catch up on what's new."

Mitchell was taken aback. He and Zack had never really been close during their Mu years. In fact, Mitchell had spent most of his time pining unrequitedly for the handsome upper-classman. "Well, uh—I guess that'd be great. Thanks."

"And, hey, Kitten," Zack added, talking past Mitchell, "why don't you tag along? If your boss here doesn't mind. Might be fun."

Kitten turned her head and, her lips barely parted, whispered, "Love to."

Mitchell could feel sweat begin pooling in his ears. "Now, wait a minute," he said. "Haven't you got a lot of *work* to do at the *office*, Kitten?" He quickly nudged her ribcage.

"Finished it," she said airily, ignoring the nudge and examining her fingernails.

"Even the *big* case file I put on your desk *just before lunch*?" He nudged her again, twice.

"Mm-hmm," she said, pushing back a cuticle. "Piece of cake."

"It's settled, then!" Zack said with a broad smile as he jumped out of the cab. "Say, Dreamweaver's, six o'clock?"

"I don't know where that is."

"I do," Kitten said delightedly.

"Actually, I'm not sure I can make it," Mitchell tried in vain.

Kitten nearly fell across his lap. "*I* can!" she trilled, waving at Zack.

He chuckled. "Well, hey, then! Shame if you can't make

it, Mitch, but them's the breaks. Kitten and I'll raise a glass in your honor.'' He gave a mock salute, then slammed shut the door.

The cabbie turned again and said, ''You folks goin' on somewhere?''

''Yes, yes,'' said Mitchell testily. ''Adams and State, please.'' Then, as the cab pulled into traffic, he said to Kitten in a stage whisper, ''You are *not* going to meet Zack for drinks.''

She crossed her arms and legs in one fluid motion. ''Am I not, then?''

''No. For God's sake! The guy was *flirting* with you. He doesn't know what he's getting himself into!''

''And what, exactly, *is* he getting himself into?'' She arched one eyebrow menacingly and awaited a reply.

Mitchell turned crimson, but dared himself to say it. ''Don't be stupid! You're—not a *woman*.''

He saw the Cocoa Puffs logo disappear from the rearview mirror, to be replaced for a split second by a pair of astonished eyes.

''I may not be a woman, Mitchell, but that doesn't mean I'm not a lady. And a lady is allowed to accept a gentleman's invitation without interference from any buttinsky-come-lately twin, thank you very much. On the subject of which, please remember we have no record of which of us came barreling through the birth canal first, so I'll thank you to stop acting like an older brother.''

Mitchell started kneading his forehead with his fingers. ''You're trying to drive me crazy, aren't you? Like Simon said you would. Just because you can. My *God*, Donald! This guy's my frat brother. Word of this gets out, I'll—I'll—''

''You'll what? Be unable to look your old Greek buddies in the face? This is not a line of argument likely to win me over, Mitchell, especially since I spent my own college years trying to avoid being beaten up by frat rats. And in any case, since you oh-so-courageously introduced me as your goddamn *secretary*, I don't see that there's any way for them to connect us beyond th—''

"That was a slip of the tongue!" he howled. "I panicked! So sue me!"

Kitten's nostrils flared. "You're getting hysterical. I don't have to take this." She clutched her purse and leaned forward. "Driver, let me out here, please."

The cabbie's eyes, wide as golf balls, reappeared in the rearview mirror. "You got it," he said, and he pulled over with an alarming lurch.

Kitten flung open the door and stuck both legs outside the cab. Just before she followed through with a complete exit, she turned and said, "Thanks for a memorable lunch, Mitchell. Let's do it again real soon. Say, June thirty-first?"

"There is no June thirty-first."

A bitter grin. "Then it's a date!" She waggled her fingers at him. "Toodles!"

She sprang out and slammed the door so hard, Mitchell's ears actually rang for a second. The cabbie wasted no time in pulling quickly away. Mitchell sat in the back, hands on the vinyl seat, reeling.

After a moment, he could hear his stomach grumbling. What a disastrous lunch hour—and not even lunch to show for it! He'd have to grab something at the deli on the corner and take it back to his desk. He'd never been there before. Maybe they had a simple croissant he could eat, or a fruit salad. He'd be able to think through this whole sorry farce if he only had something in his stomach.

" 'Scuse me for askin'," said the cabbie, interrupting his train of thought. "But—uh—was that person what just got out a guy or a chick?"

Mitchell nodded his head gravely. "Yes," he said.

chapter

14

Mitchell had a time of it at the deli. While customers and clerk alike waited with graceless impatience, he hemmed and hawed over the array of artery-clogging choices presented him, eventually settling on a chicken salad as the lesser of available evils. But when he got it back to his desk, spread wax paper over his blotter, and unwrapped the salad for consumption, he took one look at its lumpy whiteness and gave up. *I can't eat this*, he told himself glumly. And so he rewrapped it in its original wax paper, taped it up, and took it to the kitchen to dispose of.

On his way back to his office, Bereneesha stopped him. "Just got a call from reception," she said. "Your sister's on her way back t' see you."

"She most certainly is not," Mitchell snapped. "Tell her I'm out." The sheer *nerve* of Donald!

Bereneesha looked at him oddly. "Family spat or somethin'?"

He scowled at her and said, "Just tell her I'm out. Under

no circumstances is she to be permitted to see me." Then, just before he disappeared behind his door, his anger and pride made him feel rather daring, and he turned and said, "By the way, that creature is *not* my sister."

Bereneesha looked at him as though his head had just sprouted orchids.

He slipped into his office, shut the door, and pressed his ear to it, so that he might eavesdrop on the exchange that would ensue.

Shortly, he heard a muffled "Hello, Bereneesha."

"Wait a minute, there," Bereneesha called out, "he ain't in!"

"Don't be ridiculous, his door's closed. He's obviously behind it."

Bereneesha said something Mitchell couldn't make out.

"What a lot of nonsense," was the reply. "He really said that? I'm going in."

The doorknob turned and Mitchell jumped out of the way, but not soon enough to avoid being clipped in the temple as the door leapt from its frame. And there, in the doorway, stood his sister, Paula, her eyes spattered with a mixture of mascara and tears.

"Mitchell," she said. "Are you all right?"

He was holding his head where he'd been hit. "Paula!" he gasped in surprise. "I thought you—were—um—am I bleeding?" He tentatively displayed his wounded temple to her.

"Not yet you aren't." She stepped in and shut the door behind her. "What's this about you telling Bereneesha I'm not your sister?"

He sighed, went back to his desk, and sat down. "I didn't mean it, Paula. I wasn't talking about you."

Her tear-stained eyes were fiery. And with her sculpted, anthracite hair, tailored-to-kill Anne Klein suit, and no-bullshit black heels, she looked somehow gladiatorial. Mitchell in fact knew not to cross her. She had a hair-trigger temper and a voice that could shatter Teflon.

"Who were you talking about, then?" she snarled. "Veronica? There's only the two of us."

He drew in a breath. "Well, not really. It's not as simple as that."

She threw her purse onto his desk as though it were a gauntlet. "Come on, Mitch. So you're adopted. So we're not actually blood relations. That doesn't mean we're not brother and sister. Don't all the times I vomited on you count for anything?"

He smiled. "They count for something, but not in your favor."

She sat, and crossed her legs briskly. "Let's just not get all flaky, all right? Not now, when I need you most." There was a catch in her throat.

"What's the matter?" he asked, becoming aware for the first time that she was deeply upset. He leaned over the desk and opened his silver cigarette box.

She shook her head and said, "No thanks. Mitch, I just talked to Max Chafner. He said he's had no luck talking Mother out of this suicidal scheme of hers."

He slumped into his chair. So *that* was it. Mitchell had once seen a National Geographic TV special that revealed that the average shrew spent ninety-five percent of its life hunting for food. Change "food" to "money" and the description would do nicely for Paula. She'd come close to the altar with two millionaires already, but her predatory manner had sent them scampering away at the eleventh hour; and now her mother, too, was gently tugging her fortune from Paula's desperate grasp. No wonder she was frantic.

"I know, I know," Mitchell said to her now. "I spoke with Max myself two days ago. But honestly, Paula, calling Mother's behavior 'suicidal' is a bit much."

"She's giving the family estate to some lunatic religion! Of *course* it's suicidal. How can she protect herself with no money? How can she pay for health insurance? What if she gets sick? What if her breast implants rupture or something?"

He cocked his head at her. "Bit of a stretch, Paula."

She sighed and looked out the window. "I've changed my mind. I will take a cigarette."

As she lit up and took her first few puffs, Mitchell tried to determine how to handle her. It was difficult, on an empty stomach. "Listen, Paula," he said. "I'll have one more go at her myself. Okay? But let's be honest with each other here. You're only alarmed by this because Mother is divesting herself of what you perceive to be her legacy to us. Isn't that so?"

She shot a pellet of smoke his way. "I suppose."

"Well, then."

"There's nothing wrong with that, you know."

"I didn't say there was. I mean, the way we were reared—well, I suppose we've a right to have certain expectations. If Mother had intended us to clip coupons or join discount shopping clubs, she should have prepared us earlier in life."

"Absolutely." She angrily tapped her ashes into Mitchell's brass ashtray. "I'm not about to get a job as some horrible assistant photo editor or suburban wedding planner at this stage in my life. My God! I'm twenty-three! You can't teach an old—uh, person—new tricks."

"As I said, I'll try. Call Veronica and let her know I'm working on it."

"I will. She's worried sick. Imagine being saddled in San Francisco with a philandering husband while *this* is going on at home! Says she feels like she's getting it from both ends."

"Larry's still straying, is he?"

She rolled her eyes. "With anything that draws breath, apparently. Veronica says all their friends have taken to calling him 'the Mountie.'" She sniffed up a little giggle. Now that Mitchell had reassured her he'd take personal action, she calmed down somewhat. They sat in silence for a moment, a bit exhausted by the now dissipated emotional cloudburst.

"So," Paula said at last. "What's new in your life? In one of her more lucid moments, Mother said you were on the trail of some mysterious twin. It all sounds so exciting. Find him yet?"

Something lodged in his throat for a moment; when he

could again speak, he was surprised to hear himself say, "No."

"Well, when you do, bring him 'round! I'm kind of intrigued." She snuffed out her cigarette. "Be like having another brother. Although," she said, rising from her chair and coming around to him, "the one I have couldn't be sweeter."

He tilted his head so she could kiss him; then she said, "Don't bother showing me out. I'll call you later." She opened the door and, just before stepping through it, she looked back and said in a low voice, "Think about having that Bereneesha fired, won't you? I don't like her presumption."

Then she smiled brilliantly and took her leave.

chapter 15

Kitten wasn't quite certain where she was. She'd jumped out of the cab in an unfamiliar area of the Loop and stormed several blocks blinded by anger. Mitchell's arrogance was beyond belief. Who the flying, farting fuck did he think he *was?*

She'd bulldozed her way down three whole blocks, fists balled at her side, before she could bring her breathing under control. Only to have it sent into snorts and snarls again by the sight of a store window in which a pair of white, vinyl hip boots stood proudly inviting purchase. White, vinyl hip boots almost exactly like those worn by Regina Upright.

Regina herself was not of course anywhere near, but Kitten felt as if she'd been tossed from one tormentor into the scalding presence of another. It only doubled her dudgeon. She reminded herself that she'd taken Regina under her wing and ushered her into the sisterhood of the Tam-Tam, and been so devoted a friend to her that all her other friends had dropped away, like candy wrappers idly tossed from the window of a car.

Well, she was paying for it now, wasn't she? The little bitch had proven herself a real Eve Harrington, and there was no one Kitten could turn to for help or understanding who wasn't just dying to say, "Serves you right."

In her innocence, she'd thought that Mitchell might fill the gap Regina had left; but that had been wishful thinking. She should've known from her first sight of him that, twin or no, he was a self-righteous prig—certainly not someone with whom she could spend long hours on the telephone, telling secrets to. They might have shared a placenta, but it was clear they could share nothing else.

Only the glimmer of hope provided by Mr. Zack Crespin lit her darkened mood. He'd been about as obvious as a hound dog with that "Oh-and-bring-Kitten" business in the cab. It had been a long time since she'd had that effect on a man, but now that she had, she felt glamorous and powerful, and woe betide her enemies for they would yet see their day of reckoning. Regina would pay. Gordy would pay. Mitchell would pay. The great goddess Kaboodle would yet hold sway over the destinies of mere mendacious mortals.

It was in this terrible, awesome state of mind that she turned a corner and saw coming her way the man who had wolf whistled her in the Tam-Tam Club just a few nights past—the ugly little man with the alien-life-form hairpiece. It pleased Kitten that she should be given so perfect an opportunity to display her power of sexual thrall. The man had, after all, already demonstrated his interest. A flick of her head, a coy lifting of her heel in apparent demureness, and he would be hers.

Or perhaps not. The man regarded her not with lust, but with panic. Recognition emptied his face of color; his inability to acknowledge her restored it. She saw then that he was accompanied by another man, a taller, silver-haired, straight-backed sort, the kind who wore moral rectitude like collar stays. Kitten's victim looked at her and, almost imperceptibly, shook his head. Then he turned, red-faced and jovial, and began relating a boisterous story to his colleague.

Poor soul; sad, doomed soul. This was exactly the wrong moment to try anything like that on Miss Kitten Kaboodle. Of rejection and dismissal she had had quite enough, thank you. The world—the rude, insolent, traitorous world—must realize that it belonged to her. For a brief moment, she considered running up to her victim and throwing her arms around him; but no. His punishment must be excruciating; it must *linger*.

She decided to follow him.

It wasn't quite a block before he realized Kitten was on his heels. Then his scarlet face deepened to the exact shade of blood. He began talking faster and faster, as if garrulousness would help him blot her from the scene—crowd her out with words.

His colleague was looking at him increasingly oddly, and at one point stopped short and said, "You all right, Frank?" To which Kitten's victim laughed rather too loudly, and rather too long, in reply.

"Sure, sure, sure," he said, nodding his head. "Just feeling full of pep, that's all. Let's hurry back to the office so I can put it to good use." And he placed his hand on his colleague's back and pressed him into motion again—with a fleeting and, Kitten thought, dreadful look back at his pursuer.

Kitten, for her part, was the picture of nonchalance. She sashayed behind them, managing to keep pace while admiring the store window displays, basking her face in the glorious sunlight, and trailing her fingers along the smooth marble facades of the office buildings. No one would have guessed that she was in hot pursuit of the stumbling, stammering, yammering businessman a few paces ahead.

Frank and his colleague at last entered a building near Madison Street. Kitten, of course, entered it as well. When Frank half-turned and saw her patiently waiting for the elevator with them, he actually emitted a moan.

The elevator arrived. Clever Frank ushered his colleague into it, then stood right in the door, his back to the lobby, talking and laughing, as though oblivious to Kitten's desire to enter the car as well. His colleague was about to point this out to him when the doors slid shut and the elevator began its ascent.

Kitten seethed. She'd merely intended to ride up to Frank's

floor with him, then quietly ride back down; that would have been punishment enough. He'd have got the message. But now he'd thwarted her plan, and must pay a greater price.

She watched the digital monitor above the elevator as it flashed the numbers of the floors it passed, until it stopped at 14. She then extended one of her lovely, tailored fingernails and pressed the up button.

By the time the next elevator arrived at the lobby, there were a few more persons waiting to ride with Kitten. All of them got off on lower floors, so Kitten could see, to her delight, that each time the elevator door opened, it did so onto a reception-ist's desk. Clearly, this was one of those prestigious buildings in which each floor was occupied by a single, sprawling company.

At the fourteenth floor, she stepped off the elevator and lo, there was the expected receptionist—a thirtysomething woman with close-cropped hair, tight lips, and narrowed, evil eyes. Kitten had to stop herself from squealing with delight. Never had she seen anyone more likely to be an office gossip.

She approached, and said, in a deliberately huskier voice than usual, "Good afternoon. Is Frank in?"

The receptionist was regarding her with a perfect mixture of horror and thrilled fascination. "He just came back from lunch," she said. "Let me see if he's at his desk yet." She picked up the intercom phone.

Kitten reached out and stayed the receptionist's hand. "No, no, don't bother," she said. "Just tell him that—that *you-know-who* thanks him for a very, very memorable night." And then she winked, as if to supply an exclamation point.

She then retreated to the elevator, which took a very long time to return—giving Frank's coworkers plenty of time to pass the reception area and get a good look at her. Which virtually ensured that they'd all come running back to the receptionist later to ask, *Who was that?*

And the receptionist would be certain to tell them.

The goddess, having exercised divine retribution, rode the elevator back to the ground, then went to her bank to deposit her check.

chapter 16

Mitchell had Bereneesha look up the address of Dream-weaver's, and at six-fifteen he was there. It was a dim-lit place tucked into one of the more tuckable corners in Bucktown, and though the name of the place was painted on the window, the vinyl awning above the door still read LOU'S DRINKS 'N' DARTS. Inside, Mitchell noted the zebra-pattern vinyl tables, the neon jukebox blaring Melanie's "Candles in the Rain," and the seven-foot grandfather clock displaying the wrong time. On the door to the ladies' room hung an ancient film-studio portrait of Magda Gabor; on the door to the men's room, a still of Bruce Lee as Kato from the old *Green Hornet* series. The bartender was a girl who looked about twelve, wearing white lipstick and a partially devoured edible choker. Next to the cash register were three dusty volumes beneath a heaping ashtray: Camus's *The Myth of Sisyphus*, Schopenhauer's *Complete Works, Vol. II*, and *Lovely Me: The Life of Jacqueline Susann*. The tables were filled with very young persons in plaid shirts and sandals. Two of them were openly smoking marijuana. Many were of indeterminate sex; Mitchell later figured out he could tell which were men by the paisley kerchiefs they wore wrapped around their heads. He couldn't decide if this place was straight or gay, camp or hip, or something else he didn't yet know the name of. Later he would ask Simon, who would tell him, "It's just Bucktown, Mitch. Get with the program."

He found Zack and Kitten holed up in one of the more private corners, propped atop stools (Zack's suitcoat was draped over his) and cooing at each other over glasses of white wine. At the sight of Mitchell, Zack's face slipped for a split second, then snapped back to toothsome smiliness. Kitten, for her part, looked directly at him, flicked a cigarette ash his way, and said, "Sorry, no room."

Zack got up and shook his hand. "Mitch, buddy!" he said amiably. "What a surprise! Thought you couldn't make it!" He raised his arm and caught the bartender's eye. "What'll you have?"

"Oh," said Kitten, "I bet Mitch'd *love* a mai tai."

"One mai tai!" Zack called out.

"What?" Mitchell asked, confused. He'd been looking for a clean place on the floor for his briefcase, and was a beat or two behind. "What did you order me?"

Kitten brushed a stray hair behind her ear and said, "Well, I didn't think it'd work if I ordered you out, so I ordered you a mai tai."

Mitchell frowned at her and gave up his search. He borrowed a stool from a neighboring table and joined Zack and Kitten, and just kept his briefcase clutched between his knees.

Zack reseated himself, and after a few minutes of small talk said, "So, Mitch, guess you were havin' a little fun at my expense today, huh?"

Mitchell shot a look at Kitten, then said, "Wh—what do you mean?"

"Passing off Kitten here as your secretary. She just told me she's no such thing. 'Course, I *was* kind of curious how she could type with these nails." Here he took Kitten's fingers in his hand and lifted them gently.

Mitchell's face turned ashen.

Zack appeared to mistake this for protectiveness. With his free hand, he punched Mitchell in the shoulder and said, "It's okay, pal. I can understand you'd want to keep a treasure like this away from an old prospector like me."

"Mitchell is a *bit* proprietary," said Kitten, removing her hand from Zack's and stubbing out her cigarette. "Not for any romantic reasons, though. I'm sort of a sister to him, aren't I, ducks?" She gave him a smile that would've frightened small children.

"Certainly not any kind of *brother*," said Mitchell under his breath.

"What was that?" asked Zack airily as he sipped his wine. When Mitchell didn't answer, he happily continued on his own. "So what do you think of the place, Mitch? My favorite hangout in town." He set down his wine glass, loosened his tie and unbuttoned his shirt; a sprig of tawny chest hair leapt eagerly into view. Mitchell felt his heart skip a beat. "Lot of kids, but hey, who knows better where the action is? Here comes your drink."

The pint-size bartender appeared bearing a large, hollowed-out pineapple with a cocktail umbrella sticking from it. Half the bar was watching to see who had ordered it. Mitchell felt a sudden, barely controllable urge to strangle Kitten.

"Thanks," he said, his voice scarcely audible, as the bartender set the monstrosity before him. She smiled in reply, and as she made her way back to the bar Mitchell could see that she was barefoot.

"Okay," Zack said, raising his glass anew; "let's toast to old friends and new acquaintances. And may we all flourish together!"

Kitten lifted her own glass (already stained with lipstick). "Or, as they say in France," she trilled, "here's *merde* in your eye!"

Zack laughed at this non sequitur, while Mitchell worked at lifting his pineapple with both hands. After Zack and Kitten had clinked their glasses together, Mitchell tried to touch his drink to Zack's, but lost control of its weight and knocked the glass from Zack's hand and onto the floor.

"Oh, *damn* it," Mitchell said, clumsily lowering the pineapple. "Zack, I'm sorry!"

"Nice move, Mitch," said Kitten, as she helped Zack dry off his pants leg. "You haven't been out drinking already, have you?"

A thousand killer bees stung his face. "No, I have not been out drinking already. What kind of a question is that? It's not even six-thirty!"

She shrugged dismissively and balled up the wine-soaked napkin she'd been using.

Zack slid off his stool. "It's just a little blotch, man," he said, winking at Mitchell. "No big whoop. Just let me pop into the men's room and dry it under the blower."

"I'm really sorry," Mitchell repeated as Zack scooted past him and headed for the rest room.

Then he and Kitten were alone. The tension was as thick as eggnog.

A swarthy busboy scooted over to their table and swept up the shattered glass. As soon as he'd gone, Kitten said, "So glad you could join us, Mitchell. What's next? You set fire to my wig?"

"*I'm* not the one who ordered this thing," he said, flicking the cocktail umbrella with his fingers. "Makes me feel like I'm in Disneyland."

"Well, that's how I feel too," she said, hugging herself. "Thanks to Zack, that is. Isn't he *dreamy*? And does he ever know how to treat a lady!"

Mitchell groaned in frustration and dropped his head into his hands. "And what happens when he finds out?"

"Finds out what?"

He rolled his eyes. "Don't be cute."

She leaned across the table and looked him in the face. "What makes you think he's *going* to find out? You think I'm easy, is that it? Someone buys me a drink, and I just instantly drop my panties?"

He shuddered. "I don't even want to think about it."

"Then don't. And while you're at it, give me the benefit of the doubt. We're just having a cocktail and getting to know each other. Or at least we were till *you* showed up."

He tried to formulate some reply but found himself instead examining Kitten's face, now so very close to his. At this range, he could see the tiny, nearly invisible blond whiskers just beginning to peek out from her upper lip and jaw—exactly the same kind of growth that greeted Mitchell in the mirror after a full day at the firm. Occasionally these whiskers would catch the light and glint tellingly. And when Kitten leaned forward, as she was doing now, her neck craned from her scarf, clearly exposing the same kind of jutting Adam's apple with which Mitchell himself was cursed. It was all too much to ignore. Was Zack *blind?*

"Just think about what you're doing," he said desperately.

"By which you mean, don't do anything."

He took a breath, then nodded.

She looked horribly wounded for a moment, then recovered. "Okay," she said, tears welling in her eyes—angry tears, by the look of them. "Let me just say this. Let me just say that now, officially, I am sorry you ever called me. I am sorry to have met you, I am sorry to know you. And I would like you out of my life, please."

He was surprised to find himself grievously hurt by this outburst; so much so that he couldn't speak for a moment—couldn't even move. In spite of the bizarre circumstances surrounding her—*him*, goddammit, surrounding *him*—Donald was still his brother, his twin, a closer relative than he'd ever known, a closer relative than most people ever know. He couldn't simply walk away, couldn't just forget that this part of himself existed. How could he have offended Donald so badly? Didn't he know—couldn't he tell—that Mitchell had his best interests at heart?

Zack reappeared at the table, smelling of musk and heat. "What'd I miss?" he asked, slipping onto his stool again.

Mitchell looked at him helplessly, his mouth hanging open. Before Zack could grow alarmed by this, Kitten grabbed his hand. "Oh, Zack, Mitchell was just telling me the most amusing joke. Mitchell, be a lamb and let *me* tell Zack, okay?" She blew him a kiss. "Thanks! Okay, then, Zack. Have you heard about the new shampoo for dogs?"

Zack was already grinning. "No, I haven't."

"It's called, 'Gee Your Butt Smells Terrific.' *Ha*!"

Zack closed his eyes, threw back his head, and started shaking; after a moment, he leaned forward again. Tears were running down his cheek; Oklahoma was positively drenched. Mitchell remembered now that Zack had an almost silent laugh—one of the things he found sexiest about him.

Zack wiped his eyes. "*Ahu ahu ahu.* Oh God. *Ahu.* That's great."

"Isn't Mitchell just a caution?" said Kitten. She lowered her eyelids at Mitchell, then tapped another cigarette from her carton.

Zack sighed happily, then said, "Actually, I'm surprised you get that, Kitten. That's a joke only someone who watched TV in the early seventies could get."

"Well, darling Zack, how old do you think I am, exactly?" She lit her cigarette and took a puff.

He shrugged. "Twenty-three, twenty-four. Thereabouts."

She turned to Mitchell and said, "I love this man." (When she said the word *love*, she ran her tongue over her upper lip.)

Mitchell took great glee in saying, "As a matter of fact, Zack, Kitten is precisely my age."

Zack cocked his head and grimaced. "Pull the other one."

"No, no," Mitchell continued, even though Kitten was now kicking him rather sharply under the table, "it's a matter of record: we were born on the exact same day."

Zack turned to Kitten and said, "Well, you must be leading some kind of pure and innocent life, because you look ten years younger."

Kitten feinted a swoon, and Mitchell thought, *Hey! I don't deserve that.*

And here it was, he realized, only slightly less a perversion than feeling attraction for his brother: being jealous of his brother's success with another man!

But that success was limited; how long could Kitten hold Zack, once Zack learned the truth? Once he got a good look at her, outside of a dingy taxi or a dank Bucktown bar, he'd have to realize what she was. My God! Her voice had cracked four times since Mitchell had gotten here. Zack must already be close to realization.

Even so, Mitchell felt obligated to rescue him, rather than risk letting him make the discovery himself. After all, Zack was a brother Mu; they'd taken a pledge, years ago, to look after each other, till the crack of doom if need be. And Zack did need rescuing. As did Kitten—rescuing from herself. *Himself.* Mitchell recalled his vow to salvage his twin from a life of irrelevancy and buffoonery on the margin of the gay *demimonde.*

That's why he was here tonight. And that's why he stayed, through an additional hour of excruciating flirtation, not to mention four more rounds of drinks (though no more ready-mix mai tais, thank you), until the inevitable finally occurred: Kitten was forced to excuse herself.

With perverse fascination, Mitchell let his eyes follow her to the corridor to see which facility she chose. When the critical moment arrived, she stuck out her hand and brazened her way right past Magda Gabor. Figured; she'd take no chance acknowledging reality tonight, not with Zack on the hook.

When she'd been gone a moment longer, Mitchell grabbed Zack's forearm. Zack regarded him with no small alarm. "You're kind of hurting me, buddy," he said.

"Listen," Mitchell hissed, "and listen good. I don't know what you'll think of me when I tell you this, and I don't care —I have to say it. I have to tell you."

Zack pried his arm away and massaged it; he wore a look of impatient disdain. "What the hell are you raving about, exactly?"

Mitchell pitched forward, nearly spilling over his Scotch. "Zack, *lay off* Kitten. For God's sake." He leaned in even closer. *"She's really a man."*

Zack scowled at Mitchell, then shook his head and chuckled. *"Jesus,* Mitch," he said. *"I* know that. What—do you think I'm *blind?"*

chapter 17

Kitten had just finished her set, to a disappointing smattering of applause. With Gordy constantly on her case to include more upbeat material in her act, she'd acquiesced, and tonight had debuted her and Pierre's rather laconic version of "Don't Sleep in the Subway." Her audience had been unmoved. Kitten chose to place the blame on Pierre, whose glissandos and arpeggios were, she felt, rather out of place in the realm of the ginchy and the mod.

Huffing with indignation, she stamped down the corridor to her dressing room; but when she threw open the door, she found none but the Idol of Millions seated at the vanity, applying false eyelashes as big as palmetto bugs.

"I *thought* I smelled something rancid," said Kitten. She removed her stole and flung it over a chair, then plopped onto the spare chair and began unlacing her Edwardian-style boots.

Regina turned, smiled, and said with no trace of venom, "Got 'em all warmed up for me, hon?"

Kitten considered biting her tongue, but feared she might bite it off. "No," she said; "I can't honestly say that offering them the fruits of my blood, sweat, and God-given talent is in any way warming them up for fifty minutes of lip-synching to Gloria Estefan.''

Regina crinkled her nose and said, ''Silly! It's gonna be Miss Whitney tonight.''

Kitten kicked both boots across the room; one missed her rival's head by mere inches. Regina didn't flinch. ''Miss Whitney, eh?'' Kitten said, beginning to divest herself of her jewelry. ''*That* must be something to see. A black girl who's really a black boy pretending to be a white girl who's really a black girl.'' She shook her head as if suddenly dizzy. ''Multiculturalism at its most disastrously unmoored. You could probably get an NEA grant.''

Regina giggled and fixed her last eyelash into place. She had obviously decided to adopt the maddening tactic of Rising Above It All. As if to confirm this, she now said, in tones as warm as a therapist's, ''So, you never did say—did you ever actually meet your brother? Was he handsome? Was he wonderful?''

Kitten fell back into the chair and sighed. ''I don't know who you're talking about. All men are my brothers, Gina. Except the ones who're my sisters.''

Regina got up and daintily stepped into her mules. ''You know who I mean. Your T-W-I-N. What's-his-name. Milford. Milhous.''

''Mitchell.''

''There you go.''

Kitten clicked her tongue, then arched her back and began rolling down her panty hose.

''Well?'' Regina asked more insistently, hands on her hips.

Kitten let the hose fall around her ankles and dropped back into the chair. ''Well, what?''

''Well, did you ever meet him?''

She took a deep breath, held it, and then puffed it out like an adder. It wasn't easy, giving the cold shoulder to someone who refused to acknowledge it. But Kitten was determined; it was either snub Regina, or dismember her.

She shook a scolding finger and said, ''I don't think I'm

going to answer that. After all, I can't really trust you anymore, can I?"

Regina stuck out her lower lip; then she seemed to remember that she must show no sign of pique, and pulled it in again. "Trust me? 'Course you can trust me!"

Kitten nodded with sarcasm (she was proud that she alone of her circle was able to nod with sarcasm). "I'm sure I can," she said, with no less acidity. "Why, you haven't at all demonstrated your ruthless ambition to claim everything that is mine." She let her eyes drop in dismissal, then looped her dress straps down around her arms and reached over to the dressing table for a cigarette.

Regina took in a huge amount of air, then let it out slowly, as though she were trying to set the world record for exasperated exhalation. "It was *Gordy* who made that decision, Miss Kitt," she said in an edgy voice. "What was I to do? Say no to this grand opportunity, out of loyalty to Y-O-U?"

"Yes," said Kitten without missing a beat. She searched in vain for a cigarette lighter.

Regina crossed her arms. "You are without a doubt the most selfish bitch in the Great Lakes area. I am appalled by you."

Kitten sat up. "Well, long as you know that—got a light?"

Regina narrowed her eyes. "You know I don't smoke. You shouldn't either."

" 'Course I shouldn't." She arched an eyebrow. "Might get cancer and kick, and what would that do to *your* career? No one left to break new ground for you to invade and take over."

Regina snatched her vintage Dior hat from the dressing table and stormed out. "Your trouble is," she snarled as she exited, "you don't know a friend when you see one."

"I know a shit when I smell one," Kitten merrily called after her.

Then she dropped back into the chair and sighed. The trouble with being a genius at sarcasm and bitchery was, no one ever appreciated it but you.

And so she sat, amid the wreckage of her life, trying to find contentment in recalling her few well-put vulgarities. She'd almost managed a tickle of pride, but then the walls began to shake with the thunder of the outside audience's applause; this could only mean Regina had gone on. And sure enough, within seconds the entire dressing room was throbbing to the dull bass pounding of some lamentable Whitney Houston dreck-fest.

There was a knock on the door. "Kitten? You in there?"

She sighed. "Who's askin'?"

"It's Pierre."

Not *him*. Not Pierre—the man who had turned a Petula Clark hit into ersatz Rachmaninoff. "No, Pierre, I'm not in here."

She heard him laugh; then he swung open the door and wedged his great girth through its frame. He was perspiring profusely, as he always did after a set; not a pretty sight, Pierre *ápres la musique*. But his soft blue eyes were glowing and his boyish, ringleted hair still bounced above his sweat-slicked temples. It was oddly difficult not to feel lightened by the sight of the gravity-oppressed Pierre.

She thought of asking him to sit, but, looking around her, saw no chair that might support his tonnage. Instead, she offered him a cigarette.

"Oh, no, no, no, thanks," he said happily, and he leaned against a supporting beam; Kitten watched it for any evidence of give. "Listen, I just wanted to stop by and say—I know things aren't going well in the new time—but I wanted to stop and say that, well—hey—I'm glad you're sticking it out. Grateful, I mean. Really grateful."

She was surprisingly touched by this offering of thanks. "Pierre—that's so sweet. Really. But I'm not an altruist, you know. I'm not doing it for you."

"Oh, I know," he said, blushing, and he began studiously examining his fingernails. "Still, you are *doing* it, aren't you? And you don't even have to, not with your other career. You could just walk, leave the whole place behind. And I'd be out of a job, seeing as you're the last girl here who still uses me."

He grinned. "And I don't have a thing to fall back on. 'Cept my big, fat ass."

She laughed before she could stop herself. "Yes, well, it's a very *nice* big, fat ass."

"You really think so?" he asked brightly. Kitten was grateful he didn't press her for confirmation, but instead continued chattering. "I live with my mom, you know—not much of a life. She's a P.R. flak for the Department of Health. Always bringing home these grim brochures on obesity. Never mentions it, never a word on the subject, but leaves them on my nightstand. Like maybe she thinks I won't figure out how they got there. Lately, she's also been dropping these big hints about me moving out. See, she's started this crazy Amway thing and she wants to use my room as her sales office. So, you know, I'm stressed enough as it is, right now. If I didn't have the Tam-Tam, I'd go nuts. And if it weren't for you, I wouldn't have the Tam-Tam. So, like I said, thanks." He padded over to her, pecked her on the cheek, and then, to the extent that someone of his mass *could* dart, he darted away.

Kitten sat for a moment and willed herself not to cry; then, catching a glimpse of herself biting her lip in the vanity mirror, she thought, What is this, some kind of Grade Z melodrama? —and she opened the floodgates. It had, after all, been a rollercoaster of a day. Meeting Mitchell, for a start; then the impromptu "Sound of Music" number on the streetcorner (what had possessed her to do that?), followed by the interview with—what's her name—Little Miss Atmosphere; and, of course, losing Mitchell. Losing him good and hard and permanent. And *then* having to come *here*, to be insulted by a lackluster audience and a traitorous twentysomething career-snatcher. A lot to handle in one day. A lot of pressure, a lot of mistakes, a lot of heartache.

Still, through her tears, she managed a grin. Every cloud has a silver fucking lining, she told herself, and as the throbbing pulse of Miss Whitney made her head feel leaden and tired, she took solace in recalling the throbbing pulse of the inexpressibly fine Mr. Zack Crespin.

As compensations went, it wasn't a bad one.

chapter 18

"**N**ow, *here*, Mitchell," said Cyrus Trilby, holding up a finger to alert his associate that the moment was nigh; "listen to what she does with this *next* phrase."

Mitchell, slumped at his desk, managed a low whistle of amazement as he listened to a seventh-generation bootleg of Blossom Dearie singing "Put On a Happy Face" before a live audience. But in reality, he wasn't hearing any of it; his mind was awhirl with acid conjecture. I'll bet she planned the whole afternoon, he told himself. The interview, the photograph, the aborted lunch—it was all planned out.

Trilby shook his head in uncomprehending awe and sat back in the leather chair opposite Mitchell's desk. "Don't know how she does it," he said. "That kind of intuitiveness—it borders on genius."

I walked right into her clutches, Mitchell thought as he nodded at Trilby, smiling. Like an animal walking into a trap.

"What the hell," Trilby said, throwing caution to the winds, "it *is* genius. I've said so before. Why get cautious now? Oh, here's the windup."

He stared with great intensity at the tiny Sanyo tape player that sat on the desktop between him and Mitchell, and Mitchell thought, Zack couldn't have been part of her plan, but she didn't waste a second incorporating him.

Blossom Dearie held the last note of the song while a clarinet ran little circles around it, on up the scale, till it reached a discordant note and held that, too. And then there came the tin-can-avalanche sound of riotous, seventh-generation applause. Trilby sighed in rapturous exhaustion and turned off the tape player.

"Well?" he said. "What do you think?"

I think Simon was right. She's a monster.

He looked up at Trilby and said, "I think you're right. She's a genius."

Trilby grinned in satisfaction, closed his eyes for a moment, and nodded. "I *knew* you'd be able to hear it." He hoisted himself to his feet, slipped the cassette from the Sanyo, and reached across to pat Mitchell on the shoulder. "Anytime you want to give a listen to the rest of this, you just drop by and take it. Top right-hand drawer of my desk. I'll tell Cheryl you're allowed in when I'm not there."

Free access to Trilby's office, past the secretary known office-wide as "Cheryl the Centurion"? Mitchell suppressed a chuckle. If Zoe heard about this, she'd have a stroke. No; she'd run out to Tower Records and buy every Blossom Dearie CD in the house.

"Well, enough of pleasure," said Trilby, slipping the tape into his breast pocket. "Back to dull, old business."

Mitchell stood. "I've yet to find the law dull, Cyrus."

He rolled his eyes. "You young ones. All that energy. May you never change." He winked, then sauntered out of Mitchell's office with his hands in his pockets.

And then, just as Mitchell was beginning to relax, Trilby popped back in.

"Oh, by the way," he said, index finger on his chin, "Zoe tells me you've recently been reunited with a long-lost sister."

Mitchell immediately tensed up again. Somehow, Zoe must be made to burn in hell. "Well—yes," he said tentatively.

"Love to meet her. Zoe says she's quite something—a real individualist."

"She is that."

"Bring her in! Heaven's sake, Mitchell—I like to think one of the advantages of working for a small firm like ours is that we develop into a kind of family. *Share* these things with us."

Mitchell reddened and said, "I'll check her schedule."

"Fine, then. Back to work!" He winked, patted his breast pocket once more, and was gone.

Mitchell actually did *try* to get back to work, but maddeningly, the song he hadn't listened to was now inexplicably trapped between his ears. And Mitchell was of a disposition not to relish the strains of "Put On a Happy Face" playing over and over again in his head, like a looped recording on an ice cream truck. He had to do something to knock it from his consciousness.

One sure way to do that. He grabbed the receiver from his phone and punched in Simon's number.

He waited through one ring. Two. Three. He thought, If I get that ridiculous message . . .

But luckily, Simon was home, and answered on the fourth. "Hello?"

"Simon! Glad you're not working. It's me."

"Mitch? Hi, bud. Not due at the hospital till four today. Traded my shift with Brenda. She owed me, on account of me taking over her shift when she got bit by that Pomeranian and had a panic attack that it was rabid. 'Member me telling you? Thing had foam on its snout, but any fool could see it was just from nerves."

Mitchell didn't want to dwell on the concept of nervous foam, so he quickly changed the subject. "Listen, Simon, I owe you an apology."

"You owe me several. Which one we talkin' about, here?"

Simon *did* make it difficult to be gracious. But in his head, Mitchell could still hear Blossom Dearie admonishing him to take off that gloomy mask of tragedy, so he glossed over the rudeness. "I had lunch with Ki—with Donald yesterday. Although lunch *per se* never actually entered the picture."

"Uh-huh," said Simon. "What happened?"

He rubbed his nape and grimaced. "What didn't? I'll have to tell you later, when I can bring myself to speak about it. A sheer disaster from the first moment to the last, and the more I think it through, the more certain I am that sh—that he planned the whole humiliating fiasco. Even worse, my career is suffering because of him. One of my rivals for partnership is about a hair shy of figuring out that my sister is really my brother. As it is, she knows there's *something* screwy about the relationship, and she's starting to use it against me."

"I hope you're not counting on me not saying 'I told you so,' Mitch. There's only so much temptation a man can take."

"I'll do better than tempt you. *I'll* say it. You told me so. And you were right, one hundred percent right, about drag queens. They're not human. They're—they're—chaos. Walking agents of chaos. Men should be *men*, Simon. Women should be women. Confusing the two—that's an act of sedition. Of anarchism."

"*Bravo!* 'Bout fuckin' time Mitchell Sayer cashed in his 501-K and bought himself a clue."

"That's *401*-K, you pathetic denim worshipper," Mitchell said. He sketched a little caricature of Simon on a notepad and started drawing arrows in its chest. "And shut up, anyway."

"Oh, come on—you've gotta let me gloat a little. But, tell you what, I'm thinking if you're serious about this new insight you've just had, I can help you out. Lead you to the world you now realize you belong to."

Mitchell stopped sketching and held the pen still. "Wh—what do you mean?"

"Well, I've mentioned the Darklords before, I'm sure."

Mitchell actually felt the color drain from his face. "Your leather club?"

"More than a leather club, Mitchell. It's a private organization devoted to masculinism. To the fullest extent possible."

"With an entirely gay membership."

"Of *course* with an entirely gay membership. We don't have any truck with the feminine, Mitchell—the irrational, emotional, anti-intellectual feminine. To us, that's the F-word. Civilization is a *flight* from the feminine. And that means sexually, too."

"Oh, yeah? What about the Queen?"

Simon cleared his throat. "It's not so much the Queen as what she stands for. Masculine concepts like order, tradition, hierarchy. Just a hereditary fluke, Mitch, that a woman should represent one of the institutional triumphs of masculinism. Women sometimes do. Just as men sometimes represent the inertness of feminism. Think of Phil Donahue. Anyway, how about coming to the next meeting and seeing what we're about? I think you'll be surprised. Probably just what you've been looking for."

Mitchell grimaced and tapped his pen against the pad. "I don't know. I don't own any leather."

"I'll lend you some. Come on. Say you will. Be like old times, you know? Hell, if we'd have joined the Darklords in eighty-nine, maybe we'd still be together."

Simon was pulling out the heavy artillery now—bludgeoning him with both nostalgia and guilt. "Okay," he said. "Fine. I'll come to *one* meeting."

"I'm going to remind you that you said that someday, when you're president of the whole bang shoot."

"Don't hold your breath. When is this meeting, anyway?"

"Early next week. I'll call you."

That night, when Bereneesha peeked her head into his office to say she was leaving for the night, Mitchell looked up at her to say goodbye, and he saw, in her soft face, full lips, and slight shoulders, nothing less than The Enemy.

chapter

19

On Saturdays, the Tam-Tam put on its all-girl revue, featuring the full galaxy of starlets with whom its patrons had passed the work week. Even so, Kitten found herself arriving for the curtain earlier than usual—summoned, once again, by Gordy. She knew nothing good could come of this, and entered the club with her stomach roiling in dread.

She removed her sunglasses and untied her scarf. In the light of day, the club looked embarrassingly tawdry—like a showgirl wearing her stage makeup to a picnic. The harsh light also revealed the less than pristine condition of the club's chairs, tables, shelves—even the frayed red felt that lined the bar. And the mirrors were revealed to be thick with dust. Kitten felt depressingly cheap in these surroundings.

She wasn't here alone; the other girls had already arrived and were congregated around the bar. There was Raquel Dommage, the Unliving Doll, with all her Gothic accessories: black bra, black leather jacket, black full-length skirt, black lipstick, and ash-white makeup. And Tequila Mockingbird, America's

Sweet Tart, decked out in pastels and high stockings and Mary Janes, and a bright, blond Shirley Temple wig. Also May Oui, the Sultana of Sass, looking sharp in a simple blue Brooks Brothers suit, a white silk blouse, flat heels, and pearls, with her natural hair in a ponytail (May was the only one of the girls with hair thick enough to forgo a wig, and she was well hated for it).

And, of course, Regina Upright. The Idol of Millions was seated on the bar, her long legs crossed provocatively, her hair up under a baseball cap, and her tiny size 3 frame slipped into a clingy white jumpsuit. Scarcely a trace of makeup on her face, either. Nothing much about her that *should* express femininity, and yet everything did. How Kitten longed to slay her.

"Miss Kitt!" exclaimed Tequila as she ran up to her friend and bussed her on the cheek. "Any idea why we're hauled in half an hour early?"

"No, sweetie," said Kitten, squeezing her hand in solidarity, "but then, I'm currently in disgrace, and would scarcely be the first to hear."

"Oh, hon," said May, putting her hand over her heart, "don't look at it that way! We've all had our ups and downs, and yo—"

"I'm down right now, yes. Thanks ever so for the reminder." She flung her purse onto a nearby table. "So where's our august leader?"

"Right here," said Gordy from a darkened corner.

All the girls jumped. *"Christ!"* snapped Tequila. "We didn't see you there!"

"You been there the whole time?" squealed Raquel. "That's goddamn creepy!"

"Scare a girl half to death," panted May, sitting herself at a table and pressing her palm ever harder against her chest.

Gordy came out of the shadows and Kitten could see that he was grimacing. "Wanted to spy on girls and maybe get clue how girls feel about Gordy," he said.

Kitten let out a little bark of disbelief. "You—you *admit* you were spying on us?"

He took his nasal inhaler from his shirt pocket and had a quick hit. "Yes," he said. "You don't like? So what. You going to sue Gordy?"

She frowned at him and wrinkled her brow. What was he up to?

Then he broke into a smile. "Have difficult choice to make, is all," he said, popping the inhaler back into his pocket and plopping himself onto the piano bench. "Have to decide between girls for great honor. Hoped to find that one loved Gordy better than the rest. No such luck. Not even *mention* Gordy! So, must put hurt feelings aside and choose on merit. Aw shucks, right?"

They were all on alert now. Regina leaned forward, put her elbow on her knee and rested her chin on her hand. "An honor, you say? C'mon, Gordy, give. What's the B-U-double-Z?"

From his pants pocket, he produced a tattered envelope, which he waved at the girls. "Sultry vixens have bewitched one of customers," he said giddily. "Have letter here from him, wishing to remain anonymous to you all, but saying he will donate large amount of money toward putting Tam-Tam float in upcoming Gay Pride parade."

"But we've never been in the parade before," said Kitten suspiciously.

"First time for everything—especially if somebody else footing bill." Gordy swiveled on his hip in order to slide the envelope back into his pants pocket, during which maneuver his elbow slipped onto the keys and jangled an octave or two. He righted himself and said, "Float to have one star—one girl to sing on top. All others to be put on each of four corners."

"But it doesn't have to be like that," said May, who was the only girl there who really nursed no hope of being chosen as the star (her personal style was far too androgynous for the part), "you could make the float so we can *all* be on top, as equals."

Gordy shook his head. "Forgot to mention: anonymous donor has also submitted design for float. We either use it, or no moolah. So we use his design. Gordy has decreed!" Another quick hit from the nasal inhaler. "So. Gordy must choose star. Must choose among you all, each very beautiful, each good choice in own way. Very difficult. But decision is made."

A quiver of excitement ran through the club. The girls squealed and huddled into a bunch, clutching shoulders—all except Kitten, who shut her eyes and frowned. She knew instinctively what was coming.

"It's just like Miss America," whispered Tequila with breathy excitement. "Just like goddamn Miss *America!*"

"Have decided," said Gordy dramatically, "that star of Tam-Tam float in Gay Pride parade will be—"

Then he paused. He actually *paused!* The theatrical old flamer! Kitten couldn't resist opening her eyes and gazing with contempt on the four others, whose faces were rapt with anticipation, their eyes glued to Gordy's ravaged-handsome mug.

"*Shit,* Gordy, just fuckin' *tell* us!" snapped Raquel.

"*Regina Upright,* Idol of *Millions,*" he practically cried. And immediately, Regina was engulfed by her sisters, who hugged her and screeched their congratulations. She couldn't respond, however; she was too busy shaking and sobbing, tears fairly ejaculating from her eyes.

The sorry spectacle went on for a full forty seconds, during which time Kitten quietly retrieved her purse and slipped out for a smoke.

chapter

20

"**S**ister's on line three," said Bereneesha over the intercom.

Mitchell put down his sheaf of papers and reached for his phone. He paused for a second when he thought of Donald; then he shook his head, muttered "Wouldn't *dare*," and picked up the receiver. "Mitchell Sayer here."

"*Well?*" said a woman on the other end, rather abruptly.

Mitchell knit his brow. "To whom am I speaking, please?"

"*Paula.* God's *sake*, Mitch, you don't know my voice by now? So, what's going on? I'm calling for a report." She sounded even more peremptory than usual.

"Report?" He sat back. "Oh, yeah. Mother."

She emitted a little hiss of impatience. "*Yes*, Mother. What else? Mitch, you said you'd talk to her. Ow! Damn it!"

A short pause. "Paula? Are you there?"

"Yes, *damn* it. I just got my heel caught in an escalator. Pulled my shoe right off my foot. *Excuse* me, please. *Excuse* me, that's my shoe!"

"Paula, where are you?"

"Nordstrom's. The escalator's eating my shoe. *Could somebody turn this off?* Miss? Are you a manager?—*Are you a manager?*—I *am* speaking English, am I not?"

"Paula, maybe I'd better call you back."

"Don't be silly, if I can just get someone with the competence of a single-celled organism to help me, I'll be—*excuse* me, ma'am, that *is* my *shoe!*"

Cyrus Trilby stuck his head in the door. "Got a moment?" he whispered.

Mitchell covered the receiver and said, "Just a sec." Then, speaking into the phone again, he said, "Paula, I have to go. Give me your portable number."

"I want to see the store manager. Are you the store manager?—Damn it, I didn't say *department* manager, I said *store* manager."

"Paula! *Paula!*" Mitchell shrugged at Cyrus, who grimaced and departed.

"*All right*, Mitchell, calm down," said Paula at last. "I'm here. They're just getting me the store manager. I can't believe this. These shoes are Claudia Ciutis! Do you know what I *paid* for them? Honestly! You'd think a person would be safe at *Nordstrom's.* . . ."

"Paula, I have to go."

"Fine, just first tell me what Mother said."

"I haven't talked to Mother."

Another pause; this one like an Ice Age. "Mitchell, you said you would."

"I tried. I *called* the ashram. Apparently the students all live in barracks without telephones. Seems there's only a couple phones in the entire place, and those are in the administrative office. I *have* left her a message."

"I am getting just a *little* fed up with you."

"Look, Paula, what more do you expect me to d—"

"I *said* I wanted the *store* manager. Is that so terribly difficult? Shall I write it out for you?"

Trilby peeked into Mitchell's office again.

"Paula, I *have* to go."

"Mitchell—wait! This is serious. We've got to *do* something. Call the authorities. Can't you see they're mistreating Mother? I mean, really—not letting her near a *phone!*"

"That's voluntary, Paula. The students agree to it."

"Mother would never agree to that. *Get away from that shoe, please!*"

He rose from his chair and began gathering up his papers and a notepad. "Paula, we'll have to continue this some other time."

"I'm not busy, really, Mitch. I'm just waiting for the store manager."

"*I'm* busy."

"Yes, but you always are. Listen, we have to do something drastic. Do you think we should have Mother kidnapped?"

Mitchell dropped the papers, and his jaw. *"What?"*

"Have her—you know—snatched. Taken away from that place. Deprogrammed. That's the term, isn't it?"

He sat down again, appalled. "Paula, you don't deprogram someone who's cloistered herself away to study one of the world's oldest and most venerated religions."

"Why not? Watch the *shoe*, please."

"Deprogramming is only for persons who are engaged in bizarre and cultlike behavior on the fringes of society." As soon as Mitchell spoke these words, something turned in his mind. His left eyebrow rose to a telling peak.

"Are you the store manager? Well, it's about time! Your escalator is eating my shoe. And it's a Ciuti!—I said, *a Ciuti.*— Oh, very funny."

"Paula, what is it?"

"Some joker just said gesundheit. Listen, Mitchell, I— what? I *know* my ankle's bleeding. Who cares? *Save the damn Ciuti!*"

Trilby stepped into the office again, arms akimbo, looking most unamused.

Mitchell barked *"I have to go"* into the receiver, and hung up.

Trilby glowered at him. "You about ready, then?"

He nodded. "Sorry, Cyrus. Family problem."

The senior partner's demeanor changed visibly; he actually appeared intrigued. "Oh, I see! Something to do with your new-found sister?"

"Not really," Mitchell said as he gathered up his papers and started for the door. "Not yet, anyway."

chapter
21

Kitten was on a half-hour break from a sports equipment catalog shoot, and had found a comfortable corner where she could nestle and read the latest tabloids while she spooned up her fat-free yogurt.

She was partway through an article on Loni Anderson's previous life as a high priestess of Mithra in Ptolemaic Egypt, when she noticed that the constant drone of the photographer's chatter to his assistants had been interrupted. She pricked up her ears.

". . . bound to be around here somewhere," said the photographer. "Who can I say is asking for her?"

"Tell her it's her old Popsy," responded a gravelly voice Kitten recognized at once.

She leapt from her corner and bounded across the studio and into the newcomer's arms. "Pops! God, what a surprise! How'd you find me here?"

"That lady you work for—Miss Jerrold," he said dryly. Vennor Sweet, a short, red-faced man, burdened by excessive weight and excessive care, clutched her waist with both hands and gently moved her away from him—not by much, but enough for her to notice. Chastened by the gesture, she released him and stood a few inches away.

"To what do I owe this great honor?" she said brightly.

He put his hands in his pockets and, with one sidelong glance at the photographer, said, "Well, nothing pleasant. Came to tell you your mother's dead."

Kitten's jaw dropped, and the photographer whispered something to his assistants that prompted them all to file quietly to the rear of the studio.

"Oh, wow," Kitten said at last, putting her hand over her mouth. She had an uncanny feeling that she was in a movie, playing a part. Must remember to act like I feel something, she told herself. "Poor Mom. How'd she—well—"

"Highway accident," he said, and his mouth suffered a momentary spasm. "You don't need to know any details. For what it's worth, she died quick. Instantly, the medics say."

Kitten took a deep breath. The studio was suddenly too white—unbearably white, loud in its whiteness; she felt it like a hostile presence. "I think I need to sit down, Pops."

Vennor led her to a nearby stool and gave her his hand so she could climb atop it.

She pulled her lunch napkin from her sleeve and daubed at her nose. "Oh, boy," she said.

"Thought I'd best come tell you in person, seeing as how she died. If it'd been natural, in her sleep or something, suppose I'd've just called. But this is—well, it's got to be a shock."

"There wasn't any drunk involved, was there? No drunk driver or—"

"Like I said, best you don't know all the details." That was her father, always shouldering the worst of the family's burden.

The photographer and crew were looking her way; she was so far from being annoyed that she actually felt a hint of gratitude. It helped her acting to have an actual audience.

She put a hand on her father's shoulder. "This must be hell on you. *Hell.*"

"It's surely that, Doo." Doo had been her—Donald's—childhood nickname.

She bit her lip; pure theatrics. "And the other kids? How're they all—you know—"

"You're the first I've told," he said, surprising her. "Guess I thought—I don't know." He shrugged, and his eyes reddened. "You weren't real close to Mother, so I thought maybe it'd help make things right, or at least undo some of the wrong things, if I told you first."

Oh, boy, she thought, as a huge weight thumped down on her chest, like a lump of wet laundry; fuck the performance.

Suddenly, feeling something was no longer a problem. She swallowed a few sobs, then tried to say something and had to swallow a few more.

"It's a lousy thing," she said at last, her voice wavering. "Not reconciling with your mom before she dies."

"Well, don't let it ruin your day," he said; and although she knew he meant that she had a job to do and she should soldier on with a stiff upper lip, it sounded so funny after he'd said it that they both broke into wild laughter.

"Oh—huh—huhuh—oh, Doo, you know what I mean," he said, plucking her napkin from her grasp and using it to mop his forehead. "Oh, God. Thought I'd never laugh again. I thought—uhuhuh. Aha." He put the napkin over his mouth. "Got to stop this."

She slid off the stool and hugged him. "Lousy fucking world, Pops. People you think are your friends screw you, people you love disappear before you can tell 'em."

"Well, I surely love you, Doo," he said, actually returning her hug for a moment. "You're a mighty confusing piece of work, and I'm not sure I look forward to having you at the funeral, but I do love you."

"The funeral," said Kitten, furrowing her brow and breaking the hug. "Oh, damn." It was all happening too fast. She'd only just heard her mother had died, and before she could even take that in she was faced with the dilemma of the funeral. Wasn't there supposed to be some kind of decent interval in between? Some time to come to grips with all this? Say, a decade or so?

"I'm not telling you how to dress for it," Vennor said, a little defensively.

"I know, I know." She glumly tweaked his upper arm. "That's not it."

They stared at each other for a moment.

"How long are you downtown?" she asked him. "Can I buy you dinner?"

He looked embarrassed. "Just came in to see you. Now I'm driving out to Skokie to see Ronnie." He looked at his feet, and used one toe to grind an imaginary something into the floor tile. "Thanks anyway, Doo." He had too much innate grace to say that he really couldn't bear to be seen with her in public.

She kissed him. "Love you, Pops. We'll get through this."

"I know. We're tough old birds, you an' me."

He winked at her, squeezed her hand, and left the studio.

Too fast, too fast; it was all happening much too fast. Waiting for a pizza took longer than this, for God's sake. Everything was dangerously out of balance, like a high-wire walker who'd just sneezed.

The photographer and crew were making throat noises, waiting for her to notice them and give them some kind of behavioral cue. She essentially had them paralyzed until then, and she wasn't about to waste this fleeting power with a show of drippy professionalism. She'd keep them hemmed there in the back as long as she liked. All day, if it came to that.

She closed her eyes and conjured up her mother's image. Already it was fading. No, not already; it had been fading for years. Since their final break.

Too late to do anything about it now.

She cast her eyes heavenward, and thought, This is the last straw, you fucker. I'm serious! Almighty or not, you get the *fuck* off my *back*!

chapter 22

"**S**imon, I'm *cold*," whined Mitchell.

"Be there any second."

"I don't know why I couldn't have worn a shirt."

"Shirts aren't allowed."

"I could've taken it off when we arrived."

"I know you. You wouldn't have."

They continued for a few moments in a silence broken only by the clatter of their boot heels. Mitchell gathered his suitcoat around him and shivered; it was the only thing of his own he was wearing. Everything else belonged to Simon. "I thought leather was supposed to be warm," he complained. "No one ever mentions it turns all clammy when the temperature drops."

"Mitch, for Christ's sake," said Simon, spreading his arms wide and letting the brisk midnight wind embrace his near-naked, leather-strafed chest. "It can't be a fucking degree lower than sixty."

"Like I said, *cold*." He looked around him at the massing

of broken-windowed warehouses. "How much farther, anyway?"

"Almost there." More clattering bootsteps.

"Why couldn't we have parked closer?"

"Illegal. Look, shut up, will you?" He pulled ahead of Mitchell and shook his head. "Making me regret this already. Like taking along a five-year-old."

"Glad to hear that's *not* a normal practice."

"In here," he snarled, and he led Mitchell down a flight of stairs and through a darkened doorway.

"Oh, God," said Mitchell, following him into a dim corridor that smelled sharply of mildew. "What am I doing here? This is my absolute worst nightmare."

Simon laughed derisively. "I lived with you, remember? I *know* your worst nightmare." He turned a corner—barely visible in the dimness. "The one about waking up in your mother's body, isn't it?"

Mitchell stopped short. "You said you'd never mention that again! I told you that in a moment of weakness!"

Simon laughed again and kept walking. Mitchell decided he'd better follow, or God knew whether he'd be seen alive again.

"How long are these corridors?" he asked a little further on, as he felt his way along a wall. "I can't even see my hand in front of my face."

"Nearly there. Be a mensch."

Not two minutes later, he followed Simon's footsteps around another corner and was faced with yet another flight of stairs. Simon's left boot was just disappearing beyond the first landing. He dashed after it, and when he arrived at the top, he found himself in a cavernous warehouse, its ceiling thirty feet above him and its walls crowded with wooden cradles—presumably for boats. Outside, he could hear the lapping and rush of the river.

Through the hazy, mote-laden light, he spotted Simon just a few feet ahead, and raced to join him. They were immediately approached by a tall, stocky black man in a revealing leather ensemble that made him look like a cross between Cupid and

Batman. *"Simonnn,"* he said, as though this were the satisfying answer to a particularly thorny question. Then he kissed Simon passionately, nearly impaling Simon's throat on his tongue. After ending this clinch, he said, "Hell are you doing popping up at *this* end of the club?"

Simon grinned. "Brought a new recruit who's got a little too much attitude. Took him the long way to scare some respect into him."

The black man laughed, then extended his hand. "Welcome, handsome," he said. "Pernell's the name."

Mitchell, seething at Simon's duplicity, forced himself to smile and shake Pernell's hand. "Pleasure," he said through clenched teeth.

Pernell fingered the sleeve of Mitchell's hound's-tooth blazer. "Have to check that, I'm afraid."

Mitchell crossed his arms and tightened it around him.

"Oh, come on," said Pernell, "we're all brothers here. Let me help you." He scooted behind Mitchell just long enough to firmly—but gently—slip the jacket from his shoulders. Mitchell, who was wearing nothing underneath but jeans, leather chaps, and a leather choker, felt naked and ridiculous, and shot another withering glare at Simon, who appeared to be enjoying the spectacle out of all proportion.

Pernell folded the jacket over his arm and said, "There, now, not so bad, is it?" And, without a word of warning, he reached out and tweaked Mitchell's right nipple so hard that Mitchell actually screamed.

Pernell and Simon both laughed uproariously. Then Pernell said, "Just check this for you, shall I? You two have fun now!" He winked at Mitchell and sauntered away.

Mitchell, who still hadn't gotten over the passion of Pernell's greeting, asked Simon, "So, is that this week's boyfriend?"

"Who, Pernell? Hell, no. He only wants frottage." He chuckled. "Reminds me of you."

Mitchell turned to hurl a mouthful of invective at him, but before he could do so he made out whitish, lumpy forms, up and down the length of the warehouse. There was something familiar about the way they moved; something rhythmical, yet abandoned—something desperately erotic. Then he heard moaning.

"Oh my God," he said, suddenly hoarse. "My God, Simon. This is an orgy. You've brought me to an *orgy*."

"'*Course* it's an orgy," said Simon with amused derision. "What did you think we did here? Analyze geopolitical trends? Swap recipes?"

Mitchell recrossed his arms over his naked chest. "I have to leave *immediately*. I can't have anything to do with this."

Simon shook his head and sighed. "I wish you could see what a female attitude that is. We're *men*, Mitch. We have carnal desires; why not satisfy them here, where everything's stripped down to just that? What makes you think every fuck has to be a chaser to dinner and a movie?"

"*I—want—to—leave—now.*"

Simon pursed his lips. "Fine. Go find Pernell. He'll give you back your jacket and show you out. I've got bigger fish to fry. So to speak." And he stormed off.

Mitchell made his way tentatively across the warehouse, to the murky blob into which he thought he'd seen Pernell disappear. As he moved through it, entering another corridor, he could just see, all around him, men, naked but for straps and belts and harnesses, thrusting and plowing and grinding and bucking. And the noise! A low-level cacophony of pleas and pants, of breathy cries of encouragement, of begging sobs to desist—a kind of anarchic symphony of desire.

"Pernell?" he half whispered. "Is Pernell here? Per*nell*?"

Occasionally, someone stroked his leg or grabbed his ass, which caused him to jump forward like a champion leaping frog. He passed through an antechamber where a couple of guys were letting it all hang out on some otherwise innocent looking swings; Mitchell quickened his pace while they called out to him: "*Hey. Hey you.*" Soon he found himself in a room where two bathtubs had been set up in the middle of the floor; in one of these he saw a leather-cinched man standing and urinating on a leather-hatted man beneath him. As shocked as he was, Mitchell's immediate thought was of the exorbitant cleaning bill.

He'd had enough. He turned abruptly to go back to the main drag of the warehouse, and plowed right into someone's furry, rock-hard chest. "Sorry," he said, and tried to slip to the side.

But the man grabbed him, yanked his head by the hair (nearly giving him whiplash), and started kissing him in a way Mitchell had never been kissed before—as though he were starving and Mitchell was a great, big artichoke leaf.

Mitchell tried to wriggle away, but the man was too strong. It was more than a minute before he released his grip on Mitchell's hair.

"There—must be—some mistake," Mitchell gasped, pushing himself away from his assailant's chest. He could then, in what little light was available, ascertain that the guy had long, blond hair and was rather beautiful—like a broken-nosed Christopher Lambert.

This revelation caused Mitchell's resistance to weaken for the merest moment; but as soon as it did, the man sneered in recognition of it. Taking Mitchell's entire head in his two great hands, he forced him to his knees, and directed Mitchell's mouth to an area where Mitchell had never previously allowed it to stray on anyone to whom he hadn't at least been properly introduced.

"Oh, my Ga*hhugnk*," he said, as he was made to get to work.

At first he panicked, and his arms flailed, but the man would not release his head, nor allow it independent movement. Mitchell began to think of this encounter in terms of rape, and to balance in his mind the need to see justice done to his rapist against the humiliation of having to recount this scenario in public.

But then something unexpected happened. Mitchell began to warm to his task.

There *was* something exciting about it, wasn't there? Some-

thing dirty and forbidden and therefore subversively ecstatic.
And when his assailant said, "Yeah—yeah, baby—you're
magic—you're *magic*," Mitchell knew. He knew for sure. This
was what true masculinity was all about. Meeting on the field of
mutual desire—unashamed and without artifice.

And Mitchell gave himself up to the act.

And to the next one.

And the next. Each more inventive than the last.

Until at last he climaxed, and it was like every hydrogen
bomb test ever conducted on the Nevada desert all rolled into
one, with a furious harpsichord score by Scarlatti.

And then he was lying in his partner's arms, panting. They
were, amazingly enough, in one of the bathtubs. Mitchell
couldn't remember having got there. He felt a momentary
lurch of revulsion, then fought it back and relaxed—let himself
be enveloped by the ooze, the honest, unpretentious, masculine
film that covered him like an anointing oil.

I love this man, he said to himself, gazing at his cowboy, his
commander, his captain. *And I don't even know his name.*

"What's your name?" he asked, and he immediately regretted it. He had no idea what was considered proper behavior
in situations like this.

The man turned and kissed him on one of his eyelids.
"Kip," he said. "What's yours?"

"Oh—uh. Mitchell." He smiled, but inside he was shaken.
Kip? What kind of name was that for an adventurer, a man's
man, a fearless soldier of Eros? Well, not his fault; blame the
parents, if anyone. But it did sort of ruin the picture.

Kip nuzzled his neck. "You're something, you know that?"

"You're *incredible*," Mitchell replied, meaning it.

Kip bit his ear. "Wanna shower and then come back to my
place?"

Mitchell knit his brow. "You mean—go to where you live?
Your—like—*home*?"

"Uh-huh. It's not far. Fix you breakfast in the morning.
What do you say?"

Mitchell was dumbstruck. This was not at all what he expected from the man who had taken him and shaken him and shown him the love of lions. Would that kind of man *really* offer to fix him *breakfast?*

"Gee, I don't know," he said, readjusting himself so that he was just a hair farther away.

"Oh, come on," Kip said. "Be worth your while." He snapped his fingers. "*I* know how I can tempt you. Just came in the mail today. Friend on the east coast sent it. An actual videotape of the Broadway musical where Katharine Hepburn plays Coco Chanel. Circa eighty-two. A real rarity. You can't pass *that* up."

Mitchell looked at him in genuine horror. A *musical?* With *Katharine Hepburn as Coco Chanel?*

They'd even reached him here, hadn't they?—the insidious tentacles of the feminine. No matter where he went, no matter how far he fled, it had him in its coils. Bring him to the most ultra-masculine enclave he'd ever entered, subject him to a night of brute carnality, without artifice or embellishment, and *still* they claimed him.

Katharine Hepburn as Coco Chanel?

Dear *God.*

Dear God in *heaven.*

What had he done?

He was sitting in *urine.*

Without another word, he got out of the bathtub, edged his way through the darkened corridors until he found an exit, then walked the entire way home—an hour, it took him, and more—because he was too ashamed of his smeared appearance and rank odor to hail a cab.

And besides, he'd left his wallet in his jacket.

chapter

23

Mitchell now felt that his masculinity had been compromised in far too many ways: first by Kitten's teasing and contempt, then by Simon's infantilizing him, then by his molestation at the hands of that Kip person. Enough of them; enough of everyone. He knew now that the key to reasserting his manly authority, his mastery of his own destiny, lay not in recognizing his feminine side, nor in giving himself up to sexual slavery. It lay in seizing that which he could control in his world, and controlling it.

Very well, then. His vow to change Donald. A fine place to start.

What was it Paula had said? *Do you think we should have Mother kidnapped and deprogrammed?*

No. Not Mother.

It was early; seven-thirty. He was in the office, seated at his desk, facing the window as he watched the sun rise through a thicket of downy clouds, looking like an oil stain on a white rug. His fingers formed a little pyramid before his face; his legs were crossed tautly. His eyes were like braziers. When Bereneesha looked in at eight to say good morning, she must have detected something different about him, because instead of her usual recitation of the many abuses and indignities she'd suffered on the subway, she retreated in silence and shut the door behind her.

Eight-twenty. He decided to give the call a try.

His Filofax was already open to the number. And had been for more than an hour.

One ring. Two.

"Davida Sharpe." A husky woman's voice.

"Davida? Mitchell Sayer."

A brief silence. She must be paging through her memory for him. Then, "*Sayer*? Holy cow. How long's it been?"

"Graduation, I believe."

"Unbe*lie*vable. How are you? How's Simon?"

He winced. "Fine. We're both fine. And you?"

"Great! In private practice. Three years now. Family law."

"I know. I read about you a while back in *The Defender*."

She laughed. "I remember that piece. My fifteen minutes."

He swiveled in his chair and faced away from the window. "Davida, I'm sorry to be abrupt," he said; "thing is, I'm having a little family trouble, and I need a favor."

"Yeah, well, I figured you weren't looking for a fourth for bridge. What's up?"

He slowly, methodically, began pressing the crease in his trousers between his thumb and forefinger. "Brother of mine's in a bit of a fix. Got his head in a pretty screwy place. Can't get him out of it because there's this whole sick culture that's taken him in."

"Ah."

"That piece in *The Defender*—didn't it mention you'd once used a deprogrammer?"

He could hear her throat click in hesitation. "Yes," she said cautiously. "*Once.*"

"I'd like his phone number, please."

"Sayer, listen. This is a TV-movie solution to your problem.

I don't recommend hiring a deprogrammer until every other agency has been given a full shot at—"

"I'm not a client, Davida. I just want a phone number."

"I don't give out phone numbers without advice, and if I give you advice, you *are* a client." She expelled a little puff of frustration. "Don't worry, Sayer, I'm not gonna bill you."

Mitchell clenched his fist, and told himself, Just be patient. Wait through her song and dance, and she'll give you what you want. "All right," he said.

"My other piece of advice is, make damn sure you're judging this thing correctly. Deprogramming is a pretty rough business, practiced by rough people, and it's only really appropriate for deep-dish whackos. If this brother of yours has just done something a loop or two off the mainstream, like joined a Satanic rock band or become a Scientologist or started going door-to-door for Pat Robertson, it's not gonna work—and it *could* get you in major shit."

Pretend she's not insulting your intelligence, he ordered himself. "I can't really talk about Donald's problem," he said. "I *can* tell you it's not any of those things. It *is* something, however, that's given him a completely new identity. New name, everything."

"Does he still accept you as his brother?"

"Last time I spoke to him, he said no. Told me he wished I'd never been in his life."

She sighed. "Doesn't sound good. But I can't make a judgment call over the phone."

"I'm not asking you to. I'm just asking you for a phone number."

Silence; Mitchell could only imagine the clash of imperatives being waged in her head.

Finally, she said, "Hold on, I'll check my Rolodex." And the next thing he heard was a Muzak version of "Little Red Corvette."

He smiled.

chapter 24

Kitten had had quite a dilemma over what to wear to her mother's funeral. On one hand, her mother was dead, and could no longer disapprove of her youngest son appearing in full drag. On the other, her mother was indeed dead, and didn't that call for a degree of respect in saying good-bye? Yet if Kitten's mother had now joined the choir celestial, she was above such petty concerns as gender roles and dress. Yet again, if Kitten went to the funeral as Kitten, would the suburban teens in her old hometown beat her up on sight?

The moment was decided by an examination of her closet; there were choices aplenty for a Kitten Kaboodle funeral appearance, but not a single dark suit for Donald. He'd have had to wear black jeans, a black blazer, and a bolo tie left behind by one of Kitten's old suitors. Which might not be very far from what Donald's brothers might show up in, but Donald—even Donald—had his limits.

So Kitten donned a vintage black number, with shoulders so broad she could barely fit through the door, that wrapped so tightly around her knees she found herself having to take microsteps if she wanted to move at all. Atop her head she wore a flat hat with an extraordinarily wide brim that dropped an extravagant length of black lace in front of her face; she could have farmed bees in that hat.

She took a cab to the funeral parlor—costing her twenty-seven dollars!—and it was only when she arrived that she wondered how she'd be getting back.

She was, as per usual, twenty minutes late, and the service was well under way. The enormous oaken door to the chapel turned out to be much more lightweight than she'd assumed, so when she gave it a shove, it went slamming into the wall behind it, causing everyone to jerk around as though they'd heard a gunshot.

Pity that Kitten's most melodramatic entrance ever had to be wasted on her family.

She lowered her head, took several tiny steps to the last pew, and managed to simultaneously enter it and drop to her knees. She reflected that she would have made an excellent nun.

She said a short prayer—a hodgepodge of those she half remembered—then looked up to find that no one in the place had turned his or her head back to the altar yet; they were all regarding her with the kind of incredulity possible only in places where the townspeople socially ostracize others for wearing white after Labor Day.

Kitten's father was in the first row. He rolled his eyes, then turned to the front of the chapel and let his shoulders slump.

Why'd I do this to him? Kitten thought, in an uncharacteristic moment of guilt.

Then she thought, Fuck it, and stared down the rest of the mourners.

Her brother Ronnie and his girlfriend Sheila glared at her, then turned away. Tommy, her nerdy astrophysicist brother from Michigan, couldn't manage to meet her eye. He giggled and looked lengthily at his feet. Ernie, her brother from Las Vegas, had flown in without his wife and seven children; he gave

her a disappointed look, shook his head, and turned back to
the casket.

So did most of the others, now, after letting Kitten catch
their eyes for just long enough to show her they weren't afraid
of her; but Kitten bet they really were. At least, she *hoped* they
were.

Then she saw her Aunt Joline grinning broadly at her;
they exchanged a wink and Kitten felt incomparably happy.
She'd forgotten all about Aunt Joline—her mother's estranged
sister. When she was young, Donald had adored Aunt Joline,
who once gave him a suitcase full of old costume jewelry and
actually helped him try it on, telling him repeatedly he looked
"*Stun*ning!"

The organist, who had been playing some dreary, despair-
ing dirge, finished it (to Kitten's surprise—it had sounded endless), and the priest stood before the casket, his mouth hanging
open, his face red, staring dumbfoundedly at Kitten.

Emboldened by Aunt Joline's presence, Kitten leaned into
the aisle and said, "Do carry on, Father."

The priest stumbled through the remainder of the service,
and at one point referred to the deceased as "our beloved
daughter Charlie." (Her name had been Charlene.)

Kitten couldn't seem to find humor in any of it. Her
mother had died a terrible death, and the people here must be
thinking Kitten was making a mockery of this service by how
she'd dressed; and truth to tell, she herself was a little confused
by her motive. She could have chosen a more understated
ensemble—something that didn't look like she was on her way
to shoot Al Capone. Had she dressed this way to forestall grief
with glamour—to sidetrack mourning with majesty?

She hated this kind of self-analysis, and so gave it up; it was
such a bore. Why did mother-child relationships have to be so
complicated, anyway?

She thought of Mitchell, who had said of his own mother
that she was "always civil" to him; how tragic she'd thought
that, at the time. Well, how tragic was this?

Then, amazingly, for the first time since her father's visit,

she realized that Mitchell's mother wasn't really Mitchell's
mother, and that the broken woman in this casket wasn't hers.
Mitchell and Kitten had the *same* mother, and it was someone
about whom they knew nothing. What was wrong with them?
Where was their natural curiosity?

Suddenly, the whole chapel seemed filled with ugly, hateful
strangers. Kitten stood up, shimmied out of the pew, and, handling the door more gently this time, left the chapel.

She hadn't made it very far (that damned dress) when Aunt
Joline caught up with her.

"Honey pot, why'd you leave me with all those horrible
Anglo-Saxons?" she said, holding her hat to her head and
panting.

Kitten leaned into her and kissed her. "Been years, Auntie
darling! Haven't changed a molecule." This wasn't true; Aunt
Joline had gained tremendous weight, but looked the jollier for
it. She smiled, and revealed that she was still missing one of her
front teeth; she'd used to whistle through it when Donald was
a boy, to his trembling delight.

"Thank you for the sweet lie, Doo, but I know I'm a bit of
a barge these days. You, however, are looking good enough to
eat."

Aunt Joline always said things like that, affectionate things
that still managed to imply murder of some sort; it was the one
aspect of her character Kitten found faintly disturbing.

"I've rented a car," Aunt Joline said. "Let me drive you
back to the city. Hear that's where you're living now."

Kitten was overjoyed at this good fortune. "But aren't you
staying for the reception after the service?"

Aunt Joline led her to the parking lot. "Hell, no. I'm a
pariah, too, you know. No one wants to see me there anymore
than they do you. Let's just hightail it somewhere and have a
drink to Charlene ourselves, you and me. Tell each other what
a bitch she was and admit we loved her anyway."

Aunt Joline drove down the Eisenhower Expressway at
about thirty-five miles an hour. Other drivers passed her while
laying on their horns, an endless chorus of Doppler-shift

shrieks. Kitten thought, *If she doesn't speed up, we're gonna be involved in a drive-by shooting.*

But she puttered on, oblivious. "After Fivos left me—that's my third husband, the Greek musicologist—did you get the invitation to the wedding? I asked your mother to forward it—anyway, after Fivos I bought a farm in Scotland and that's where I live now, just outside of Edinburgh, which is a really cosmopolitan city in most ways, except of course there's no place any civilized human being can eat unless you like Indian food, which of course I do. But you can't like Indians themselves, see, which is the paradox, because I sort of adopted a young Pakistani girl named Chandu and when people in town found out she wasn't my housekeeper but my foster daughter, well, they showed how cosmopolitan they are, which is not very."

"Oh, I'm sorry about that," Kitten said, fascinated anew by Aunt Joline's boomerang course through life. "Maybe you should pull up stakes and go back to the villa in Tuscany. You loved it there."

"Oh, honey, I had to sell that," she said. A mile or so ahead of her, a groundhog ran into the road; Joline slammed on the brake as though she'd been on top of it. The Audi behind her almost rear-ended her; its driver now blared his horn at her in vain. "See," she continued, creeping forward, "I was living with this Israeli for a while in the eighties, and he got into some kind of trouble in Brussels, I didn't know what exactly, but he needed money to help him out of it; and after I wired him the proceeds from the sale of the villa I learned that the trouble involved some kind of terrorism so I thought, Enough of *him,* and I went to live in Hong Kong for a while because I got a job offer to teach a course in Milton at a secondary school there, which is pretty funny 'cause I'd never read Milton. Had to read him on the plane. A little too Puritan for me, but I liked his portrayal of the Devil a lot. Reminded me of my first husband, who was for sure the best of the bunch. 'Member him—Uncle Sasha? Back when you were just a cute little Doo that we wanted to squeeze to death? Anyway, when I got to Hong Kong, the school had closed because the headmistress had fled in the big 'brain drain' that's going on over there in anticipation of Beijing rule, so I took a job running a karaoke machine at a Japanese bar, which is where I met Fivos, who used to come in and sing Okinawan folk songs he'd learned phonetically. Swear to God. I mean, how was I not supposed to fall in love? Bastard. Anyway, once I'd finished with *him*, I went to Scotland to start a family. You should come and meet Chandu, you'd like her."

They'd been driving for twenty minutes and hadn't even reached the city limits. "Aunt Joline," said Kitten, "can I ask you something?"

"Oh, you're so polite I could smother you! You know you can ask me anything."

"I've always wondered: Why did Mom stop speaking to you?"

She pursed her lips and stared at the road ahead. "Well, she blamed me for you turning into a drag queen, dear."

Kitten felt her face boil. "I thought so. That's—that's just ridiculous."

"Is it?" Aunt Joline gave her a slightly deflated glance. "I guess I always thought I *was* part of the reason."

Kitten realized with astonishment that this was a point of pride with the woman. "Oh, hell," she said, "I'd have been a drag queen no matter what. You just made sure I was a *glorious* one."

Joline smiled brilliantly, and actually sped up a little; when they sailed past the WELCOME TO CHICAGO sign, Kitten noted that they were doing a bracing forty-four m.p.h.

chapter

25

Gil Begley displayed the self-important air of someone who couldn't count on respect from any other quarter. Davida was right; he did look rough—fiftyish, hefty, balding, and jowly; but he also had a veneer of sophistication that Mitchell could see through like Saran Wrap. His habit of trotting out sixty-dollar words, for example; they sat in his South Side sentences like a Cadillac on a dirt road.

"It's all *scientific*," he said, leaning into Mitchell's desk and arching an eyebrow. "Our methods, our approach, our results. Incontrovertibly scientific. Our success rate is ninety-five percent. You name a cult, we've done a rescue." He sat back proudly and adjusted his tie with both hands. One hairy wrist bore a two-tone Rolex.

"Maybe you could *explain* your methods to me. Briefly," said Mitchell. He swiveled back and forth in his chair, not quite comfortable with his visitor.

"Sure thing, Mitch. Well, we start off with the complete

isolation of the brainwashed party. This almost unexceptionally incorporates physical restraint."

"Physical restraint?"

"We tie 'em up. In a chair."

Mitchell began tapping his pen against his knee. "I see."

Begley looked at his cuticles, as if he had to rattle off this spiel every other day. Mitchell could've sworn he saw him stifle a yawn. "Then, see, Mitch, we deprive the party of sleep, to actuate a state of weakness and suggestibility. Once we've got 'em where we want 'em, we start gradually wearing down the programming by constant recapitulation of some basic facts that they need hammered at 'em. They resist at first—you better believe it—but if it takes weeks to get 'em to come around, then fine, we take weeks. If we have to, we use physical threats and emotional abuse to subjoin the main attack."

Mitchell bit his upper lip and nodded. "Uh-huh."

Begley crossed his legs and smiled; the fabric of his suit was so shiny at the knees that Mitchell could have fixed his hair in it. "I think, Mitch, beyond that, the less you know, the better. For your own peace of mind."

"How thoughtful." He sat back in his chair and sighed. "Okay. You said a ninety-five percent success rate. I suppose that's documented."

"I am perfectly capable of proffering you references."

"Hmm." He tossed his pen onto his desk. "All right, then. Let me tell you a little bit about the subject in question. My brother. Donald Sweet."

"The defection of a family member is indeed occasion for acute prostration," said Begley, sounding as though he'd said it a million times before. His tiny diamond earring caught a sliver of light.

"Yes. Well. He's a transvestite, living under the name Kitten Kaboodle, and spends a great deal of his time in the company of other men who have adopted female identities— or, as they are rather appallingly called in the vernacular, 'drag queens.' "

"Ah-hah," said Begley, displaying for the first time a hint of dismay.

"I should tell you, Mr. Begley, that I have yet to s—"

" 'Scuse me, Mitchell," Bereneesha interrupted him via intercom.

"Not now, please," he snarled back at the machine. When he was certain Bereneesha had rung off, he continued. "As I was saying, I have yet to see my brother in his natural identity. We were separated just after birth, and I've only recently found him. My problem is that I found him as he is: in women's clothing, maintaining a female persona." Noticing Begley's increasing discomfort, he said, "Are you with me so far?"

Begley was about to respond when Cyrus Trilby opened the door to the office, his face crimson and a fearsome vein between his eyebrows that looked like someone had taped a scarlet pipe cleaner to his forehead. *"Do* forgive me, Mitchell," he said in a voice roiling with venomous politeness, "but it appears you did not allow your secretary to announce me."

Mitchell surprised even himself by turning to Trilby, narrowing his eyes, and saying, "I'm afraid that's because I can't admit you at the present moment, Cyrus. Please excuse me, and accept my assurance that I will see you as soon as I am able."

Trilby looked as though someone had yanked his pants down. He muttered something unintelligible, then quietly retreated and pulled the door shut behind him.

"Now, then," Mitchell said without emotion, as he turned back to Begley; "I believe you were about to say something."

"Uh—yeah," Begley replied, taking one last astonished look over his shoulder. "Say, was that guy your boss?"

"Yes. You were about to say something?"

"Right. Uh . . ." He resettled himself in his chair and took a reappraising glance at Mitchell. "Thing of it is, Mit—Mr. Sayer—uh—I mainly work with brainwash victims. You know, kids who fall into cults and stuff. Your brother—he lives with these other transvestites?"

"No; I believe Donald maintains his own apartment."

"Right. Then—uh—he counts on them for his income?"

Mitchell shook his head. "He earns the bulk of his money independently of them."

Begley sighed and slapped his hands on his thighs. "Gotta be honest with you, Mr. Sayer, this just isn't the kind of thing I usually handle. Like I said, I deal mainly with brainwash victims, not gay people. I can't change your brother's sexual orientation."

Mitchell sighed and turned his head to one side for a moment, as though seeking a sympathetic glance from someone invisible; then he turned back to Begley and said, with barely disguised patience, "I'm not asking you to change his sexual orientation, Mr. Begley. I'm asking you to restore him to his true identity. I don't care if Donald is gay, as long as he's Donald."

Begley was beginning to sweat. "Still a bit out of my line." He wiped his forehead with his sleeve.

"Why is that?"

"Well, it kind of sounds like he's just mixed up, not brainwashed."

Mitchell fixed a gaze on Begley that might almost have burned a hole through his head. "Your mistake, Mr. Begley, is assuming that brainwashing is something that must be performed with intent. I maintain that brainwashing can be phenomenal; it can result from an unfortunate synthesis of cultural accidents. Consider my brother's case. It's clear he was imprinted by an endless succession of movie musicals on late-night TV, plus an available supply of cheap fashion magazines, for which we may fault the negligence of his parents, but certainly no more malevolent agency. And yet, it's brainwashing all the same, isn't it? I submit to you that stripped of this faulty socialization, he will rediscover his male persona—gay or straight—and go on to lead a more productive and fulfilling life."

Mr. Begley cocked his head. "Well, you make a good case."

"Argue against it, if you can."

Begley sighed and threw his hands in the air. "What the hell. Business is in the crapper, and I like a challenge. You know my fee?"

"Know it, and accept it."

He shrugged. "Fine. When do we begin?"

Mitchell pursed his lips. "As soon as possible."

Begley shifted in his seat again. "Real go-getter, aren't you?"

Mitchell said nothing.

"Well, push comes to shove, I could be ready tomorrow."

Mitchell nodded.

"How we gonna arrange it?"

Mitchell pressed his fingers to his lips. "I'll arrange for Kitten—I mean, Donald—to meet me tomorrow, at lunchtime, at the west entrance to this building. You'll be waiting."

Begley pulled a small notepad and a pen from his inner jacket pocket and began scribbling. "I'll—be—waiting," he recited as he wrote.

"You'll know Kitten because she'll be the gaudily dressed woman who meets me at the entrance. After which, I'll arrange somehow to separate from her—to get her on her own. At which time, you will apprehend her."

"At—which—time—I—will—ap—pre—hend—her," he said. He lifted his head and said, "Two p's in apprehend, right?"

Mitchell nodded and grinned. "Just one more thing."

Begley sat with his pen poised. "Shoot."

"I don't want Donald to know I'm the one responsible for this abduction. Not 'til the deprogramming is a success."

Begley smiled and waved a hand at him. "No problem," he said, and he tucked the notepad back into his jacket. "Your name won't ever come up."

"I know it won't. I've just stipulated that it won't."

Begley laughed nervously, then got to his feet and said, "Well, then, Mr. Sayer, I'll see you—or rather, I *won't* see you —tomorrow afternoon. Let us hope for a fortuitous outcome."

Mitchell shook his hand and said, "I think we'd better do more than hope."

Begley's sweat was running down his temples now, and his upper lip looked like an oil slick. "Right, then. I'll show myself out."

"Nonsense," said Mitchell, who accompanied him to the door of the office. Begley tripped over the carpeting on the way out, and then appeared mystified at which way to turn to find the reception area.

"That way," Mitchell said, turning him by his shoulders and giving him a gentle shove.

When he was out of sight, Bereneesha leaned out of her cubicle and bleated, *What the hell did you say to Mr. Trilby?*"

He looked at her in bewilderment. "Why do you ask?"

She wheeled her chair into the hallway, and whispered to him, "He came outta your office saying that whatever it was made you so tough suddenly, he liked it. Said all you lacked as an attorney was a little backbone, and now you had it."

Mitchell felt himself go quite weightless. "I'm sure you shouldn't have been eavesdropping, Bereneesha," he said, hiding his giddiness.

She scowled at him. "He was sayin' it to *me*, fool!"

"Whatever. Back to work, now!" He returned to his office and shut the door.

And then he called Kitten.

chapter 26

Kitten had seen Aunt Joline off at the airport, dashed home, and pulled herself together with admirable speed; she was putting the final touches on her face when the doorbell rang. She took a quick glance at her wristwatch: 7:14. Zack was early, damn him. She got up, squeezed her way past her mountains of furniture and bric-a-brac, and buzzed him into the building. Then she reached into the hallway and gave the doorknob a twist, letting the door fall open for him.

When he swept into her apartment moments later, she was just capping her eyebrow pencil, having finished her makeup in record time. Of course, tonight she had deliberately applied far less than usual.

"Hey, beautiful!" Zack said as he kicked the door shut behind him.

He was thin enough to slide right past her dresser and wig stand, and then he jumped onto her bed like an ape and thrust his big, wide, midwestern face at her. His birthmark was as red as a beet. She turned her own head at the last minute, allowing him to kiss only the area directly below her left ear; to salve his pride, she simultaneously pursed her lips and made an affectionate, smacking sound.

"Hell of a kiss," he complained, kicking off his shoes.

She patted his head. "Don't be greedy. Yet." She popped open her lipstick and made a little show of making herself up in her vanity mirror. It was strictly unnecessary, of course; she looked exactly the way she wanted to. But she desired that Zack should think this state of perfection was merely a matter of a few lightly applied strokes.

Zack, for his part, was paying her keen attention, even as he plopped onto the bed and stuffed a pillow under one arm. "Something different about you tonight," he said. "Not that I've known you real long, or anything. But am I right?"

She turned, put her hands on her hips, and bent one knee slightly. "It's the outfit," she said. "Like it?"

He squished his mouth to one side and raised an eyebrow. "It's certainly a look."

"Belonged to my mother. Stole it from her cedar chest when I left home." She ran her hand down the side of the snug-fitting lavender cocktail dress. "Comes with this, too." She slipped on a ribcage-hugging jacket with elbow-length sleeves. "And just wait—the final touch." She pulled on a pair of white gloves, then lifted her hands in the air. "You like?"

He rested his head on his knuckles. "Well. It's a *mite* conservative."

She patted her brunette wig, which had been combed into a straight fall until it executed a gravity-defying flip at the shoulders. "That's just the point. Here, help me with the pearls."

"*Pearls*, even." He clambered across the bed on his knees. "What's the occasion? Big D.A.R. social or something?"

She handed him the necklace and hoped he couldn't tell the pearls were fake. "No. It's because of Mitchell, believe it or not."

He snorted. "I choose not." He laced the pearls around her neck and fumbled with the clasp at her nape; she helpfully lifted a flap of hair to give him room.

"Listen, Zack, there's something I have to tell you."

"If it's about you and Mitch, I don't want to hear."

"It's not what you think."

"I haven't said what I think."

She gave him an I'm-disappointed-in-you look over her shoulder. "He's my *brother*, Zack."

His fingers went momentarily still. "Mitch?"

She nodded. "*Twin* brother, actually."

He shrugged and continued his efforts with the clasp. "Never told me he had a twin."

"Well, back when you knew him, he had no idea. We're orphans, separated at birth. I only actually met him for the first time a week ago. Same day I met you, actually."

"There," he muttered as he let his hands drop. "All set."

She lowered her flap and turned to him. "How do I look? Honestly."

"Like Jackie Kennedy in the motorcade. Minus the blood."

She giggled. "Oh, you're so sweet!" She turned to get her purse.

He sat on the bed, seemingly unwilling to move until he'd heard the whole story. "I still don't get why Mitch being your twin brother has anything to do with you dressing so young-matronly tonight."

She shouldered her purse. "Long story. Tell you in the car."

"First let's have a kiss."

She felt a surge of erotic glee, then leaned over and mashed her lips into his—careful not to upset her wig. Then she stood up and smiled. "Okay?"

"Now let's have a hand job."

She hit him with the purse.

"That's not a hand job," he said, leering.

She grabbed his shoes from the floor and quickly squeezed her way out to the hallway.

"Come back with those, please," he called after her.

"You come and get 'em!"

He made a lunge for the door, and with a shriek she fled down the stairs.

She hadn't quite made it to the first landing when she heard him come pounding after her; and when she dared venture a look, she saw him bearing down on her with mock fury on his face. She gasped in delighted terror and threw the shoes at him, then flew down to the next landing, where she nearly toppled old Miss Frobisher from 3-A.

"Oh! Sorry, dear," said Kitten, almost meaning it.

"You shouldn't run on the stairs," said Miss Frobisher with a tremor in her voice. She clutched the handrail and appeared deeply frightened.

" 'Course I shouldn't, I'm just—" At that moment, Zack rounded the stairs like a quarterback, emitted a triumphant yell, and grabbed Kitten by the shoulders.

Miss Frobisher nearly toppled over the railing.

"Oh, sorry, ma'am," he said, seeing her for the first time. He released Kitten (whose wig had been jarred nearly a centimeter out of place), then reached over to steady the old woman's worsening footing on the stairs.

"Don't touch me!" Miss Frobisher croaked in terror. *"I have leprosy! I'll give you leprosy!"*

Kitten decided this situation could only get worse, so she took Zack by his jacket sleeve and pulled him down the stairs. He hopped after her, trying to don his shoes as he descended.

"She be all right?" he whispered, tossing his head up toward Miss Frobisher.

"Oh, yeah. Probably."

They reached the vestibule and he held the door open for her. "She really have leprosy?"

Kitten shrugged. "Dunno. See any body parts back on the stairs?"

They laughed together, then exited the building and began the short walk to Zack's car. Kitten had no sooner hit the crowded street than she went rigid and alert, preparing for a possible confrontation. It was second nature; a reflex of self-preservation.

He didn't know her well enough to understand her sudden tenseness. "You okay?" he asked, pulling his keys from his pocket. "I didn't do anything wrong back there, with the leper?"

She shook her head and forced a smile.

When they were safe in the car, she allowed herself to relax again. Once they'd fastened their seatbelts, she reached over and grabbed his crotch.

"Yow!" he cried. "Don't do that when I'm driving!"

"You're not even in gear yet."

He winked at her. "Kid, when you're around, I'm *always* in gear."

She rolled her eyes. "That's the most appallingly B-movie line I've ever heard come out of a real person." But of course, she was secretly thrilled by it.

When they were under way, he said, "Okay. Mitch. Tell."

She sighed in resignation. "It's like this. When we found each other after all these years, things didn't go well. So I made a little vow to loosen him up—"

"He could use it," said Zack, absently picking at his ear.

"—and I did *try*. That afternoon we met you. Tried to show him life could be spontaneous and colorful and *fun*. But all I did was make him hate me. Okay, maybe I overdid it a little. But when he started to come down on me, I pretty much told him to take a hike."

"Ah." He eased the car onto Lake Shore Drive and accelerated.

Kitten leaned back into her seat and continued. "I felt bad about it afterward, but what's done is done. Or so I thought. Then he calls me today and asks if I'd like to have lunch tomorrow. Another chance to just, you know, start over. I thought that was so wonderful of him. Made me think he really *does* care, really *does* want to understand."

"Mmm." Zack was staring at the strip of road ahead of him, bounded on one side by the choppy expanse of Lake Michigan, and on the other by the imposing edifices of the Gold Coast.

"So, I thought I'd meet him halfway," Kitten continued, perplexed by Zack's cool demeanor. "He obviously wants me to be something I'm not—wants me to be Donald." She shuddered at the thought. "Well, I can't do that, but I *can* tone myself down—make Kitten a little more compatible with his world." She looked at Zack. "That's why I dug out this old ensemble. And that's why you're taking me to The Waterworks for dinner."

"Oh, is *that* why?"

She nodded. "I figure, if I can handle myself at a posh joint like that, I can handle anything Mitchell Sayer throws at me."

He said nothing; they drove in silence for a while.

When they sped off the Drive at LaSalle Street, she was compelled to say, "You don't seem to approve."

He chuckled in disdain. "Well, I don't."

She pivoted on her hip. "Oh, Zack, why not? I thought you'd think I was being so mature and conciliatory about this!"

"Conciliatory? By changing who you are? By letting Mitch tell you how to live your life?"

"He's not doing that," she said in a small voice.

He nodded with sarcasm, and Kitten was thrilled to see that another human being actually possessed this skill. "No," he said, "he's not doing that at all. You just look like this because you like it, right? Come on, Kitten! Let me tell you a thing or two about Mister Mitchell Sayer. After all, I've known him a little longer than you have."

A sudden realization hit her. "You don't like him, do you?"

"Not really. Never have. I'm sorry, but it's true." He changed lanes abruptly, almost skimming another car; Kitten felt her heart jump. "Guy's anal-retentive, passive-aggressive, and a control freak. Everyone in the frat house hated his guts. I know he thought it was because we'd all caught on he was a fairy, but it wasn't that. Hell, half the guys in the frat have given head to a brother during one drunk or another. No—reason we couldn't stand Mitch was, he's a pain in the ass."

She looked at her hands. "Oh. Poor Mitchell."

"Poor Mitchell!" he repeated with a bitter laugh, and he shook his head. "Just watch out for him, okay? Watch your step around him. He'll hurt you, if he can."

She desperately wanted to change the subject, so when they

came to a stoplight she reached over and pretended to brush something from his cheek. "So it wasn't tough for *you*, then? Being gay in the fraternity?"

He whirled, and looked at her in complete astonishment. "What are you talking about?"

She leaned back, surprised by his vehemence. "I merely asked if y—"

"I heard what you asked. Christ, Kitten! *I'm* not gay."

She felt everything in the world go liquid for a moment; was she losing her marbles, or was there a seriously mind-altering paradox at work here? "I beg your pardon?"

"*I'm not gay.* I love women. *Love*'em." He shrugged. "Probably more than any guy you'll ever know. Been with all kinds—fat, skinny, black, white, old, young. Hell, it's tough for me to think of a type of chick I *don't* want to screw." He turned to her. "Which is pretty much why I'm with you, kid. To me, you're just one more kind of chick—a chick with a dick."

Kitten found herself short of breath; she tried to control a sudden surge of emotion.

After a few moments, when she'd regained a measure of self-possession, she stared lovingly at Zack and said, "That is the single sweetest thing anyone's ever said to me."

chapter 27

Evening was just beginning to spread shadows like wet laundry across the landscape when Zack pulled up in front of the Envoy Imperial Hotel, in whose confines was located the prestigious and decades-old Waterworks restaurant. An acne-scarred valet opened the passenger door and helped Kitten exit the car without looking anything other than bored by the task. *A perfectly glorious omen*, Kitten told herself.

Zack held the door for her and smiled so handsomely that she thought she might faint. If it weren't for his birthmark, he'd be forbiddingly perfect; as it was, she had to keep herself from asking silly and damaging questions like, *What is he doing with me, of all people?*

They passed through the lobby, which at this hour was filled with serene couples of the best sort—lithe, red-faced men with thinning hair and eight-hundred-dollar suits, and rail-thin women with hair pulled back so that their faces were actually taut, each wearing a simple sheath or slacks and a sweater. Kitten was ravenous with envy at their ability to look so unquestionably feminine in such shapeless and largely ill-defining garb.

She looked up. The ceiling was crowned by a chandelier bigger than her entire apartment, with bronze cherubs cavorting around its base. She looked down. Her sensible flats were crossing an antique Oriental rug that looked like it had been left out in the rain for a century.

It was the first hotel lobby into which she had ventured where there was no sign of a TV set.

She balled her fists and fought off a full-frontal assault of anxiety. Then she took Zack's arm and tried to appear natural, although she was keenly aware that nearly all the women were looking her way. *If only I'd worn a different wig,* she scolded herself.

She looked to Zack for a reassuring wink, but instead found him beaming his brilliant grin at all and sundry. Suddenly she realized who, exactly, all the women were looking at, and she felt immeasurably better.

The entrance to The Waterworks was just across the lobby; they were there in a jiffy.

The maître d' was a tall man with the most obvious comb-over Kitten had ever seen, and she'd seen a few. He affected a French accent, but even Kitten could tell it was a sham. "Good *eev*-aneeng, ma'amselle, miss-*you.* 'Ave you a rizzer-vass-*yawn?*"

"Crespin. Party of two," said Zack authoritatively.

While the maître d' checked his leather-bound log, Kitten peeked around him at the restaurant itself. It was filled with a golden light that spilled over every plate of food, over every pair of shoulders; there was a real honest-to-God pianist, and he wasn't playing anything Kitten even recognized—no regurgitated mealworms from Billy Joel or "Miss Whitney." This sounded like something classical. She decided it must be Chopin, if only because she liked to say "Chopin" and would enjoy doing so in relating this story to the gang at the Tam-Tam.

Next to almost every table was a silver bucket on a stand, and in each bucket was a green bottle with a label even she could recognize from a distance. That orange one was Veuve Clicquot. That white one was Perrier-Jouët. That dark green one was Dom Pérignon. How odd to see so many people drinking all this out of honest-to-God crystal flutes, *à deux*, instead of out of plastic

cups in a crowded apartment! Look at them—in groups of twos
and fours—every table either boy-girl or boy-girl-boy-girl—looking gorgeous and chiseled and—and burnished, like copper—
or gold—

Her breath started coming harder. She was aware—had
always been aware—had *boasted* of it, for God's sake—that living
as a manwoman, living as Kitten, she had had to make sacrifices.
Well, sacrifices were one thing when they were in the abstract;
they were even kind of enjoyable, in a way—*Ah, yes, there are joys
in life I will never know, simply because I have chosen to be true to
myself*—but they were quite another when they were right there
in front of her, in all their splendor, laid out like a banquet she
could only hope to crash. She actually licked her upper lip.
Three words were all she could conjure, all she could tell herself, over and over, like a mantra: *I—want—this.*

She was only half aware of the way the maître d' kept glancing up from his book, taking longer and longer looks at her.

Finally, he nodded and said, "Wun mo*mah*, please," and
stepped away from his station to where another man, this one
older, grayer, more distinguished, was standing with his hands
behind his back, surveying the restaurant. The manager, Kitten
presumed.

"What's going on?" Kitten whispered.

Zack shrugged.

The maître d' tipped his head, ever so slightly, in Kitten's
direction, and the manager then craned his neck almost un-
noticeably and had a look at her himself. Then he turned back
to the maître d' and initiated a flurry of hushed conversation.

Zack looked at her and grimaced helplessly, as if to say,
What can you do?

"Maybe they gave away our table by mistake," she said. She
silently recited a little prayer that this was the case. The alter-
native didn't bear thinking of.

Yet think of it she must. For when the maître d' made his
way back to his station, his face wore an expression Kitten
couldn't possibly misread: the haughty, impervious demeanor
of the sentry before a pariah. She steeled herself for an attack.

He cleared his throat, ran one hand over his open book,

and took a swift, appraising look at Zack. Then he fixed his gaze on the pocket of air between Zack's and Kitten's heads and said in a low, firm voice, "I'm zorry, but eet ees the policy of zees restaurah not to admeet gennlemen wizzout zhackets."

Zack pulled open his blazer with both hands. "What do you call this?"

The maître d' pursed his lips. "Eet ees not of you zat I am speaking."

Kitten's face filled with blood; her tongue swelled up in her mouth. The room dissolved, melted away. She had to concentrate on standing upright.

Zack put his hands on his hips. "Well, then of whom exactly *are* you speaking?"

"Zack," she said, but her voice was too hoarse to be heard.

The maître d' nodded at Kitten, eyeing her surreptitiously. "Your companyuh, miss-*you*."

Zack shook his head in disbelief. "What the hell's the meaning of this?"

Kitten grabbed his arm. *"Zack,"* she said, this time more audibly.

"I want to know what the fuck this is about," said Zack, his birthmark turning bright red. People in the restaurant were starting to turn and stare.

"It's okay, hon," she said, tugging on his sleeve. "Let's just go. It's nothing I'm not used to."

"You talking about the *lady*? Huh?" Zack demanded, ignoring her. *"That* it, buddy?"

The maître d' took a step back. "Zat ees no lady."

Rejection was one thing; repudiation, quite another. Kitten felt something in her brain twinge and snap. "Listen, you goddamn fake Frog," she hissed, "I'm every *inch* a lady, with five miserable exceptions."

"Six," said Zack. *"Surely* six."

She lurched forward and slammed her own hands onto the precious reservation book. *"Where the hell do you get off treating me like this?"*

The manager stepped in from the sidelines. "Bernard is

not the author of this restaurant's policy," he said, in clipped, oily, American cadences. "I am."

Kitten hauled off and slapped him across the face, astonishing even herself with her show of bravado and her impeccable theatricality. "Then that's for you, asshole," she sputtered. As a follow-up line it wasn't much, but she'd write a better one in the car—pure staircase wit to juice up the story for the Tam-Tam gals.

If she could bring herself to tell them about this at all.

Suddenly, she felt as if she might cry. She managed to emit a tremulous "Take me home," then let Zack lead her to the door, his hand on her back.

She'd almost made it to the lobby when a new and important thought occurred to her. She whirled back on her stunned oppressors, grabbed her lapel, and with every drop of venom she could summon, hissed, "Just for the record, you fucking troglodytes, this outfit *does* have a jacket."

There, she thought. *No need for staircase wit now!*

And then the dam broke, and Zack had to guide her out of the hotel by her shoulders while she howled and sobbed, covering her face to spare herself the far extremes of mortification.

As luck would have it, the valet hadn't even had time to move Zack's car. Kitten crawled in and collapsed, then had a look at her face in the rearview mirror. Appalling; mascara everywhere. Like a map of the Martian canals. When Zack got in and buckled up, she turned away from him.

"Don't let it get to you," he said as he started the ignition. "Couple of assholes."

"Couple of *free* assholes," she wailed as he pulled into the street. "Couple of assholes who can go anywhere in the world they want."

"Everyone's got chains, hon," he said. "Theirs are just less visible. Tell the truth, I think *you're* the one who's freer than most." They came to a stop; she felt his hand on her shoulder. "You don't *let* yourself be shackled."

"Fat lot of fucking good it does me," she said, then gasped back a few more sobs.

He accelerated again; Kitten saw a green light flash over her hands. "Whether it does you good isn't the point," he said. "You know that."

Amazing, this man. Amazing of him to understand such a thing. No one else understood it. Her parents. Mitch. "You're right," she said with a sigh. She summoned up her courage and looked him in the face.

He glanced at her momentarily, then laughed as he returned his eyes to the road. "You're incredible," he said. "You should see yourself. Like an artist's ideal image of a suffering woman."

A wave of comfort and warmth swept over her. "Mister Zack Crespin," she said, her voice catching. "You are too goddamn good to be goddamn true."

He snickered. "Hell with that."

"I mean it." She took his hand.

He squeezed it. "Listen, Kitten. I like you a lot. I'm not trying to break up with you or anything. Not now. But there hasn't been a woman yet who's been able to keep me for long. Just understand that, okay?"

She felt a twinge of pain. "Oh, I knew *that* about you from the *start*," she said merrily, almost as if it were true.

"So let's enjoy it—enjoy *us*—while it lasts."

She put her hand over her breast, as if amazed that he thought it necessary to say this. "Why *else* do you think I'm here?" she said, a little laugh in her voice.

But it was the last straw; the final defeat. No more of them—and no half measures, either. Zack was right about one thing. "I've made up my mind," she said a few moments later, as they sailed back up Lake Shore Drive. "Tomorrow, when I meet Mitchell for lunch, I'm gonna be my big, bold, brassy self. And he can take a flying leap into the pavement if he doesn't like it."

He squeezed her hand again. "Atta girl."

"Now, please, Zack, just take me somewhere for a quick bite so I can get home early and kill myself."

He chuckled all the way to the Fullerton exit.

chapter 28

Kitten found herself downtown and ready for lunch twenty minutes earlier than she should have been, so she'd decided to go shopping. The object, after all, was to make Mitchell wait for her, not vice-versa.

She'd clip-clopped her way up Randolph Street to the venerable facade of Mason's Department Store, her favorite since childhood, now, alas, fallen on hard times. The store had once maintained a presence in virtually every major midwestern mall; now, only the original store was left. It had a sort of deathbed air about it, but Kitten liked it because its buyers were clearly insane and bought stuff only a drag queen could appreciate (even when they ordered Ralph Lauren it somehow arrived looking like Bob Mackie), and because they were so hungry for business that she could go in with a two-day beard and no one would act the least bit snooty.

She was feeling particularly bold today, and had it in mind to look at some lingerie. But she'd only just stepped off the elevator when she was virtually accosted—there was no other word for it—by an enormous middle-aged woman with a wedge of gray hair that resembled depression brick, a suit that looked as though Vivienne Westwood had designed it as a Sherman tank cozy, and an aura of perfume so thick that Kitten could feel it ooze into her ears.

"I know how to get rid of those unsightly wrinkles," said the woman with all the fervor of a fundamentalist Christian. She clutched Kitten's arm and her nails felt like a bear trap.

Kitten was both astonished and affronted. "I beg your pardon," she said, in her loftiest, Margaret Dumontest manner.

"Just two weeks and they'll be gone, *zammo!*—guaranteed, so you bet," said the woman.

"Zammo?" Kitten said.

"Just like zammo," said the woman. "Here, you will permit me to show you. Nothing to pay for any demonstration, eh? So you bet."

Because of the woman's odd way of speaking, Kitten guessed she was an East European refugee of some kind—arriving in America in midlife, uncertain of how to dress or groom herself, but lucking into a job in the only department store in town that would have her.

Her heart melted, as it only did in the presence of another outsider, another soul trying desperately to become her dream of herself. How could she not help?

"Please do show me," she said brightly. "Show me how to get rid of—" She swallowed gamely. "—these unsightly wrinkles."

The woman's jaw dropped a little, as though she couldn't quite believe her ears. Then she tightened her grip on Kitten's arm—Kitten actually yelped—and pulled her over to a counter bearing an illuminated chrome sign that read ALTAVENUS.

The woman released Kitten's arm, picked up a mud-brown bottle bearing the same name, and started to speak, tentatively, as though she were a fourth-grader reciting a Victorian poem from memory.

"So. As the ancient Greeks of women once used oils and unguents favored by the goddesses to be making their skins healthful and glowing, so—so—ummm—healthful and glowing." She stopped, and took a deep breath. "Altavenus now has the same recipes for today of women, to smooth our skins as though we were of classical Greek statues of Athena or Venus. What, you ask me, is in Altavenus skin products? Only all-natural oils and unguents is what my answer to you."

She appeared blissfully relieved to have made it this far. With great reverence, she unscrewed the bottle and placed the metallic cap on the counter. Kitten watched with what she considered appropriate awe, and thought, *Well, she does have beautiful hands.*

"If you will permit me, I will rub a little Altavenus Moisturizing Lotion onto your madame's cheek, and you will then feel the glorious warmth of ancient oils and unguents enriching your skins and erasing age with—um—ancient oils and unguents." She poured a little glob of the fecal-appearing ooze onto two of her fingers, then held it up to Kitten and said, "You smell, okay?"

Kitten leaned forward and the acrid, sooty-cinnamon odor entered her nose like a shot. The odor itself wasn't unpleasant, but it had the sharpness she associated with electrical short-circuits and dirty diapers. She jerked her head back, and then, noticing the look of alarm that the woman wore, smiled and said, "Oh, but that's quite something, isn't it?"

"So you bet!" said the woman, extending her hand toward Kitten's face. Kitten flinched, then steeled herself and allowed the woman to work the jelly-textured matter into her cheek. Within seconds, it was drying like Elmer's glue. Kitten endured it all by conjuring up an image of the woman's early life in Poland, wearing a thin cloth housedress and wooden shoes that didn't match.

"You feel it?" asked the woman as she wiped her fingers onto a handkerchief. "You feel the wrinkles vamoosing?"

"I do, I feel a sort of tightening," said Kitten quite truthfully.

"Already your skins is looking more supple, more youthful. Perhaps I may show your madame some more . . . ?"

Kitten tried not to show the horror she was feeling. "Oh, there's more, is there?"

The woman opened her arms wide, to encompass the

length of the counter. "Oh, yes! A full line of Altavenus products, just new to this store, so you bet! Bath oils, shampoos, cosmetics, deodorants, a full line indeed!" She put her hand to her neck and leaned forward conspiratorially. "All," she said, "used by personally me. I am very one hundred percent of Altavenus products."

Kitten looked at her watch. "Oh, heavens. If only I had the time, I'd *love* to see more. But I'm due to meet someone for lunch in exactly five minutes, so—well, alas, and everything." She shrugged her shoulders.

The woman looked at her with a frozen, devastated smile. "Perhaps your madame will permit me to give up my card?"

"Oh, yes, certainly," said Kitten.

The woman scouted around behind the counter for her card; clearly, she was not often given an opportunity to present it to someone. Kitten checked her watch again. She should really leave now if she wanted to meet Mitchell on time. But she couldn't just walk out on this poor soul.

The woman finally emerged, triumphantly holding aloft a dog-eared card. She handed it to Kitten, who immediately looked at the name: SOFIA TRZWRCZKA.

That name was like a dagger through her heart.

"Oh, the hell with it," she said to Sofia. "Gimme the works."

Sofia spent a few frightening moments hyperventilating, and Kitten seriously thought she might have to call the store manager to ask for oxygen. But Sofia recovered and busily began ringing up and bagging the complete line of Altavenus products.

As she hurried back into the elevator, laden with the signature purple-and-gray Mason's shopping bags, she found herself, oddly, looking forward to telling Mitchell this story. She'd have had to tell him anyway, as an explanation for her being late—but she actually felt herself *wanting* to tell it to him, because of who he was. It was a nice feeling.

As for what she was going to do with the full, lethal line of Altavenus products—well, wasn't Raquel Dommage's birthday coming up?

chapter

29

The day had to be gloomy, didn't it? And worse; at ten to twelve, it started misting. Mitchell took his portable umbrella from the shelf in his office closet where he kept emergency supplies (flashlights, bottled water, a first aid kit, travelers' checks) and rode the elevator to the lobby, which he crossed, his heart pounding, to the west entrance of the building. People jostled him—people busily on their way somewhere or other, blissfully mindless of anything beyond the moment. Mitchell, mindful of the consequences of every step he took, both envied and despised them.

He exited the building and flapped up his umbrella; as he did so, he caught his thumbnail on the catch (damn the cheap thing!) and tore a little piece of it off; the exposed skin beneath it started to seep blood. He considered going back upstairs for his first aid kit, but he'd told Kitten twelve noon, and while she was probably the type to be late, he couldn't take a chance. He scanned the street on either side of him; one of the illegally parked vehicles belonged to, and contained, Gil Begley. He didn't know which. Better that he didn't.

As if it weren't irritating enough to have injured himself opening the umbrella mere minutes after having left his first aid kit, he now decided that the umbrella really wasn't required; the misting might be visible, but he was the only one on the street who had allowed it to push him to the extreme of an umbrella, and he was loath to appear in any way unorthodox or alarmist. He took his finger from his mouth, shuttered up the umbrella, and stood silently waiting, sucking on his wound, while a gentle fizz settled over his face. Soon, he was feeling miserable and damp. After a few minutes, he spotted a couple of people on the opposite side of the street with umbrellas in full sail, so he felt it safe to reopen his, but more carefully this time.

He checked his watch. 12:03. He scanned the traffic on the street again, looking for Kitten. Funny, him not really knowing when to expect her. Was she always late, or was this an anomaly? He really *didn't* know her very well, did he? Well, it was to be expected. How many times had they actually met? Twice? No— wait. Not even twice. There was the aborted lunch, and then drinks at Dreamweaver's with Zack. Two occasions, certainly, but separated by only a few short hours—surely that had to count as one meeting, not two. Oh, he'd seen her before that, in the Tam-Tam Club, but they hadn't spoken then; he hadn't been ready.

It must be that his preoccupation with her—to the extent of almost all else these past several days—had made it seem to him that their relationship was of much longer standing. Not to mention their bond of blood, which made it feel as though their connection was in fact a matter of decades. But of course, it wasn't—not even close. What, then, was he doing here, pursuing this course of action against a person of whom he had virtually no knowledge at all? Certainly Kitten hadn't lived up to his expectations, but his expectations, he reminded himself, had been ridiculously high—a juvenile kind of hero worship in advance. Hadn't he wanted Donald to be a superior version of himself? So Donald hadn't lived up to that—had in fact done just the opposite. That wasn't his fault. How dare Mitchell decide that Donald must pay for Mitchell's naivete—and after only a single day's acquaintance?

Suddenly, he became aware of the full extent of his monstrous arrogance. How dare he presume that his fraternal relationship gave him the right to uproot Donald from the life he had built for himself? Is this what he saw as the essence of the masculine prerogative—trampling the intricate web of laws and principles that formed civil society? Kicking them to shreds in pursuit of his own ill-considered power over others?

And he, a lawyer!

He began to feel sick to his stomach. He couldn't accept that he was really such a monster; it was too wretched a thing to face. He leaned against one of the building's eroded marble columns and decided that he must, instead, have fallen prey to some kind of temporary insanity, brought on by the shock of Donald's revealed nature and by the failure of Simon's so-called masculinism to provide him with anything but debasement and disappointment. Again, though, these were *his* failings; it wasn't fair for Donald—for *Kitten*—to pay for them.

He began to fear for Kitten's appearance. He couldn't see her, but he reminded himself that Begley was somewhere in the vicinity, watching as well. Watching for a gaudily clad woman who would stop and speak to Mitchell, after which Mitchell would ditch her so that she could be snatched.

In bold daylight. Off Franklin Street. My God! He must have had balls of brass to plan this foolhardy adventure.

Never mind—the solution was obvious. When Kitten appeared, Mitchell would steer her into the lobby of the building, away from the street, where she would be safe. He'd then take her to the opposite entrance, where he'd personally hail her a cab and see her safely into it. Even better, he'd get in with her. Really, truly take her to lunch. Live out what had until now been a ruse.

He was just beginning to consider the details and fine points of this new plan when he was interrupted by Zoe Briggs's emergence from the building. She looked at him, then turned away as if she hadn't seen him; but then, apparently deciding that her eyes had met his too directly to accommodate this fak-ery, she turned back and said, "Oh, Mitchell! I almost didn't recognize you."

"Why not?" he asked, deciding not to go easy on her. "Same gray suit I've worn twice a week for two years." Which is more than he could say for Zoe; she was clad in a lime-green checked jacket studded with carbuncular brooches and pins, all of which made her look like a photonegative of an Italian tabletop.

She laughed nervously and said, "I'm just not used to see-ing you sucking your thumb, that's all. Took you for an over-sized toddler. And what's with the umbrella? Sky's clear now."

Mitchell did a slow burn and didn't answer. He folded the umbrella and turned to look for Kitten, not wanting Zoe to distract him from spotting his twin as soon as possible.

Zoe shifted her hefty briefcase from one hand to another. "Listen, Mitchell, I have to apologize again for not getting the Wrolen file to you. But there's been so much going on, I haven't even had time to go through it myself!"

"You could always just get Bereneesha to make a copy for me," he said out of one side of his mouth, not even bothering to remove his thumb from the other.

It was her turn to redden. "Well, yes, but—see—Wrolen specifically asked that we not copy his originals." She erupted into a gold-toothed grin, apparently pleased with her quick thinking. "Because of the sensitive nature of the documents. Afraid of copies finding their way out of the office, I guess."

He rolled his eyes. "How very Cold War."

She sighed, as if agreeing with him. "I know, but what can you do? The client is king." She shifted the briefcase again. "Anyway, I *promise* to get the file to you before the weekend. 'Kay?"

"Whatever," he said, not even looking at her. He was scouring the street for Kitten.

She cleared her throat and said, "Well, anyway. I'm off at meetings for the rest of the day. See ya." And she turned and trotted away, a wedge of lime-green in a sea of dark blue and gray.

Mitchell checked his watch. 12:11. So Kitten *was* the type to be late. Maybe he knew her better than he thought. The notion pleased him, in some strange way.

Noise of a commotion roused his interest; he turned in the direction Zoe had just gone, and discovered, through a crowd of startled onlookers, that there was a tussle going on just up the street. Thinking Kitten might be involved, he took a few steps toward the trouble, squeezed through a knot of suits and ties, and saw that Zoe, of all people, was at the center of it; she was vainly trying to fight off a man who had hold of her arm. Her briefcase was lying on the sidewalk behind her.

Mitchell recognized the man. Gil Begley.

Why on earth was Begley harassing Zoe? Did he know her from somewhere?

He felt a little lightning flash of anger. The man was *supposed* to be watching for Kitten. Never mind that Mitchell no longer wanted Kitten abducted; it was the principle of the thing. He wasn't paying Begley to go bothering anyone else.

It wasn't until Begley pulled Zoe into a car and sped off, that Mitchell realized what had happened.

"Oh. My. God," he said, and he stood staring after the fleeing car as though he might somehow stop it in its tracks through sheer force of will.

Then it skidded around a corner and was gone, leaving the crowd of onlookers to break slowly apart and go guiltily on their way.

Mitchell went and collected Zoe's briefcase. The latch must have been snapped open during the tussle, because when he picked it up, it fell open and its contents tumbled onto the street.

Still in a stupefied daze, he crouched down to collect the papers and files and put them back in the briefcase. And he stopped and stared at one particular file for a full twelve seconds before he realized what it was.

The Wrolen file.

It had writing all over it. Post-It notes. Phone numbers. Dates. Figures. He flipped it open and found faxes to Zoe, from Benjamin Wrolen. And copies of Zoe's replies.

He looked up and peered into the distance, as if he might be able to call up some vision of where the car was now.

His mind was a whirl.

A moment later, a police car rounded the corner, siren blaring petulantly.

He gathered the briefcase under his arm and crept quietly back into the building.

chapter 30

It was all the Golden Girl's fault, really.

Just as the doors to the elevator had been closing, with Kitten contentedly inside by her lonesome, the Golden Girl had appeared in a fury, prying the doors open and squeezing into the car, after which the elevator had whined in anger for a minute or so, then descended four yards and stopped dead.

"Damn," said the Golden Girl. She kicked the control panel with an expensive Italian shoe. There was a bandage around her ankle, and a little gold chain around the bandage.

Kitten had seen women like this before: all sharp angles and hard edges, tailored suits and tailored hair—the kind of women so powerfully beautiful they could actually afford to act mannish. Kitten, who spent her life trying to soften her rough spots and round out her square ones, was completely in awe of these gladiatorial women—they were beyond her comprehension, like Roman goddesses.

Thinking of Roman goddesses made her remember "ancient oils and unguents," and she couldn't suppress a giggle.

The Golden Girl whirled on her and said, "Glad you find this so amusing. We're *stuck* in this thing, you know."

"Oh, I don't find it amusing at all," Kitten protested in her highest, most musical voice. "I'm supposed to be meeting someone for lunch, and I'm already running late."

The Golden Girl jabbed at the CALL button several times, then leaned into the corner, directly beneath a sign that read SMOKING PROHIBITED BY LAW. "Mind if I smoke?" she asked casually.

"Not at all," said Kitten, who would've liked a cigarette herself but now felt unable to partake, as though the Golden Girl had declared it her exclusive province—like mineral rights, or something.

She produced a Salem, then a silver Tiffany lighter, and was soon puffing away. She looked in Kitten's direction but appeared not to see her; it was as though she were looking through her, not at her.

"This is what I get, you know," she said, expelling a tangle of smoke from one side of her mouth. "This is my punishment for trying to economize."

Kitten nodded. "Yes. Well."

"I mean, for God's sake. My mother goes fruit-loops and gives away my inheritance to some kind of, I don't know, swami or something, and I get into a legal tiff with Nordstrom's, so I put two-and-two together and think, 'Well, maybe it's time to examine some of the lower-end stores.' *Hah.*" She sucked in another mouthful of smoke and released it through her nose. "Never again, you know? Just never fucking—I mean, look at us!"

Kitten felt compelled to take in the entirety of the elevator cabin. "Yes. I see."

The Golden Girl slipped her foot out of her shoe and rubbed her bandaged ankle with one hand, holding her cigarette aloft with the other. "I guess if you have to economize, the thing to do is, buy fewer things at the good stores instead of the same number of things at cheaper stores. Then you don't have to put up with crap like this."

Kitten nodded. "That makes sense."

"Either that, or find a man rich enough to make it a non-issue." She released her foot and flexed it back and forth. "Correction: a man rich enough *and* with enough backbone to not freak out over a woman who knows what she wants and isn't afraid of saying so. In other words, forget the whole thing." She tucked her foot back into her shoe and eyed Kitten's bags. "Big day for you, huh?"

Kitten didn't want to admit to having bought anything here after the Golden Girl's blistering screed against it. She looked down at her Mason's bags as though they'd wilfully betrayed her. "Oh, these are just some things I bought for my mother. She likes it here." *Why did I mention my mother?* she thought guiltily. *Must still be on my mind after all that drunken eulogizing with Aunt Joline.*

The Golden Girl took one last drag of her cigarette and shook her head. "Time was, my mother wouldn't be caught dead in a place like this." She flicked the butt to the floor and ground it beneath her heel. "Now, of course, she'll probably end up in a hut in the Himalayas personally sewing half the textiles they sell here. Is sixty too young for senility? Do you think?"

Kitten winced. "Kind of."

"The betrayal of *trust* is what really gets me," she continued, jabbing the CALL button again. "Sends me to Stephens College and then expects me to be able to work for a living. I mean, I majored in equestrianship. Seen the want ads lately?"

"No, I'm afr—"

"Not a lot of call for skilled horsewomen. So, do they ever actually *fix* this damn thing?" She gave the control panel another kick.

"Maybe they don't know we're trapped here yet," Kitten offered helpfully.

The Golden Girl looked stunned by the possibility. Then she put her hands to her mouth and called through the roof of the cabin, *"Hey! Hey, geniuses up there! You've got two ladies and a lawsuit stuck down here!"*

They listened; nothing.

The Golden Girl put one hand over her face. "Okay. I give up. You win."

Kitten raised an eyebrow. "Who—who are you talki—"

"*Life.* The universe. It's all out to get me."

"Hon, believe me, I know *exactly* how you feel."

The Golden Girl turned toward her, and Kitten thought for a second that she might actually *see* her; but in the next moment, the elevator gave a little mechanical burp, and set itself in motion again.

Twenty-three seconds later, the doors opened onto the ground floor.

The Golden Girl said, "Good day, now," and strode out into the store.

Kitten knew instinctively that if the Golden Girl were called upon to turn around right now and point out the woman she'd shared the elevator with, she wouldn't be able to pick Kitten from the half-dozen others who loitered by the bank of elevators.

Well, in a way, that was a kind of victory.

Happy, Kitten bustled out the door to meet Mitchell, with any luck within a respectable margin of lateness.

chapter 31

Mitchell hadn't returned to the office, because had he done so, he would have been morally obliged to tell the members of the firm what had happened to Zoe. So he'd called Bereneesha from the lobby, told her he'd taken ill (not a falsehood; he felt sick to his stomach), and asked her to cancel his appointments and shut down his PC. Then, fretting over his briefcase, which he'd left sitting open next to his desk, he asked her to shut that as well, spin its rotary combination lock, and put it safely in his closet.

Then he'd driven home, bandaged his thumb, and tried Gil Begley's phone number for a panicked half-hour, getting an answering machine each time. And each time he'd hung up rather than leave any incriminating evidence on tape.

He sat now in his armchair, staring at Zoe's briefcase, which he'd set on the floor near the fireplace. And his mind didn't know where to fly first. To Gil Begley's rather disastrous error? Zoe's apparent betrayal of him? Kitten's undoubted fury at having been stood up?

It was all a cauldron of poisonous brew. *Something* had to bubble up and burst. But he'd do no further stirring himself. He'd done too much already. If some consequence was bound to happen, then let it. He'd wait.

And wait he did. Soon, it was dark outside; his night light switched on automatically.

So much for the man of action, he thought. *Reduced to immobility in an armchair.*

The doorbell rang.

Mitchell's heart caromed off his breastbone.

"Who is it?" he shouted at the door.

"Your mother," came the muffled reply, "who taught you better than to yell indoors."

He leapt out of his chair and dashed out of the living room and across the foyer, where he almost wiped out on the freshmopped slate. Then he flung open the door and stood face-to-face with Bettina Gladding Sayer Hutsell Varney—or someone very like her, with short-cropped hair—and an unknown companion, a tall, pale, droopy-haired young girl with a patrician nose, who grinned at him furtively.

Mitchell ignored her. "You've cut your hair," he said to his mother.

"Yes." She leaned into him and kissed him. "Don't stare, dear. And don't stand with your mouth open. This is my friend, Helena Wold-Manning. I was at school with her mother. Helena, this is my son, Mitchell. Mitchell, your *mouth.*"

He stared at her. "You've cut your *hair.*"

"Yes, and I'm wearing brown. Are you going to invite us in?"

She *was* wearing brown; a smocklike thing with a shawl. And sandals. Who *was* this woman? "Come in," he said.

She swept past him into the foyer. "Come along, Helena," she commanded. "Don't be shy." As the girl followed, giggling wildly, Mitchell could see that she was similarly garbed.

He shut the door, then followed his guests into the living room. He turned on the overhead light and found his mother standing, arms akimbo, looking at the Chinese rug.

"You've got rid of your coffee table," she said when he'd joined her.

He nodded. "You told me it was hideous and Scandinavian."

She shook her head. "Honestly, Mitchell, if you'd only let on I have that kind of effect on you, I'd have been so content I'd never have had to join the ashram. May we take a seat?"

"Please. I'm sorry. Forgetting my manners."

They sat, and Bettina folded her hands in her lap and smiled. Helena was still giggling nervously and darting glances about the room.

Mitchell took a small breath and said, "You've cut your hair."

Bettina nodded yet again and said, "This is obviously of some import to you."

"No, no," Mitchell protested. "It's just that—it's *short.*"

"It was short before."

"But now—it's so—so—"

"Helena tells me the current term of choice is 'buzzed.' "

"Yes. That."

She leaned back into the couch. "Mitchell, I didn't come here to discuss my hair. I cut it off so that I would no longer have to deal with it. Hence, I do not wish to deal with it here."

He nodded frantically. "I see."

"Now. I got the message that you called. Sweet of you. First of my children to do so, though I have had the pleasure of receiving a handsome pair of attorneys who represent Paula."

It was Mitchell's turn to fall back into his chair. "Oh, no. I didn't know she was going to do that."

"Glad to hear it. Anyway, I sent them packing." She paused. "May I use your lavoratory, darling?"

"Certainly." He rose. "You know where it is."

She made her way down the corridor. "Helena, tell Mitchell how you came to be in the ashram. I'm sure he'll find it most enlightening."

Then she was gone, and Helena was staring at him, her

eyes wide, like a rabbit in the path of the Tianaenmen tanks. "I—ah—" she said, barely audibly.

Nothing more emerged from her mouth; she sat in stunned paralysis until Bettina came back several minutes later, rolling down her sleeves.

"Mitchell, what are you still doing with your neighbor's copy of *Glamour*?"

He blushed bright red. "I just haven't got around to returning it yet."

She resumed her seat. "Well, you can hardly return it now. It's all curled up at the spine. Have you been reading it?"

"No, no," he said, blushing even more deeply. "That's from being on the radiator."

"Well, I don't know what it's doing in the bathroom at all," she said airily.

They sat in a kind of formless silence for a moment.

"I'm a bit thirsty, dear," Bettina said at last.

He jumped up. "Sorry. I really *am* forgetting my manners. Scotch?"

"Water will be fine, thank you." She turned to her companion. "Helena, would you be a dove and fetch it for me? I'd like to speak to my son in private. Kitchen's down that corridor."

Helena jumped to her feet. "Of course."

Mitchell held out a hand in protest. "Oh, there's no need, I—"

"You don't mind Helena in your kitchen, do you?"

"Not at all. Help yourself, Helena. But I'd be more than willing t—"

"Helena is seeking humility in servitude, aren't you, Helena?"

Helena giggled rather demonically, and skittered out of the room.

When she was gone, Mitchell shrugged. "Seems like a sweet girl."

"Heroin addict," said Bettina. "And a Sarah Lawrence alumna on top of it! There are no guarantees in this world, Mitchell."

"I thought that's what you were seeking. Guarantees."

She crossed her legs and smiled. "Maybe I was. Childish of me. I know better now."

"So you're learning a lot?"

She lifted her shoulders. "A little. Mainly I'm busy *un*-learning. Lot of that to do before the main event."

"But you're happy?"

"Oh, sweetheart!" She waved her hand in the air. "I don't have the words. Happy! More like I finally see the *road* to happiness."

He sighed, and picked at an imaginary speck of lint on his trousers.

"You don't believe me."

"Not that." He shrugged. "Suppose I'm envious."

She leaned forward. "Now, Mitchell. What cause have you to say such a thing?"

Helena popped around the corner. "Mitchell," she said, her voice fluttery and high, "might I have some water, too?"

"Yes," he said. "I thought I'd said help yourself."

"Then might I have some Oreos, as well?"

He laughed. "Anything."

She squealed, but Bettina raised a cautionary finger. "Helena, dear; Oreos are made with lard."

A look of dread crossed the girl's face. "They—they are?"

"Yes, dear. And we're vegetarians now."

She looked down at her hands. "But—Bettina. *Oreos.*"

Bettina cocked her head. "Now, I know your mother, dear. She never gave you Oreos."

Helena dragged her foot back and forth. "No. Got hooked at college."

Bettina looked at Mitchell and shook her head. "Oreos *and* heroin. And at Sarah Lawrence! If I hadn't found Buddhism, this would've done me in." She turned back to Helena. "You know you shouldn't have Oreos, dear."

The girl pouted. "You wouldn't tell on me for just one, would you?"

Bettina sighed. "How many times do we have to go through

this? There's no one to tell! It's up to *you* to look after your own karma.''

"I guess." She turned to the wall. "Wish you hadn't told me about the lard."

"Now you know that's not true."

She disappeared around the corner again.

Mitchell shook his head. "What's her story?"

"Didn't she tell you? I told her to tell you. Poor, damaged thing. Been through a lot in her young life. Now she wants to work toward *real* joy. Her ambition is great, but her weaknesses are many. She had to come back into town to see her parole officer, and I vo—"

"Wh—what?" Mitchell interrupted. "That woman is a felon?"

"Mm-hmm. And I volunteered to escort her, to be her touchstone, so to speak—her link to the ashram." She paused. "And to see you and Paula, of course."

Mitchell got to his feet and looked toward the corridor. "Do you have any idea what my silver is worth?"

Bettina clicked her tongue. "She's not a thief, Mitchell. She's a drug addict."

"All the same," he muttered, and he started for the kitchen.

At the corner, he nearly collided with Helena, who grinned in apology, then craned her head around him and said to Bettina, "Fig Newtons?"

"Fig Newtons are fine," said Bettina grandly.

Mitchell was too embarrassed to follow her now, so he returned to his chair. He smiled sheepishly at his mother, who raised an eyebrow at him and said, "I'll resist the urge to ask what *you're* doing with Oreo cookies in your cupboard, and instead ask why you imply you're not happy. Is it because I plan to sell all my things? Are you and Paula in league against me?"

He shook his head. "No, no. Course not. They're your things to sell."

"Thank you, darling. And to not sell, as it happens."

He blinked. "What was that?"

"I'm not selling them. I'm giving them to you and the girls.

I never meant to give them to the Dalai Lama in the first place, you know. I don't know where Paula got that idea. I was simply going to sell them, get them out of my hair. I wanted to be unencumbered by material possessions. I can accomplish the same objective by just signing them over to you. I believe you'll have to pay some fierce capital gains taxes. Check with Max on that."

"Mother, you needn't do this. I don't want your things."

She smiled. "Dear Mitchell. You'd better take them. If you don't, Paula will."

He pursed his lips and nodded. "I suppose she would." He chuckled. "She must be ecstatic."

Bettina grimaced. "Paula has never experienced ecstasy. She'll have a brief moment of empty euphoria when I tell her, then immediately begin plotting how to get the bulk of my jewelry before Veronica can stake a claim. She's yet to learn the value of *being* as opposed to *having*." She sighed and wove her fingers together. "Now tell me, dear. Why aren't you happy?"

"Oh," he said, "it's all to do with that twin brother of mine."

"You found him!" said Bettina, and she clapped her hands. "Does he really look like you?"

"I hardly know. Never seen him without a wig and makeup."

"I'm sorry?"

He felt his face contort, and before he could stop himself, he was spilling out the whole sordid story. "Mother, he's a transvestite! He calls himself Kitten, and he wears dresses and wigs and performs at a club as a female singer, and—and—well, that's the bulk of it, anyway. Every time we get together—well, it's only been twice—*once*, really—it's like daggers drawn. I can't get close to her. *Him.* I can't tell you—I had such high hopes. And now—"

She stopped him. "Mitchell, you realize that your hopes are irrelevant to this situation."

"I—know that now." He took out a handkerchief and wiped his forehead.

"I must warn you against anger and pride. In regard to

this, as in all else. That's one thing I *have* learned. They can only lead you astray."

"Actually, I just kind of learned that myself." The hard way, he thought, as he stole a glance at Zoe's briefcase.

She put her chin in her hand. "Mitchell, try to understand that your brother has a spirit that is in many ways the same as yours. It's just the clothes you can't get past."

He shook his head. "The clothes are just the *point*, Mother. They're the outward sign of what he is—a whirlwind of social and cultural confusion waiting to inflict itself on someone. Lately me."

Bettina did something she had never done before. She got up from the couch, went over to Mitchell's chair, sat on the arm, and stroked his hair. "Or maybe he's someone desperately trying to find a corner of the world where he can fit," she said, not acknowledging this sudden intimacy. "Someone who shows more courage every time he walks down a street than you or I have ever had to show in our lives. Someone who was born different and has made the difficult decision to *stay* that way. Because to him, if to no one else, it's real." She bent close to him and kissed his ear. "Help him, Mitchell."

"How?"

"*Love* him."

She stroked the hair behind his ear a few more times, until he could bear it no more; a little longer and he'd be weeping like a baby. He looked at her and said, "What on earth is keeping Helena with that water?"

She winked at him. "Go and find out, shall we?"

They discovered her in the kitchen, her mouth and hands stuffed with fig Newtons, staring at Mitchell's tiny five-inch TV.

"Helena?" Bettina said in a gentle, inquiring tone. "Is everything all right?"

"It's *great*," the girl said, chewing maniacally. "Jake left Amanda and went back to Jo."

chapter
32

A few hours earlier, Kitten had stomped up the stairs to her apartment. When she reached the second floor landing and saw Miss Frobisher peering out a crack in her door, she stomped even louder and hissed at her, so that the old woman gave forth a little hiccup of fear and slammed the door on her.

She was so angry, she almost couldn't handle her keys; she fumbled them into the lock by sheer chance, then flung open the door, threw her purse across the room, dumped her Mason's shopping bags on the floor, and kicked the door shut.

And then she gave forth with a full-throttle, Sally-Bowles-at-her-best scream.

The phone rang.

Kitten pounced on it, grabbed the receiver by its neck, and yanked it to her ear. *"What!"*

"Um—Kitten, honey? That you?"

"Who's askin'?"

"Just me. Tequila."

"Oh." She sat down and hurled one leg over the other. "What do *you* want?"

Tequila Mockingbird giggled. "That time of the month, sweets?"

"Don't be a bitch." She reached over to the lamp stand and got a cigarette from a gilded box. "I'm in a *foul* mood."

"How come?"

She hung the cigarette from her lower lip and grabbed a matchbook. "Had a lunch date with my twin brother."

"Oh, how'd it go?"

"*Didn't*. Fucker *stood me up*." She struck a match against the bottom of her shoe, then lit the cigarette.

"Habit of doin' that, don't he?"

"*Had* a habit. Not getting the chance again. *Finished* with that asshole."

"Wish you wouldn't do that, Miss Kitt."

"Do what?" She puffed out a dagger-shaped cloud of smoke.

"Use *asshole* in the pejorative. To some of us, an asshole is a very pleasant thing indeed."

Kitten rolled her eyes. Tequila was also the only one of the Tam-Tam drag queens who insisted on being called a 'gender illusionist.'

"You still there?" Tequila asked.

"Sorry; I just couldn't talk for a second. Politically correct terms always trigger my gag reflex. Listen, you called for a reason."

"Yeah, I was by to see you today."

"I wasn't here."

"I know, I know. Got into your building anyhow—ducked after some old gal while she was letting herself in with her grocery cart. Almost had a seizure when she saw me on her heels. Told me not to come near her 'cause she's got bubonic plague or something."

"Leprosy. Why'd you want to get in here if you knew I wasn't home?"

"Slipped something under your door I knew you'd want to

see first thing. New issue of *OUTlandish*, got an article with you in it.''

Kitten's anger felt suddenly, miraculously lightened; this could only be the promised profile by Skye Armitage. She stubbed out her cigarette. "Tequila, you angel cake!" She got to her feet. "Thanks a mil. Gotta go now, give it a gander.''

"Sure thing, hon. Shouldn't get real excited about it, though. I'm warning you in advance.''

"Jesus, Tequila, never figured *you* were one for sour grapes.''

There was a strange silence. "Well, it ain't sour grapes, sugar. Ain't any kind of grapes at all. Maybe a raisin.''

Kitten clicked her tongue, said, "Call you later,'' and hung up; then she dashed back to her front door, where she found a slightly trampled copy of the new *OUTlandish*, with that adorable naval officer Keith Meinhold on the cover—another of the seemingly interminable series of he's-in, he's-out, he's-in stories. *I'll give him in and out,* thought Kitten lasciviously as she returned to her sofa.

She sat down and flipped through the paper, looking first for the photo of her in Mitchell's lap (which, she was delighted to reflect, would cause him acute embarrassment). But she made it through the paper without having seen it.

Maybe the photo had been cropped. She flipped through the issue again, looking only for her own magnificent mug.

Not there.

Well, maybe the story had run *without* a photo, although that seemed inconceivable. She flipped through the paper yet again, scanning for her name in a headline.

Nothing.

Flustered, she decided to go through once more and at least look for Skye Armitage's byline.

Ah.

There. On page 5.

CHICAGO DRAG QUEENS ENTER THE MAINSTREAM, by Skye Armitage.

And next to it, a great, big glamorous photo of **Regina**
Upright. In a bubble bath.

Kitten's heart came to a cold, dead standstill.

She read on.

> The sizzling sisters of Chicago's drag community
> are stepping out of their fabulous closets and into the
> limelight in ever-increasing numbers. Most notable is
> the gal known to Tam-Tam Club regulars as The Idol
> of Millions, Miss Regina Upright, who this week signed
> a six-month contract with independent TV station
> Channel 48 to host a late-night movie show, "Mistress
> Regina's Fabu-Flicks."

> "It's sort of a cross between Elvira and 'Mystery
> Science Theater 3000,'" said the irrepressible Idol of
> Millions, caught by this reporter at her Lakeview home
> enjoying a keep-fit breakfast of Grape Nuts, apple
> wedges, and coffee with "about seventeen teaspoons"
> of Sweet & Low. "The show will be hosted by me, and
> I'll give a rundown on the truly immortal grade-B star-
> lets who grace each film, such as Beverly Garland and
> Vera Hruba Ralston. Then we'll show the film itself,
> with me and a different pair of guest snap queens each
> week sitting in and giving our insightful, wise and in-
> variably kindly meant comments."

> "Mistress Regina's Fabu-Flicks" is scheduled to air
> at 3:30 A.M., not exactly prime-time, but still an un-
> precedented foothold on the airwaves for a midwest-
> ern manwoman of Regina's stature. Channel 48
> Program Manager Glenn Yardley comments that, "We
> don't really consider that we're burying Regina. We're
> going after the midnight-movie audience, and most of
> them are still up at that hour; and those that aren't—
> or who haven't gotten home yet—can always tape her.
> We have a feeling she's going to be big in this town,
> and when that happens, we'll consider moving her up,
> maybe to an 11:30 slot. But that's the future."

In the meantime, Mistress Regina vows to down many multi-vitamins in order to keep up her pressing schedule as both Tam-Tam celebutante and television hostess, not to mention pursuing her more "physically demanding" hobbies, which she prefers not to name. "It's not gonna be E-A-S-Y," she says with a sigh worthy of Bernhardt, "but I know I can succeed. After all, I've got Wessonality."

The Idol of Millions isn't the only drag Cinderella in the public eye. *OUTlandish*'s own advice columnist and gal-about-town Glori Bea has recently guest-hosted several segments of WJJC-FM's Saturday-night sex affairs show, "On Getting It On." And Regina Upright's fellow Tam-Tam performer, Kit N. Kabudle, boasts a long and prosperous career as a successful women's hand model with the Jennifer Jerrold Talent Agency.

By the time she got to the last line, Kitten was having a hard time reading the print; she was clutching the paper too tightly and shaking too much.

It seemed that all she had done for the past two weeks was endure indignity after successive indignity. Even from Zack, who, sweet as he was, had essentially told her she was a novelty act. A curiosity.

And now this.

Hadn't she vowed, no more humiliation? No more mortification?

She was trembling so violently that her cheap brass bracelets were clattering like the sidecars of a freight train.

She got up, and even though nearly blinded by rage, managed to navigate across her debris-strewn apartment to her bedroom, where she removed her wig and makeup, donned a Gap t-shirt, and took to her bed. There, shorn of the accouterments of the beleaguered and bedeviled "Kit N. Kabudle," she began, slowly, to relax. And this indeed was the measure of her despair: that for the first time in her life, she felt more comfortable as Donald.

chapter

33

As Kitten entered the Tam-Tam to prepare for her supper-hour performance, she was yanked—literally *yanked*—aside by Carlotta, the enormous, broad-chested bouncer.

She regained her footing—momentarily lost under Carlotta's whiplash grip—and blinked in surprise at Carlotta's demeanor, which was fearsome. Her face was gnarled with anger, her lipstick smeared up onto one cheek, and her rat's-nest wig (she owned only one; all the girls at the Tam-Tam were sure she slept in it) was extending fibrous strands above her head, making her look something like a cockatoo in full display. Through her threadbare t-shirt (which read, inexplicably, I'M WITH STUPID), Kitten could see her pectorals heaving indignantly up and down her chest.

"Evening, Carlotta," Kitten said genially. "Am I right in guessing you'd like a moment of my time?"

The bouncer, who still clutched one of Kitten's arms, emitted a low growl and said, "I want you to let him go."

Kitten felt a fleeting thrill; this was almost exactly like a

scene from one of the lurid old movies she'd loved as an ado-
lescent. The only thing spoiling it was that she had no idea what
Carlotta was talking about. "I beg your pardon," she said, smiling sweetly. "Let *who* go?"

"You *know* who," burbled Carlotta, and she gave her a
shake.

Kitten felt her teeth rattle and her wig jar. Suddenly
alarmed, she cast her eyes around the bar, but found that no
one was paying any attention whatsoever to her and Carlotta's
little tête-à-threat.

"Carlotta, darling, I don't mean to provoke you—in fact,
over the course of my long years I've developed the kind of
fondness for my face that would inspire me to go to any lengths
necessary to prevent you from conceiving that you might have
cause to alter its basic structure—which in turn is the principal
reason you should believe me when I aver that I do *not* know
of whom you speak."

As Kitten had intended, her rather verbose response had
caused Carlotta a moment of confusion—and thus a dilution
of her anger. When the strapping girl had at last waded her way
through to the sense of what Kitten had said, she leaned into
her and said, "I mean *Pierre*. Who else?"

Kitten was truly astonished. "Pierre? What about him?
What have I done to him?"

Carlotta gave her another shake. "You're holding him
back, that's what! You've got to let him go!"

Now that Kitten knew she was being accused unjustly, her
own feisty, terrierlike temper flared to life, and she actually
managed to wrest her wiry little arm free of Carlotta's oven-mitt
hands.

"If Pierre wanted to leave the Tam-Tam, I certainly
wouldn't stand in his way," she said, thrusting her chin up to
where Carlotta's own face snarled down at her. "But as it happens, Pierre not only does *not* want to leave, he's actually *grateful*
to be here, and grateful to me for keeping him employed when
all the other girls don't use him."

Carlotta crossed her arms. "And you *believe* that?"

She hoisted her purse over her shoulder as if this ridiculous discussion were delaying her. "Why shouldn't I? He wouldn't lie to me."

Carlotta surprised her by grabbing her once again. "Of *course* he wouldn't lie. But he's also too sensitive to tell the whole *truth*."

"And what's the whole truth, pray fucking tell?"

Carlotta stuck out her lower lip. "He wants desperately to leave! He feels useless here. The girls make fun of him. The patrons call him names. He only has anything to do when you come in to sing, and you do your sets in the worst possible time on the schedule."

"Fuck you very much for reminding me."

"And when he went to thank you for being the only one who justified his staying here, what he was *really* doing was trying to get *you* to realize that you're the only thing holding him back, so that you could do the right thing and insist that he go."

Kitten shook her head. "What are you talking about? He doesn't *have* anywhere to go. He told me so!"

"Of course he doesn't! That's *why* he wants to go. Because if he's suddenly out of a job, with no prospects, he'll *have* to find something else. He'll never be motivated to do that while he has even the bare minimum of stability and security here."

Kitten shut her eyes and laughed in astonishment. "And I was supposed to infer all that from his coming to my dressing room to tell me I'm wonderful? Come on, Carlotta!"

The bouncer released her grip on Kitten's arm and shoved it back at her; Kitten almost fell off her heels. "No, I guess I couldn't expect *you* to read between the lines. Not someone so shallow. *You'd* never notice that Pierre finishes every set by coming to my station and crying on my shoulder, because he's so unhappy."

"That's hardly fair! After a performance I'm too tired and wrung out to—"

"Wrung out? *Strung* out is more like it."

Kitten felt her scalp start to itch with real anger. "What's *that* supposed to mean?"

"As if I have to spell it out! The whole club knows about you and your heroin habit."

"M—my—my—"

"*Heroin habit.* I'm not afraid to say it, like everyone else is."

Kitten was feeling quite faint. "That—is a *filthy* lie. Who told you that?"

"Everyone knows. Everyone's been talki—"

"WHO TOLD YOU THAT?"

In the silence that followed, Kitten realized that she'd lost too much control; all chatter in the bar had stopped, and she could feel the eyes of every single patron and employee searing into her.

And yet, something in her voice must also have told Carlotta that this was not a matter she took lightly—that it could in fact be a slander of the very first order.

The bouncer took a step back and said, in a low voice, "Regina told me. Regina told everybody."

Kitten felt, actually *felt*, the knife wound in her back.

"Thank you, Carlotta," she said. "Everything that's gone wrong in my life now makes a great deal more sense."

That, too, was a line worthy of B-movie immortality, but as Kitten strode to her dressing room, she could manage to find no pleasure in it.

chapter

34

Kitten rushed through her set, then threw on her coat and tried to slink out of the bar; she didn't dare risk running into Regina in the dressing room—her face would show everything. And she didn't want Regina to know she was on to her until she'd taken some time to analyze this monstrous betrayal.

Unfortunately, Regina was just coming through the door when Kitten reached it. Kitten ducked into the shadows next to a pay phone and waited for the bitch to pass. There was someone with her, she noticed now—another queen Kitten faintly recognized. Where had she seen that queen before? A young thing—cross between Bjork and Wednesday Addams. There couldn't be two like that.

"You don't *know* what an inspiration you've been to me," the queen was telling Regina, who bore the aspect of a particularly condescending empress of Russia. "When I was a kid, I used to sneak out of my family's house in Barrington and take the train a whole *hour* just to see you."

"Actually," said Regina with an acid smile, "I've only been performing here six months."

The youthful queen didn't miss a beat. "Well, I just moved out this summer."

That's who it was. That bitch from Barrington—what had her name been? Barbarella Fitzgerald. Fed Kitten the same line, not more than two weeks ago. Which was probably ancient history, in her nappy little head. She'd clearly hitched her wagon to a brand new star. The star of the moment.

Feeling physically wounded, Kitten waited till they were well into the club before leaving the shadows and limping home.

She lay now on her couch, a bag of Pepperidge Farm Orange Milano cookies propped open on her chest, and as she sorted through the whole mess, she devoured cookie, after cookie, after cookie.

Regina, it was clear, had been undermining her for some months now. She could probably date Gordy's sudden displeasure with her from the time Regina had joined the club. The heroin story was probably just the tip of the iceberg—the crowning lie among the many that had caused Gordy to promote Regina over her.

And then there was the matter of the *OUTlandish* profile. She'd told Regina about her interview with Skye Armitage, Regina must've then called the paper to offer her own, more sensational story as the profile's new focus.

And come to think of it, what *about* "Mistress Regina's Fabu-Flicks?" Where had *that* come from? She'd spoken to a couple of other girls at the club, and no one they knew had ever auditioned for Mr. Glenn Yardley of Channel 48. How had he managed to find a star for his late-night drag show without interviewing any actual drag queens? Something fishy there, too. Like as not, Kitten wasn't the only girl to get screwed over by Regina. Shrewd little bitch . . .

The telephone rang. Kitten stared at it, as if willing it to stop; but each ring seemed more insistent than the last, so she gave up and leaned over to answer it. With any luck, it would be Zack.

She sighed into the receiver, then listlessly said, "Hello."

"It's Mitchell. Don't hang up."

She had the receiver halfway back to the cradle before his words registered; then she hesitated a moment and brought it back to her ear. "What do *you* want?"

"To apologize."

"Too little, too lame, too late, Mister Yuppie Scum. Sayonara."

"I love you."

She dropped an Orange Milano cookie onto the carpet.

"What did you say?" she whispered.

"I said I love you. You're my brother. My twin brother. My *sister*. Whatever you are, I love you. And I'm sorry we've had to do such a hat dance before reaching this point."

Kitten was stunned. "I—I am, too."

A minivan-sized silence followed.

"I'm not offering any explanations," said Mitchell. "For lunch this afternoon, I mean. Explanations just seem to muddy the waters between us, somehow."

"Yes," said Kitten.

"The truth is, we don't understand each other. We *let* ourselves misunderstand each other."

"Yes," said Kitten.

"What it amounts to is pride. Well, I've been proud and lonely for a while now. I think I'd like to try it the other way for a change."

"Yes," said Kitten.

"There's been a lot happening in my life, lately."

"Mine, too."

"A lot of searching. A lot of conflict."

"Me, too."

"It—I don't know how to put this. I think I was looking at you as being the problem. You were never the problem."

"No."

"*I* was the problem." He paused. "Or a large part of it, anyway."

"Me, too. Well, me and someone else."

"Really? Yeah, there's someone out for my blood, too. Rival
I didn't even suspect. I kept thinking *you* were my rival. Isn't
that ridiculous? Rival for what? And all the time I had this *real*
rival, right under my nose—"

"Me, too. Never suspected a thing. And all the time—"

"I was so obsessed with you, I didn't see that she—"

"—was stabbing you in the back, stealing your career? Tell
me about it."

He whistled. "Bizarre, isn't it? We've been in pretty much
the same place all this time, but instead of joining forces, we've
been fighting each other."

"And letting *them* win."

"Exactly!" Mitchell laughed. "Pretty pathetic, aren't we?"

Kitten grinned widely, and found to her surprise that the
grin was squeezing tears from her eyes. "Uh-huh."

"Tell me about yours. Your rival, I mean."

She heaved a wobbly sigh. "Oh. Not much to tell. Another
girl at the club." She paused. "You understand what I mean by
girl, don't you?"

"Sure. I've come *that* far, at least."

"Well, this girl—she's been telling lies about me behind
my back. God knows how long. Got the whole place against me.
To the point now—I mean, my stage career is almost over. It's
a joke."

"Well—don't give up yet."

"I won't."

"And you know, even if the worst happens, you've still got
your hand modeling career. You won't go hungry."

She shook her head. "But that's just a job. Starring at
the Tam-Tam—being the Doyenne of Despair—Mitchell, that's
me."

"Then don't quit. *Fight.*"

"All right, then. Help me. Tell me how you're handling
your rival."

A long silence. "Gee. Kind of complicated."

"Never mind. Probably wouldn't work for me."

"I—wouldn't think so. I've kind of botched things, actu-

ally. Pretty badly. Best if you think up your own way to handle
—what's her name?''

''Regina. Regina Upright.'' She put the bag of cookies on
the floor and sat up. ''Soon to be the star of 'Mistress Regina's
Fabu-Flicks' on Channel 48.''

''Wow.''

''Yes, wow. Course, her real name is Rondell Davis, and
without her makeup and slut duds you'd never look twice at
her.'' She grimaced. ''Although I suppose the same could be
said of me.''

''Not a chance. Not if you're as handsome as I am, underneath it all.'' He laughed.

Kitten drew her knees up in pleasure. ''You might be
surprised.''

''Actually, I'd really like to see.'' He cleared his throat.
''Listen—would that be possible?''

''I don't know, I—''

''Be great if we could just start over, you know? Clean slate.
What if I come over tomorrow, after work, and we just go out
for a couple of drinks? With you as you.''

''You've already *met* me as me.''

''You know what I mean. With you as *me*, then.''

She squirmed. ''I don't know. I'm not really comfortable
in that identity.'' She snickered. ''Hell, I *hate* that identity.''

''I know you do—but it's my strongest connection to you.
It's my frame of reference. I'd love to see you as Donald. Just
once. Personal favor, never to be repeated. Please?''

She frowned. ''Well. All right.''

''Terrific!''

''But we *stay in* and have drinks.''

''I'll bring over champagne.''

''Veuve Clicquot, then. I insist.''

''Of course.''

''Gold label.''

''I'll make it the Grand Dame.''

''Ooh, you do know how to live!''

''Shall we say, six o'clock?''

"Glorious. You've got my address?"
"Uh-huh. I'll see you then."
"Bye. And—uh—"
A spell of weighty silence.
"What, Kitten?"
"Just—I love you, too."

chapter 35

Mitchell was jarred awake by a call at four-thirty in the morning. He lunged for the phone, got his right arm tangled in a sheet, and had to pick up the receiver with his left.

"Hello?" he said, his voice cracking.

"I don't know you, and you don't know me," said a man at the other end of the line. "We never met." And then he hung up.

"What? Who is this? Wait!" Mitchell listened to the dial tone for several heartbeats before hanging up the phone.

His sleep disturbed, he got up to prepare for the day; and it wasn't till he was in the shower, lathering his hair, that he realized the voice on the phone had belonged to Gil Begley.

He arrived at work at just after six o'clock, still disturbed and confused by the call, and was waiting for the elevator for a full fifteen seconds before he realized that the stooped, ashen figure in front of him was someone he knew. That disheveled lime-green jacket was a dead giveaway; the same one she'd worn yesterday, if quite a bit the worse for wear.

His heart racing, he leaned forward and touched her shoulder. *"Zoe?"*

She turned to face him, and her eyes were ringed and hollow. "Oh, *Mitch,*" she moaned, and she grabbed him and hugged him. "You have no idea what I've been through in the past twelve hours!"

The other two persons waiting for the elevator tilted their heads ever so slightly toward Zoe. Mitchell laughed nervously and looked at the LED indicators over the two elevators. One of them was descending rapidly. Eleventh floor, tenth floor, ninth . . .

"I was *kidnapped,*" said Zoe with a catch in her throat. "I'm not joking! Like some kind of bad movie." She clutched Mitchell's arm, wrinkling his suitcoat. "Some Neanderthal nabbed me right off Franklin Street—in broad daylight! Just after I'd talked to you!"

"My God—was it—was it horrible?" Fourth, third, second . . .

"Worse." She bit her lower lip, and the elevator bell rang. "Mitchell, these three men—the Neanderthal and two gorillas of his—they blindfolded me and hog-tied me!" The elevator doors slid open, and the other two workers filed into it, clearly reluctant to get out of earshot of Zoe.

Mitchell held her back. "Let's get the next one," he said. "More privacy."

The doors slid shut and the elevator sailed away.

Zoe leaned into him. "Mitchell, they *molested* me." A tear slipped out of her eye.

He was stunned. "They did not!"

"Swear to God! Well, sort of. They took me to some filthy abandoned office in a building next to a railroad track. I tried to pay attention to what lines passed so I could help the police find the place, but I couldn't make them out. Anyway, then these three thugs, they started calling me Donald and asking me why I wear women's clothing and I kept saying, 'My name is not Donald,' and they kept saying, " 'Yes it is.' " And then they started showing me fashion magazine layouts and when I'd look at them they'd suddenly switch to pictures of gutted animals and then they'd flash a light in my face and scream at me. It was terrifying! And finally, after hours of this, when I was a completely broken woman, one of them did it—felt my crotch." She shuddered. "And then they *all* felt my crotch, and they started looking really scared—maybe because they knew they'd gone too far—and they tied me back up and put me in the car. I thought they were going to take me somewhere and rape me, but instead they asked me where I lived and when I wouldn't tell them they dropped me at Wabash and Ontario."

A new elevator arrived; Mitchell hustled her onto it before anyone else could enter the lobby and rush to share it.

The doors slid shut and Mitchell heaved a sigh of relief. He pressed the fourteenth-floor button and the elevator started its ascent.

Zoe took a well-used handkerchief from her breast pocket and daubed her nose. "I didn't have any money because it was all in my briefcase, which I lost. And I couldn't walk home from there, obviously—I mean, I live in Evanston—so I walked here instead, and waited on a bench for the building to open."

"For God's sake, Zoe, don't you have any friends you could've called?"

She sniffed. "Not really." She looked at her feet. Then, fiercely, she snapped her head up and said, "I'm gonna find the bastards who did this to me, and I'm gonna make sure they rot in the slammer. I swear to *God* I'm gonna do it."

Mitchell knew the time was now. Now, or he'd lose his nerve and have to live in fear for the rest of his life.

He reached past Zoe and depressed the red lever that brought the elevator to a dead halt.

She looked at him, confused. "Mitchell, what is this? What are you doing?"

He rubbed his hands together. "We have to talk."

She backed away from him. "About what? And why here?"

He grinned nervously. "Look, Zoe—about the 'Neanderthal' who kidnapped you. The thing is—he works for me. *Worked* for me."

Her lip curled into a snarl. "For *you*?"

"He's a professional deprogrammer; I hired him to—well, to apprehend my twin brother and to cure him of his delusion that he's a woman."

She looked at him with complete consternation. "You mean—that wasn't—"

"That wasn't my sister you met, no. Introduced himself as Kitten, but he's really Donald. I hired a deprogrammer to make him realize that. Arranged to meet him outside the building, for a lunch date; he was supposed to come up and talk to me, so that the deprogrammer would know who he was, and then I was supposed to somehow get him alone, so he could be snatched. When you came up to talk to me, before that could happen—well, I never realized that they'd think that—that you—"

"They thought I was a drag queen?" she said in a voice that could've cut through a banshee's wail.

He nodded. "I saw what happened, and I tried to call them afterward, to tell them what a mistake they'd made, but I couldn't get through." He shrugged and turned his palms to the ceiling. "Sorry."

She balled her fists and shook her head. "You're gonna pay for this, Sayer." She flicked her wrist and snapped the red lever back into position; the elevator started to move. "Soon as the partners get here, I'm marching straight in and telling them what you did to me."

"In the first place, I didn't *do* anything," said Mitchell, snapping the lever down again and bringing the elevator back to a halt. "In the second place, you're not mentioning this to the partners at all."

She babbled out a derisive laugh. "How exactly you planning to stop me, buster?"

He raised an eyebrow. "Zoe, I found your briefcase. I've got it at home."

A flicker of worry crossed her face before she could manage to hide it. "So—what does that—does that mean I'm supposed to be so *grateful* or something, that I'm supposed to forget this whole disas—"

"I saw the Wrolen file."

She narrowed her eyes at him. "You looked through my personal belongings."

He cocked his head and gave her a get-real look. "Let's not start mounting our moral high horse, shall we? Not after what you've done. Gone behind my back. Pretended not to have familiarized yourself with Wrolen's case file, when you've been corresponding with him for days."

She was flexing her hands now, like she was preparing to leap at him and strangle him. "I was going to tell you."

"When? My birthday? Christmas? The next presidential administration?" He shook his head. "The situation is this: my personal family problems accidentally ensnared you—a perfectly understandable if unfortunate mischance. *You*, however, are guilty of insubordination, sabotage, and just about every breach of ethics one associate can commit against another." He reached over and gently flicked the red lever upward; the elevator continued its climb. "Now, at lunchtime, I'll run home and retrieve your briefcase. And at, say, two o'clock, you and I will get together and decide how we're going to divide up the work on the Wrolen job. This morning, I suggest you get some money from petty cash, take a cab home, and change clothes."

She glared at him for the remainder of the ride, until the doors opened on the fourteenth floor. Then she stepped out of the elevator, whirled on him, and said, "Understand this, Sayer: you may have beaten me on this thing, but you and I are now enemies."

He laughed. "Considering the way you conduct your friendships, I can't see that that'll make for much of a change." He dug his keys from his pocket and unlocked the back door to the office. "But if you want some free advice—"

"I'd rather vomit blood."

"I'm giving it anyway." He held the door shut, refusing to open it until he'd had his say. "Zoe, the way to make partner is not to cut the legs off everyone who's in competition with you. You do it by being a team player. By gaining the support and trust of your peers. Don't you know what it means to gain power at the expense of others? Never ends well. Reread your Shakespeare! *Henry the Fourth, Macbeth,* for God's sake—"

She groaned in disgust and pushed her way past him; the door flew out of his hands.

He sighed, then stood for a moment and collected himself; an upsetting confrontation, all told, but a productive one. He *had* beaten Zoe—stalemated her, really, but to Zoe it would amount to the same thing—and even been graceful about it. If she wanted to pursue her self-destructive career path, at least he had the consolation of knowing he'd tried to stop her.

It wasn't until a few hours later that a less worthy thought struck him, and he realized how effectively he'd ended his rivalry with Zoe. Just like that. She might double-cross the other associates, but she didn't dare cross him—not now, not at any time in the future; his knowledge of her wrongdoing was just too dangerous. She'd never risk him spilling the beans.

And it was all because of Kitten, in a way. Without Kitten, it never would've happened.

He leaned back in his chair and thought, Well, if Kitten was indirectly responsible for my victory over my rival, maybe I can be a little more directly responsible for a victory over hers.

He rolled his chair up to his desk, flipped through his Filofax phone directory, and found the number he needed. Then he picked up the receiver and dialed.

After a half dozen rings, he heard a child wailing, followed by a woman's harried voice. "—ake care of you once and for all, young lady, just as soon as I'm off the phone." A breathy pause, then, "Deene Detective Agency."

Mitchell smiled. "Cora? Mitchell Sayer here. Got a moment? I've got a quick little job for you. . . ."

chapter

36

Mitchell left work early to run errands, the first of which was to buy a bottle of Veuve Clicquot Grand Dame at a wine discount store on Clark Street. Even wholesale, it set him back a nice piece of change. Never mind; he owed it to Kitten, after all the craziness he'd put her through. Hell—if it came to that, he owed it to himself for the same reason.

This brought to mind his disastrous night at the Darklords' "meeting," which in turn reminded him that his walk to his car would take him past the veterinary clinic where Simon was employed. He stopped to consider whether he wanted to continue on this path and risk Simon seeing him out the window. This provoked a spate of obscenities from an enormous, greasy-faced homeless man who was trying to pass him, his arms filled inexplicably with battered old Andy Williams LPs.

Mitchell held his breath while the foul-smelling bum made his way around him, muttering something about yuppies who think the fucking world is their fucking oyster. Mitchell grinned when he realized that this wasn't radically different from what Simon would say in the same situation.

This made him reflect fondly on Simon, and even miss him, so that he decided to stop avoiding his old friend and drop in on him. After all, Simon had been nice enough to messenger him the jacket he'd abandoned at the Darklords' headquarters, wallet intact and no questions asked. Mitchell had never even called to thank him; hadn't in fact spoken to him since.

The clinic was bustling today. There were the usual half dozen weepy twentysomethings bearing cardboard cartons containing mewling cats, but there was also a ferocious-looking younger man with a tattoo of a flaming skull on his shoulder, who had a muzzled rottweiler on a leash, and a couple of elderly women in faded hats who sat huddled over a bichon frise with an eyepatch. Mitchell spotted Simon at the reception counter, sporting a leather armband beneath the sleeve of his hygienic white work shirt; he was engaged in a heated exchange with a slender black woman who punctuated her sentences with nibbles on her fingernails.

"Do you really have to put him to *sleep* just because his *teeth* are dirty?" she asked.

Simon confused her by shaking his head back and forth at the same time he answered in the affirmative. "Dog of that size, it's the only way."

"*What's* the only way?" Nibble, nibble.

"Putting him to sleep."

She shook her head. "I can't allow that, I'm sorry. I really don't know why you can't just clean his teeth. I really don't know what is the big deal about it."

Mitchell noticed Simon's working-hard-to-remain-calm demeanor—a look he knew only too well from their years together. "Ma'am, a Dalmatian that size—believe me, four of our best hands couldn't hold him down. He *has* to be knocked out."

"Knocked out?" she asked.

"Yes. That's what we're talking about."

"You said before, put him to sleep." Nibble, nibble.

"Same thing. Knock him out, put him to sleep—six of one."

"But I thought—when I was a kid, my mama would threaten—" Nibble, nibble, nibble. "I mean, when I didn't take

care of the dog, she'd say she was gonna put it to sleep. Like
—it meant that—'' She ground to a halt.

Simon turned bright red, and Mitchell could tell his friend
had slid from frustration right into barely suppressed laughter.
"Ma'am, your mother was using the term differently than we
do. She was using it as a euphemism for putting the dog down.''

"Putting it down where?''

He shook his head. "I mean terminating its life.'' He
waited for a reaction and got none. "Having it *killed*.''

The woman let her hand hang limp before her mouth for
a moment. She looked absolutely mortified. "I knew that,'' she
said a bit too defensively. Then she swept up her purse and
said, "Okay, fine, put him to sleep. If you're sure it's safe.''

"It is,'' said Simon, grinning. "You can pick him up after
four.''

She grinned sheepishly and darted from the clinic.

When she'd gone, Mitchell stepped up and said, "Hey,
Simon.''

"Mitchell!'' He pointed after the fleeing Dalmation owner.
"Did you hear that?''

"Mm-hmm.''

"Oh, thank *God*!'' he said dramatically. "No one would
ever've believed me without a witness. Like the time that crazy
lady with the hairnet brought in her springer spaniel to be
spayed, and asks if it would cost less if she supplied her own.
Her own what? I ask. And she pulls out a fucking garden
spade!''

"I remember,'' he said, smiling. "I still don't believe it.''

"Hell of an anesthetic we'd've had to use on the poor
bitch.'' Simon wiped tears away from the corners of his eyes,
and sighed in merriment. "Oh, God. So what brings you here,
anyway? Haven't heard from you in—shit. Days.''

"No, no you haven't.''

He spotted the Grand Dame. "That for me?''

" 'Fraid not. Listen, Simon—''

An attractive Hispanic man in a lab coat leaned into the
room behind Simon's counter. "Next up,'' he said.

Simon winked at him, then turned to Mitchell and said, "Just a sec." He ran his finger down his check-in chart and said, "Rowella?"

"That's us," said one of the old women, looking uncertain as to whether she should stand, or wave, or both. "That's our girl."

Simon nodded in the direction of the adjacent hallway. "Examining Room Three, dear. Doctor'll be with you shortly."

The women rose from their chairs with all the pep of a beach eroding, then ambled down the corridor fussing over Rowella, who panted happily.

Simon turned back to Mitchell and smiled. "Big date tonight?"

"Of a sort. I've finally worked it out with my twin."

Simon's face fell into a scowl. "Oh. The drag queen."

"Yes. I just came by to tell you, you were wrong about her."

"Oh, it's 'her' now, is it?" He rolled his eyes. "Well, Mitch, last week you told me I was *right* about 'her.' Now suddenly I'm wrong. Getting a tad flaky in our old age, are we?"

One of the boxed-up cats began howling like a baby being boiled. Mitchell winced at the sound. "Maybe for a while, but that's all over. I just wanted to tell you that—well, I had a bad experience with Kitten, then I had a *really* bad experience with your men's group, but now—"

"You know, you never did tell me how it went that night."

Mitchell balked. "No. And I never will."

"Don't have to." His eyes twinkled. "Heard all about it, anyway. You put on quite a show, you know. Guys were talking about it for days afterward. Said you turned into a complete animal."

Mitchell felt his face burn, and hoped no one in the waiting room was listening. "That's just the point, Simon," he said, lowering his voice. "I don't want to *be* an animal."

"We're all of us animals, Mitch."

"You've been working in this place too long. Some of us are actually proud to be human."

Simon crossed his arms and smirked. "Guy you were with that night—Kip—he's been asking after you."

Mitchell guffawed. "Oh, you mean the Coco Chanel fan? Sterling example of brute masculinity *he* turned out to be."

"So he's a little conflicted. Happens to the best of us.

What, he's not good enough for you, Mister Irons-His-Pocket-Squares?"

"He's the crucial figure in the most humiliating experience of my entire life, and if it weren't for you—"

"Oh, sure. Blame *me*."

"I'm not blaming anyone anymore. That's what I'm trying to tell you. I'm making my own decisions from now on. Making up my own mind about things."

Simon shook his head. "*Bad* idea."

The owner of the howling cat called out, "Listen, he's in pain. Couldn't someone see him now?"

Simon leaned over the counter and sweetly said, "No."

The woman let loose an affronted gasp. "This is *really* unbelievable."

Simon pointed to the endtable next to her chair. "I suggest you take that copy of *Harper's and Queen* and read the article on the life of Princess Michael of Kent, which I've taken the trouble to mark with a Post-It note. She sets a fine example on how to bear life's misfortunes and indignities with grace and good humor."

The woman turned her head angrily, but the tattooed rottweiler owner grabbed the magazine at once, turned to the page in question, and started reading avidly.

"Simon," said Mitchell, "we've been friends for too long to let anyone else or any*thing* else come between us. I'm going to build a relationship with my twin. I want you to be happy for me, and I want to be able to tell you about it. Just like I tell you everything else. I *need* that."

Simon grimaced. "Okay. Deal. Under one condition."

Mitchell shrugged. "Name it."

"Tomorrow morning, when you call me all upset about what a disaster the night has been, I get to say 'I told you so.' "

Mitchell almost laughed. He extended his hand and said, "Agreed!" As they shook, he couldn't help snickering and saying, "Boy, are you going to feel silly when you hear how off base you were!"

chapter 37

All the other doorbells had names by them—Magnuson, Riege, Frobisher, Brenner-Costello, Tsaligopoulou. Mitchell rang the remaining one—the one adjacent to the legend HERSELF!

The speaker crackled to life. "That you?"

"It's Mitchell, yes."

The door buzzed angrily; he pushed it open and found himself in a musty, dim-lit vestibule, then raced to push open the next door, to the stairway, before the buzzing ceased.

He made his way up one flight of stairs, and was on his way to the next when he heard, "You in?"

"Uh-huh. Thanks."

His heart was leaping into his throat. Why? Why was he nervous? It was silly to be nervous. *Stop being nervous!*

Another corner, another landing, and there he was. In the doorway.

Donald.

Mitchell wasn't prepared for the sight; he stopped short,

one hand on the railing, one hand clutching the Grand Dame.

My God, he thought.

They stared at each other for a moment, like strangers.

"You're—you look wonderful," Mitchell said at last, his voice threatening to break. "Very handsome."

Donald blushed, then snorted. "Sure, *you'd* say that."

He was wearing a raspberry Esprit sweatshirt, jeans with the knees out of them, and clogs. He had a leather strap around his wrist. His hair was longish, and tucked behind his ears. He looked amazingly, astonishingly, like Mitchell. So much so that Mitchell couldn't think of a thing to say that wasn't some unfunny reference to this fact.

Donald gestured past the door. "You want to come in?"

Mitchell nodded, climbed the last two stairs, and made his way to the door; he wasn't more than two steps into the apartment when he turned and kissed Donald on the cheek. "Hello, brother," he said tenderly.

"You melodramatic *thing,* you," said Donald, now completely crimson. "Did you rehearse that? Be honest."

He shook his head.

Donald shut the door and took the Grand Dame from him. "Ooh, it's *chilled* already! You're one of those think-of-everything types, I know. A real detail queen. Well, lucky for me! I'll just grab some glasses and we can crack the old witch open." He scooted around a corner and was gone.

Mitchell took his first look around the place. It was tiny—not much bigger than an efficiency apartment. It had the look, though, of the storeroom for a summer-stock theater. Shoes, gowns, capes were everywhere, strewn over everything. There were two floorlamps, each with a wig atop it, like something from a Disney theme park; Mitchell thought they looked just seconds away from breaking into song.

He stepped further into the apartment and caught his reflection in a wall mirror; it stopped him in his tracks.

Donald reappeared with two glass tumblers and a dishrag, which he'd wrapped around the Grand Dame's curving neck. "Here she *cooomes!*" he trilled, before catching sight of Mitchell before the mirror. "What's up? Come on, make yourself comfortable." He kicked aside a red velvet frock. "There's a couch under here, somewhere."

Mitchell said, "Come here for a second."

Donald hesitated a moment, then joined his brother at the mirror. They looked at their reflections, side by side.

"Uncanny," whispered Mitchell. "Like seeing double."

Donald half turned, lifted his shoulder to his chin, and pursed his lips. "Which twin has the Toni?" he cooed.

Mitchell fingered his brother's thinning hair. "You're receding, too, I see."

Donald gasped. "Lousy bitch!" He swung the Grand Dame into Mitchell's hip.

"Oh, come *on*," Mitchell said, laughing. "If you can't admit it to me, who *can* you adm—"

"I'm not admitting anything! Now sit down and shut up!"

Mitchell gingerly felt around the mounds of clothes until he discovered something that resisted his probing; he swept aside a pile of sweaters, and there was an easy chair. He climbed into it.

Donald had put the tumblers on the window sill and unwrapped the foil around the bottle's cork. "There she is!" he cried, showing Mitchell the revealed portrait of Nicole Ponsardin on the metal cap. "Pug-ugly as sin, yet so beautiful to behold." He tried to twist open the wire cage holding the cork in place, but his lengthy fingernails kept getting in the way.

Mitchell reached over. "Allow me."

"Ooh, you big strong man, you," said Donald as he passed the bottle to him.

Mitchell grabbed the ball of the cork and, with a heroic-sounding grunt, gave it a swift tug. The resultant pop set Donald whooping with glee, which segued into shrieks of hilarity as foam spilled over the spout and onto Mitchell's trousers.

Donald shoved both tumblers at Mitchell. "Fill 'er up."

Mitchell giggled and did so.

Then they lifted their glasses high and said, simultaneously, "Here's lookin' at you," which caused them both to scream with laughter.

"Admit it," said Donald; "you rehearsed *that*."

"I'll admit it if you will."

They each took a sip. Mitchell felt the champagne go down his throat like electricity conducted through burnished copper. *"Mmm,"* he said.

Donald licked his lips. "She do taste fine."

They smiled at each other, feeling happy and slightly uncomfortable, unsure of what to say next.

Mitchell took another swallow, then shifted in his seat. "Well, I suppose maybe I should apologize, just to get it out of the way."

Donald shook his head. "Don't be silly."

"Well, I've caused you some grief."

"Likewise. Can't we just forget it?"

"I just want you to know I never really intended any harm. And I never really looked down on you." He managed a smile. "You were a curve ball, that's all. I never expected anything like you."

"That's because there *isn't* anything like me. I'm *sui generis.* You'll just have to learn to appreciate that." He topped off his glass, then did the same for Mitchell's.

Donald's Latin-dropping jogged Mitchell's curiosity. "So, uh—did you ever go to college?"

"Oh, hell, yes." He sat on the floor and crossed his legs. "Four miserable years."

"What was your major?"

"Renaissance history and literature."

"You're kidding! My minor was Fine Art, but I specialized in the Renaissance."

"This was during the Animal Husbandry phase, was it?"

"Well—yeah." He could feel his face flush. "Don't you think it's amazing that our areas of major interest are so similar? That can't be coincidence."

"Well, we *are* twins, you know. Still, I have to say, I can understand *my* interest in the period, but not yours."

"I was just about to say the same thing."

"Oh, please! Mitchell! How could I *not* have been interested? I felt so out of *place* in that frat-rat, beer-swilling world.

Naturally I became obsessed with the worlds that came before
—the ones I'd missed out on." He put his tumbler on the floor
and leaned back, resting on his elbows. "I mean, like most
queens, I was already mired in the Golden Age of Hollywood.
You know, devouring all those great Davis and Crawford and
Dietrich movies that taught American women how to be indi-
vidualists. Or pretend to be, anyway. But *unlike* most queens, I
started to think about *why* they were the way they were. See, the
great American *actors*, like Gary Cooper and Spencer Tracy and
Jimmy Stewart, they were all so natural, whereas all the great
actresses were these tremendously mannered types. Outra-
geously theatrical. Ever see a Tracy and Hepburn movie? He's
so salt-of-the-earth, and she's this Fabulous Creature. Like she's
from another planet."

He reached over for another swallow, then wiped his
mouth with his wrist and continued. "Okay, so here's my pat-
ented theory on why this was the case: See, the great male actors
had this tradition of male iconography that went all the way
back to Homer. Right? They all grew up with the stories, the
heroic legends, so they just sort of naturally grew into the kind
of personas that fit that mold. But, honey, the *women*! They had
to build themselves from scratch! There *was* no female iconic
tradition."

"Uh-huh," said Mitchell, who was very much afraid that
Donald was about to present him with a cultural justification
for drag, and that he'd buy it.

"Now, by this time I was in college, and I was researching
this pretty heavily. I mean, I was determined to find a forgotten
iconic tradition for women, and hon, it was *just not there*. I mean,
except for the Virtuous Wife and the Whore. Octavia and Cle-
opatra. Agrippina and Messalina. The Virgin Mother and the
Magdalene. See what I mean? Kind of limiting, ain't it? Women
were generally held back from any sort of accomplishment beyond those two realms, so the few women who *did* achieve any
real influence or power over the years had to invent themselves
from scratch—just like the great Hollywood actresses. I mean,
Hatshepsut, Eleanor of Aquitaine, Joan of Arc, Catherine the

Great—titanic self-creations, just like Davis and Crawford and Dietrich. That's why we queens love them so much. We're misfits in the male world, so *we* have to create ourselves from scratch, too. And who can we look to for inspiration, for ideas on how to do that? No one but the great women of history—from Nefertiti to Marie Antoinette to Miss Diana Ross."

Uh-oh, thought Mitchell. This is making sense to me. He finished off his tumbler and poured himself some more.

"Anyway, by the time I'd reached my junior year, I'd sort of fallen into Renaissance history as a major, by default. Because I was spending so much time anyway reading about the great age of self-created women—Mary Queen of Scots, all those Medici broads. And Elizabeth the First. She's been my *real* obsession. Probably the first great drag-queen role model in history. *Everything* about her was the most fabulous artifice, and she carried it off like some legendary Warner Brothers movie idol. With a whole country not just as her audience, but as her fan club! I mean, Mitchell, they *adored* her. When she was almost seventy—this crooked, wrinkled thing with rotten teeth—she dressed like a fucking homecoming parade float, and the people were enraptured. They called her 'Gloriana.' *That's* inspirational. I've read nearly everything that's ever been written about her. I even did my senior thesis on *The Faerie Queene*." He winked. "Then I got my diploma and became one."

Mitchell suppressed a burp. "Funny, I've got an ex-lover who's obsessed with Elizabeth the *Second*."

Donald snorted in derision. "Frump, frump, frump. Not a self-creation *at all*. Or if she is, it's too frightening to think about. Say, do we need crackers here, or something?"

"Maybe. What kind you got? Carr's?"

"Ritz."

He wrinkled his nose. "Pass."

They each had another swallow of the inestimable Widow.

"I guess my next question, then," said Mitchell as he wiped the bubbles from his upper lip, "is why you didn't—you know —go all the way."

"All *what* way?" asked Donald, rolling over onto his side and propping his head up on one hand.

"You know." He made a little scissor motion with two fingers.

Donald blanched for a moment, then recovered. "Why do people always ask that?" he said, seeming genuinely baffled.

Mitchell shrugged. "Well, isn't it the obvious next step? You dress like a woman, adopt a woman's identity—why not actually, physically become a woman?"

Donald dropped back and laid his head on the floor. "Okay. Well. Let me try to explain. First of all, Kitten Kaboodle is—well, she's my creation, right? *I* made her. Whatever she is, she comes right out of me, and no one else. In her entirety."

"I understand," said Mitchell, as he surreptitiously slipped off his shoes.

"So, she's totally mine. She's totally *me*. I take a measure of pride in that, you may be surprised to learn."

"Not really. I can see why you'd be proud. I *like* Kitten."

He rolled onto his side again. "You do not!"

"Do so." Mitchell laughed. "Took a little time, that's all."

Donald smiled. "That's so sweet! She's very pleased to hear it."

"In fact, as happy as I am to see you, Donald, I find—and I'm amazed to be admitting this—I find I actually kind of miss her."

Donald put his free hand on his elevated hip and said, "Well, don't get all moony about it, she ain't that far away!" Then he lay back again. "Anyway, like I was saying, Kitten was one hundred percent my creation. So, why would I want to get some surgeon involved, make him partly responsible for her? Share in the glory that is she? Not to mention electrologists, pharmacists—I mean, it seems so unnecessary."

"I understand."

"So—*excessive.* I mean, I kept dressing and acting out until I reached a point where I felt like me—the point where I became Kitten. And once you reach that point, why *bother* going any farther? Just 'cause some straights can't deal with it?"

"No, honest, I underst—"

"Plus, I guess—I guess I have a problem getting rid of something that can't ever be replaced." He lifted his head again and gestured around the apartment. "As you may be able to tell, this particular pathology extends to items well beyond my penis."

Mitchell sighed. "How'd we get on this, anyway?"

He rolled over, lifted himself, and sat on his haunches. "*You* brought it up, Miss Thing. And I'm not drunk enough yet to tell you to quit being so fucking Montel Williams about it. Here, give me your glass." He took the bottle and topped off first Mitchell's tumbler, then his own. Then he lifted the bottle to the window and said, "Hell, we're killin' off the old girl in a hurry."

"Well, we can always go continue this at a bar."

"Dressed like *this?*" Donald shook his head. "I'll never be *that* drunk." He leapt to his feet. "See what I've got in the fridge." He scooted around the corner again.

Mitchell gazed around the room to pass the time, his eyes alighting on a Klimt poster, a faux Tiffany lamp, and an etagere bearing a half dozen dying houseplants. Then, from a distance, he heard Donald yell, *"I've got half a bottle of good Chardonnay and a whole bottle of really bad White Zinfandel."*

" *'Bad White Zinfandel' is redundant,"* he shouted back.

"Which one should I bring, then?"

"Both."

The Widow was soon gone, and then the Chardonnay, and then even the White Zinfandel. At which point Donald remembered a bottle of Scotch his father had sent him for Christmas five years before, which he'd used to prop up a collapsed shelf in his ancient rolltop desk. He fetched it with one flick of his wrist, letting the paper-laden shelf fall to pieces.

They were well into the Scotch, and had traded life stories, when Mitchell, now on the floor next to Donald, again looked him in the face and, shaking his head, said, "I still just don't get it."

"Get what?"

"This—*need* you have. I mean, in some ways, we're so alike, and in others—I mean, the way you run away from who you really are—it just doesn't compute."

Donald's face darkened. "You're right, you still *don't* get it. This *isn't* the way I really am. *Kitten* is the way I really am."

"I don't understand that, either."

Donald sat up, accidentally tipping over his tumbler. He appeared not to notice. "What's not to understand?" He grabbed the front of his sweatshirt. "Look at me! I'm just this ordinary nothing of a man. Someone you'd never look at twice, if you saw him in the street. A big gray absence of a person."

"Hey," protested Mitchell. "Those are *my* looks you're dissing."

Donald ignored him. "Now, why would I want to be this way," he continued, letting go of the sweatshirt in disgust, "when I can put on a little makeup, a wig, and some attitude, and become this showstopper? This attention-grabber? Someone who walks into a room and brings that room to a standstill?"

Mitchell tried to see it but ended up shaking his head. "It's just beyond me. Forget it."

A frightening kind of light filled Donald's eyes; it was a gimlet look—a spider's look. "Maybe the best way to make you understand is to have you see it from the inside."

Mitchell chuckled nervously and downed another mouthful of Scotch. "How can you possibly do that?"

Donald looked toward a row of wig stands. "Gee, I *wonnn*der . . ."

Mitchell felt the room go suddenly cold. "No," he said, barely audibly. "No, Donald. Absolutely not."

But he had already been lifted to his feet, and was being dragged bodily toward Donald's vanity.

chapter 38

"**T**his is kind of spooky," said Donald as he applied the first layer of foundation to Mitchell's face. "Like I'm somebody else, making me up." He sang the "doo-doo-doo-doo" introduction to the "Twilight Zone" theme, and cracked up.

Why am I submitting to this? Mitchell wondered as he gazed at his reflection in the mirror. His eyes were dull and his mouth was hanging open. Is it because I'm too smashed to resist? Is that all?

"You've got a real fine beard, like me," said Donald gaily as he worked the foundation into Mitchell's jawline. "Hardly visible at all, except that it's gumming up the works, here. Got to be real precise with it. Wish I'd have thought to shave you, first."

Or am I humoring Donald because I owe it to him? Am I just being a nice guy? Maybe it's both. Maybe I'm too drunk to resist, *and* I don't want to, because it's making Donald happy.

"Stop looking so worried! What, are you scared of my nails?

Don't be. They may be lethal, but I do this every day. Yet to poke an eye out.''

I bet if I asked him to stop, right now, he'd stop. I bet he would. All I have to do is just say it. Just open my mouth and say, Stop.

"All right, now let's have a look at those eyes. I'll spare you the eyebrow plucking—you're welcome—but we'll have to go heavy on the mascara and eyeliner to take some of the weight away from those big, bushy brows of yours. Like a couple of caterpillars crawling across your forehead. Close your eyes, now.''

Whoops! Hard to maintain my balance with my eyes shut. God, I really *must* be wasted! Hope I don't fall over. Maybe I can just go to sleep till this is over. Except I shouldn't be *letting* this happen. I know I can stop it. I know Donald would understand. It's gone too far, as it is. A joke is a joke. I mean, really.

"There we go—looks beautiful. You've got great skin. Really porous. Just drinks this stuff up. Do you use a moisturizer? I don't suppose you've had your colors done. What am I saying? We're twins! You're obviously a winter, like me. I can use anything from my palette. Here . . .''

Kind of soothing, though. The gentle pressure against my eyes, my eyelids, my temples—it's like Shiatsu, or something. Kind of relaxing. Therapeutic. Feel a little bit like I'm floating . . .

". . . tilt your head a little. Take the shine off that forehead . . .''

Floating above, what, floating above a big forest . . . being tickled by the trees . . .

". . . to try an understated, subtle shade . . . close your mouth . . . let me brush it on y . . .''

. . . caught in a tree . . . tickling my lips . . . bird's nest . . . river in the distance . . . pink clouds . . . Titian nude and . . . over where . . . a Ferris wheel . . . I'm on a . . . upside-down . . . falling . . . wind caressing my head . . . my hair . . . pulling my h— "What? Wh—''

"Mitchell, you were sleeping! You were honest-to-God sleeping!"

He was disoriented; he panted. He didn't know where he was.

Wait a minute. Donald's apartment. In front of the vanity mirror. Was it a mirror? Where was *he*, then? Why wasn't *he* reflected? There was Kitten, there was Donald, but—

Wait—something wrong—Kitten *and* Donald?

"I'm just gonna put a cap over your head, okay? For the wig to sit on." Donald stretched something over Mitchell's skull, while in the mirror he stretched something over Kitten's.

Mitchell gasped for breath.

"Hold still!" Donald snapped.

I . . . I'm Kitten! he realized with horror.

"Hold *still*, I said! Why are you so squirmy? You're either dead asleep or jumping out of the chair. Like some kind of—"

"Donald, stop this, I don't want any m—"

"Don't be silly, we're practically fin—"

"I can't even look at myself!"

Donald shoved him back into the chair. "Now just hold your horses, Jezebel! This'll take two seconds, and then we can take it all off, if you want. But this is *scarcely* the time to chicken out." He reached behind him and produced a brilliant platinum wig, with extra-length bangs and about seven inches of curls arching skyward.

"Get ready to be amazed," said Donald. "This is the glue that holds it all together."

And he set the wig on Mitchell's head. Mitchell was still disoriented; for a single, surreal moment, he felt like a monarch being crowned. In his head, he actually heard a chorus triumphantly singing Handel's "Zadok the Priest."

And then Donald took his hands away.

Mitchell recognized nothing in the mirror. Nothing except dazzling, spellbinding, intoxicating beauty.

"My God," he said, his voice hushed. "I'm—I'm *gorgeous*."

Donald clapped his hands. "Ain't it the truth?"

Mitchell began hyperventilating and put his head between his knees. "I really think I'm going to throw up now."

Donald rubbed his shoulders. "Don't hurl, girl! We still got to get you in a posh frock."

"Oh, no, no more!"

But Donald was not to be denied. He danced across the apartment to a ramshackle antique wardrobe, and threw it open; on the inner doors were dozens of clippings from fashion magazines, adhered to the woodwork with yellowed cellophane tape. *"Just let me see if I can pick out something you'll like,"* he called out. *"If I don't, then we'll call it a day, okay?"*

Mitchell grunted in reply, leaned back in the chair, and tried to control his breathing. He couldn't seem to take his eyes off the mirror. He really was *beautiful.* It felt—well, peculiar, certainly, but beyond that, it felt curiously *lightening.* As though he'd been given some kind of spiritual boost. Ascended to a higher plane. How could that be? How could it possibly be?

There was so much going on in his head, so many bells and whistles, that for a moment he didn't recognize the buzzing of his cellular phone.

"That yours?" called Donald as he rifled through the wardrobe.

"Yes," cried Mitchell. *"Where's my jacket?"*

"Right below you."

Mitchell snapped his head to the side (the weight of the wig surprised him; it almost gave him whiplash) and saw that his jacket was hanging daintily over the very stool on which he was perched. He got up, pulled the jacket into his arms, retrieved the flip phone from its left pocket, and pressed TALK. He then tried to bring it to his ear, but a big flap of wig was in the way; he dropped the jacket and used both hands to maneuver the phone beneath it.

"—ello? Anyone there?" It was Cyrus Trilby's voice.

"Cyrus, yes, hello! It's me, Mitchell!"

"Mitchell! Is something the matter?"

Mitchell's heart did a little somersault. Was the wig affecting his speech, making him sound like a woman, too? He deepened his voice and gruffly said, "Well, hey, no, big fella. Not a damn thing. Why do you ask, pal?"

There was a slight pause; then Trilby continued. "We were

expecting you at the restaurant. When you didn't show, I thought something might be the matter. That's all."

"Restaurant? I don't know what you—"

"You mean Zoe didn't tell you?"

"Um—no. Afraid she didn't."

Trilby sighed. "Don't know what's got into that girl. Been acting squirrelly all day. I thought you and she had reworked the division of labor in the Wrolen matter."

"Well, yes—we did that this afternoon."

"And it was my understanding that based on that, you were taking her place at tonight's dinner with Wrolen and me."

Mitchell's heart was now sinking. "I'm sorry, Cyrus. There appears to have been some kind of misunder—"

"Well, it's a little embarrassing, Mitchell. I've just sat here and had an entire dinner with Ben all by myself. And an empty chair between us."

"I'm sorry, sir."

"Did you and Zoe discuss this meeting at all?"

"We did, sir, and I—"

"Well, who did you decide would be here?"

The answer was Zoe, of course. Mitchell cursed her; apparently she was still capable of a few final jabs against him. But he straightened his spine and said, "Cyrus, I accept full responsibility for the misunderstanding. I'd prefer to go no further into it, except to say that I'll take whatever measures necessary to make sure nothing like this happens again." That sounded good; he was virtually pointing a finger at Zoe, while shouldering the blame himself, like a good manager should. Cyrus would easily read between the lines; Zoe's attempt at sabotage would only end up making her look bad.

Trilby made a grumbling noise. "Well, how soon can you get down here?"

Mitchell felt faint. "What?"

"There are some new documents I want to have you look over during the weekend. Don't want to let them wait till Monday. We're just finishing up here. Where are you now?"

"Uh—well—I'm in the Lakeview area, sir."

"Splendid! We're at Mia Francesca on Clark Street. Shouldn't take you five minutes to get here. See you then."

"Found something wonnnderful," Donald sang across the apartment as he held up a glittering emerald floor-length number.

"What was that?" Trilby asked.

"That? Uh—a friend of mine. I'm at his house."

"That was a *he*?"

"Did I say he? I meant she."

"Well, tell her goodbye and scoot over here, Mitchell. Ben's looking itchy, I'd better get back to the table."

"Cyrus, I—"

A dial tone stung his ear.

He dropped the phone onto his jacket and looked at himself in the mirror. He wanted to scream. "My *God*," he said, pressing his hands to his face. "There's no *way* I'll get all this goop off my face in time! Jesus God *almighty*! I'm—I'm—" He felt a whirlwind of anxiety and anger whip up inside him like a funnel cloud; he was almost rocking on the stool. "I'm *FUCKED*!"

The sound of this completely uncharacteristic expression, delivered with all the force of Krakatoa on one of its more ornery days, brought Donald hopping back over to the vanity, the emerald gown draped over his arms. "What's wrong, hon?" he asked, his brows knit.

Mitchell was staring at himself in the vanity, shaking. "It's —it's *over*. My career. I have to meet my boss at Mia Francesca in, like, five minutes. Donald, this gunk is going to take half an hour to get off, isn't it?"

"Oh, at least."

He felt panic grip and shake him. "What do I do? What do I *do*? He's *waiting* for me!"

"Oh, tell the old asshole to stick his finger up it for a while. Call the restaurant back, have him paged. Then you tell him just that. Hear? You listen to Donald."

Mitchell whirled, his eyes blinking in fury and despair. *"Listen to Donald?"* he shrieked. "If I hadn't listened to *Donald*, I wouldn't be *in* this—*FUCKING*—*MESS* right now, I'd—'' He stopped short.

Through his anxiety and his stubborn tears, he was getting another good look at Donald. And he found himself possessed of an idea.

He grabbed his brother's arm. ''All right, now, you listen to me and listen good.''

Donald let out a little peep of alarm. ''What? Mitchell, you're hurting me!''

He stood, not releasing his grip. ''You are the only person in the entire goddamn world who can save the career I've spent half a decade building. You understand? You read me?''

''Yes, yes! Jesus, girl! Don't get your tits in a twitter! I'll do whatever I can!''

Mitchell released him and picked up his jacket. ''Put this on, then, and go down to Mia Francesca's and pick up an envelope from my boss.''

Donald looked confused. ''I still don't see how that solves your problem. I mean, if he's expecting *you* to show up, then why would—'' He stopped short, choking on an epiphany. ''*Oh*, no, Mitchell! I'm not even comfortable *looking* like you, I'm certainly not gonna try and *be* you.''

Mitchell shoved the jacket at him. ''You just said you'd do whatever it takes.''

''I lied. Leave me alone.'' He backed into a corner.

Mitchell hemmed him in. ''All you have to do is pretend to be me for five minutes, say hello to my client, get an envelope from my boss, and come right back here. That's it. And my career is saved. Tell me you won't do that. Look me straight in the eye and tell me you won't.''

Donald was the one trembling now. Slowly he lifted his head, and when his eyes met Mitchell's, they were watery and defeated.

''My God, but you're a bitch,'' he said. ''I could almost be proud of you.''

And he grabbed the jacket.

chapter

39

Mitchell looked out the window in time to catch Donald wandering dazedly up the street. He thought, Am I out of my mind? Sending him out to pretend he's me?

After all, Donald might be his identical twin, but his behavior made him a closer match to Pearl Bailey. And although he wore Mitchell's understated hound's-tooth blazer, the rest of his attire was more than a trifle fey.

Still, all he had to do was exchange pleasantries with Trilby and Wrolen, pick up the documents, and scoot right back here. What could possibly go wrong?

Mitchell felt a shiver of fear, as if he were tempting fate by even wondering such a thing, and he made a quick check of his wristwatch. If Donald weren't back in ten minutes, he'd have to do something—find some way of helping him escape the restaurant. Phone in a bomb threat, maybe.

He swept a little clump of lingerie from the arm of one of Donald's chairs, then took a seat, deciding to make himself as comfortable as possible for the duration of this agonizing wait.

He leaned back into the cushion and sighed. He was feeling a little winded; the wig was proving heavier than he'd expected, and warmer, too. Suddenly he wondered why he hadn't just taken it off. And once he wondered that, he had to wonder why he *still* wasn't taking it off.

But he wasn't to be allowed the luxury—or perhaps the peril—of too much introspection. Donald's telephone jangled him out of it.

Donald had left explicit instructions to answer all calls, as he was expecting both Zack and Jennifer Jerrold to ring him. So Mitchell reached across the coffee table and grabbed the receiver, and had it up against his ear before he could be amazed at how natural it felt now, to sweep away the flap of hair to accommodate it.

"Hello," he said pleasantly.

There was a spate of incoherent stuttering at the other end, followed by a semi-obscene torrent of rage—punctuated, inexplicably, by occasional bouts of what sounded like sniffing. "Dumb bitch! Stupid bitch! Guess who miss her *entire show* tonight? (*Snf, snf.*) How many times I tell stupid bitch to not be late? Huh? A billion, I bet! And how many times (*snf*) I get same answer—'Oh, Gordy, I not used to new time, I keep forgetting.' Well, you not forget anymore. You now fired! (*Snf, snf, snf.*) Gordy has decreed."

Mitchell tried to interject. "I'm sorry, but I'm afraid you're mistaking me fo—"

"No mistake! No mistake! Gordy just decreed that Gordy has decreed! (*Snf, snf.*) You late once, you late twice, and didn't I say, you late once more, you fired? And you say yes Gordy, but then tonight, you show up not even late, you show up *not at all*! No, no, no—no mistake!"

"That's not what I meant. I mean I'm not Kitten."

"I not kiddin' either! Had enough grief from you already, and now, by golly, it ends. (*Snf.*) Get ancient ass over here *tonight* and pick up all crap that could remind Gordy of you tomorrow, or it get thrown in street for homeless peoples, except maybe they got too much taste to want it. *That's all!*"

Mitchell found himself listening to a dial tone.

Wow, he thought.

He hung up the phone and sat in bewilderment, his mouth hanging open. Donald—Kitten—had been fired from the job that meant nearly everything to her, and hadn't even been here to make a case for herself. Mitchell had stumbled into that role instead, and blown it. Blown it good.

He fell back into the chair and glumly thought, Well, I got her into this mess. After all, he'd been the one who insisted that she meet him tonight as Donald, submerging the strong, confident Kitten identity beneath one that was insecure and tentative. He'd been the one to then ply Donald with liquor until he didn't know which end was up, so that he completely forgot his—Kitten's—performance. And he was the one who then sent Donald on a ridiculous errand so that he wasn't here to defend himself when this Gordy person called and axed him.

He gritted his teeth and thought, Well, if I got him into it, I'd better damn well try to get him out of it. He got to his feet and felt the fighting spirit well up in him. He didn't even feel drunk anymore; the searing fear he'd felt after Trilby's call had burned all the alcohol out of him. He felt he could march right into the Tam-Tam, find this Gordy person, and assault him with such a barrage of threatening legalese that the poor fool would probably offer to rehire Kitten on the spot.

He trotted over to the vanity and sat down. All I have to do, he thought, is get this gunk off my face, and I can head over there.

He looked around for some Noxema (That's what one uses, isn't it? he asked himself), and as he was looking, he had a wonderful, rather terrifying idea: wouldn't it be even more astounding if all the threats of civil action came from Kitten herself? A confident, legally savvy Kitten who wouldn't take any shit from some petty, abusive bar manager? And wouldn't it be better if, instead of *offering* to hire Kitten back, he could just do it right then and there?

It was worth a try—if only because it'd be so satisfying to be able to report all this back to an amazed and eternally grateful Donald.

A voice inside Mitchell's head, tiny and barely distinct, tried to tell him that maybe there was another reason he liked this plan so much, but Mitchell refused to listen to it. He was far too busy.

He carefully removed his shirt, socks, and trousers, folded them neatly, and set them on a chair. And then, like Columbus embarking for the new world, he put on the emerald gown. This wasn't as easily managed as he'd thought; Donald was a hair thinner than he was, and he had the devil's own time zipping himself up in back. In fact, he almost wrenched his right arm out of its socket. Then he had to unzip himself again, as he'd forgotten to fill the breast folds with tissue and they'd just hung down like donkey ears.

When he'd got the dress in place, he noticed his arms. While no one would ever have described Mitchell's body as in any way hairy, he had to admit that the downy fuzz covering his forearms and wrists was just visible enough to look jarringly incongruous in the wall mirror. He searched through Donald's closet and drawers till he found a pair of black full-length gloves; he donned them immediately.

He then put on a pair of low-heeled black pumps, tried them out by walking up and down the apartment, and decided that they posed no real threat to life or (especially) limb. Then he pilfered through Donald's jewelry box and by sheer luck found a single pair of clip-on earrings—dangly things that looked like disco glitter balls. He fell in love with them, attached them to his lobes, and went to survey himself in the mirror.

Not quite the genuine Kaboodle, but close enough to take his breath away. He was a beautiful woman. He *was*.

After admiring himself a moment more, he took his wallet and keys and put them in a pocketbook he found lying atop a dog-eared copy of Camille Paglia's *Vamps and Tramps*. And then he swept out the door.

As he made his way down the stairs, he wondered if maybe he should have left a note for Donald, who would surely return to the apartment first. Unfortunately, he couldn't afford the time to go back now.

On the first floor landing, he met an elderly woman who

was descending the stairs with some difficulty. He took her elbow and said, "Need a hand, dear?"

She looked at him in trepidation. "You better not touch me! I have leprosy!"

He almost laughed. "Never mind. Anything that could fall off my body probably wasn't there an hour ago anyway." And he helped her maneuver the rest of the stairs.

chapter

40

The glare of the setting sun was like a bucket of cold water in Donald's face.

When was the last time I was out in this identity? he wondered. If he could just recall that, he might not be so terrified. He stopped at a corner to wait for the streetlight to change, and tried to remember.

There'd been a couple of after-midnight trips to the White Hen for cigarettes, hidden beneath a baseball cap and an overcoat; an infrequent morning jog; an occasional leap into a cab for a full makeup session at the Tam-Tam. But that wasn't what he meant; when, exactly, was the last time he'd gone somewhere *as* Donald, to *be* Donald?

He couldn't recall.

Of course, he wasn't going anywhere as Donald, now. He was going as Mitchell.

The light changed; the WALK signal illuminated. He tried to comply, but fear made him immobile, so that he had to be pushed into motion by the harried, hurried crowd behind him, on their way to—where? Dinner engagements, most probably. Like Mitchell's boss.

Mitchell's boss. He knew the man's name, but how was he supposed to recognize him? They'd never met.

What was he *doing* out here?

He turned up Roscoe and headed toward Clark Street. Mia Francesca was on Clark, wasn't it? He'd never eaten there, but he was pretty sure.

His heart was pounding. His feet felt funny. He looked down and gasped. Clogs! Mitchell had sent him out in clogs. What would his boss think? And why did he *care?*

And these fingernails! Had Mitchell considered *them?*

He stopped in the middle of the sidewalk and gazed at his outstretched hands. His nails were at their lengthiest—strong, thick, and beautifully tapered. His pride and joy. No, *Kitten's* pride and joy. Mitchell's doom and damnation. How the hell was he supposed to hide them?

He dropped his hands to his side and peered up Clark Street. The ebony awning of Mia Francesca was within sight. Just run up there, Mitchell had said. Get an envelope from his boss. Then come right back.

Okay. Here goes.

''Mitchell?''

A woman's voice—from behind him. Just keep going, he told himself, picking up speed. Don't look back.

''Mitchell *Sayer*!'' Spoken with enough authority to stop an Islamic jihad in its tracks.

Oh, God, he thought. And he turned around.

Among the crowd on the sidewalk was a lone woman standing and looking at him, hands on her hips. Young—mid-twenties at most—and gorgeous, too. Tall, leggy, with the kind of bouncin' and behavin' hair Donald would've gladly given a year of his life to have. And dressed to the nines in a pajamalike pantsuit. Sonia Rykiel, unless he missed his guess. Which of course he never did.

The sun was behind her, so he couldn't quite make out her face; but there was something about her that was oddly familiar. It wasn't until she strode up to him, smiling widely with huge, utterly carnivorous teeth, that he recognized her: the Golden Girl from the Mason's Department Store elevator. Mitchell knew *her*?

Just before she reached him, he stuck his telltale hands into his pockets. "Surprise, surprise," she said, and she astonished him by leaning right into him and planting a kiss on his cheek.

He tried to look unruffled, but she noticed his abashment. "Oh, come on," she said, giving him a punch in the arm. "I know this is a gay neighborhood, but your reputation's not going to suffer if you're seen getting a kiss from a woman now and then. Especially one who's your sister."

Sister? Mitchell had only briefly mentioned having sisters. Was the Golden Girl really one of them? His head was spinning. He grinned sheepishly and said, "You are correct! No homosexual could object to me kissing a woman who is my sister!" Then he tried to laugh heartily, and succeeded rather too well.

She furrowed her brow at him but kept smiling. Then she said, "Heading south? So am I." And she made as if to walk with him.

"Actually, um, I'm heading north." He turned in the opposite direction.

She grabbed his arm. "Stop being such a clown. I *saw* you walking south. Now come on, I want to talk to you."

He gave up and walked beside her, down Clark Street.

I'm going to kill Mitchell, he vowed. As soon as I get back. Rip out his throat with my bare hands, and I don't even care if I break a nail.

And the ebony awning loomed ever closer.

"I want to thank you for interceding with Mom," said Mitchell's sister. "I beg her, I beseech her, I plead with her, I even send lawyers after her, and she doesn't budge. I get Max to work on her, to no avail. But I ask *you* to have a word with her, and next thing I know she's handing over the entire estate to m—us." She cleared her throat. "I just wanted to say thanks, and also that, uh, I know I was kind of hysterical about this

whole thing, and I realize I may have acted a little—immaturely.
Well, a lot immaturely. Sorry about that. I know I put you
through the wringer."

Donald nodded and tried to look understanding.
"Ummm—sure," he said. Then turned his head and pretended
to be interested in the window of a swimsuit store. He was terrified that at any moment she'd take a good look at him and
realize he wasn't who she thought he was.

"Now, don't be that way," she said, tugging on his arm.
"I'm apologizing, and I don't do that often. Don't shut me out.
You're the only brother I've got. I want us to be friends."

He looked at the ground, shrugged, and tried to smile.
"Fine."

She clicked her tongue. "All right. Be that way." They
walked another few yards in silence. "Listen, are you free for
dinner? I just left my new shrink's office, and I'm famished.
Maybe we can talk through our problems over dinner. Been
ages since we did that. My treat. Mom's money hasn't come
through yet, of course, but I got a nice cash settlement from
Nordstrom's over my little mishap." She daintily lifted her pants
leg and displayed the bandaged ankle. Then she dropped the
hem and peered up the block. "Mia Francesca is just ahead.
How about it?"

"Oh, nooooo," he said, laughing nervously. "Thanks very
much, and all, but—um—it's just not—I can't take the r—well,
just no." He inhaled sharply and felt faint.

She shook her head. "Really putting the screws to me,
aren't you? You know, this session I had today, with Dr. Forbes-
Dimenti—it was a lot about you."

"Oh?" The Mia Francesca awning loomed overhead. He
stopped.

She followed suit, then turned and put a hand on his arm.
"Well, you *and* Mother *and* Veronica. See, the resolution of this
whole financial mess—I mean, it's left me feeling kind of—
empty. And I find that the money isn't all that I want. The jewels
and furs and the real estate—I want what goes *with* it. The family connection." She shivered. "Imagine that!"

Donald tried bestowing a big-brotherly smile of approval on her. "Very commendable," he said.

She pursed her lips. "When did you become so sarcastic? Honestly, Mitchell, I just want us to be closer. I never *see* you. That's not good. Had to do a double-take before I even recognized you just now." She touched his temple. "You're wearing your hair longer. I didn't even know."

So she *had* taken a good look at him—and still didn't realize he wasn't her brother! Donald recalled the way she'd looked right through Kitten in the Mason's elevator; maybe this woman was just too self-obsessed to ever *really* see anyone else clearly.

He was about to respond when someone from outside the restaurant called his—or rather, his brother's—name. "Mitchell? Mitchell! Over here!"

A leprechaunlike man in a navy blue suit was standing by the Mia Francesca window, waving him over. Could this impish figure possibly be the fearsome Cyrus Trilby? "We just came outside to get some air," he said jovially. "Crowded as all getout in there. You remember Ben Wrolen." He nodded his head in the direction of an Ichabod Crane–like man standing next to him—tall, gaunt, and of a more humorless mien than Donald had ever seen. Twelve faces like that on a jury, and you could find yourself hanged for a parking ticket.

Wrolen extended his hand and said, "Evening, Sayer."

Here it was. The crucial moment. Mitchell's revered client waiting for Donald to shake his hand. Donald thought of his fingernails, which only two days earlier had been photographed while tracing the delicate curves of the Maybelline logo.

Thinking quickly, he pretended to have been knocked off-balance by a passerby. He stumbled a little—never removing his hands from his pockets—then he turned and barked at the faux assailant. "Watch where you're going, buddy!"

The man turned to face him in some bewilderment, and in so doing revealed a clerical collar. *Oops!* thought Donald. He turned quickly back to his companions and said, "Can't count on manners from anyone these days." And he saw—what a relief!—that Wrolen had withdrawn his hand.

But Mitchell's sister was at his side now, beaming her irresistible toothy smile at Trilby and Wrolen. So blatant was this silent interjection that Trilby was forced to say, "Mitchell, why don't you introduce us to your lovely companion?"

He looked at her as if he'd completely forgotten her existence until now, and said, "Oh, of course! How stupid of me. Cyrus Trilby, Ben Wrolen, I'd like you to meet my sister—uhhm—yes, my sister." Damn! He didn't know what to call her!

Wrolen cocked his head and, after a few uncomfortable seconds, said, "Does she have a name, Sayer?"

Donald cackled at the ridiculousness of the question. "Of course she has a name!" Then he fell silent again, and pretended to have suddenly stepped in something unpleasant. Which of course drew all eyes to his clogs—not at all what he'd wanted.

Fortunately, Mitchell's sister took matters into her own hands, and introduced herself. "Paula Hutsell," she said, and she stepped up and shook Trilby's hand.

"I've been looking forward to meeting you," said Trilby enthusiastically. "I keep telling Mitchell to bring you to the office, now that you've found each other after all these years!"

Paula looked momentarily confused. "I've been to the firm many times, Mr. Trilby," she said graciously. "How is it you escaped me till now?" She then moved on to shake Wrolen's hand—although she first had to recall his attention from Donald's clogs, which seemed to fascinate and appall him.

"I ran into Mitchell on the street," said Paula. She took Donald's arm. "Happy coincidence. In fact, I'd just asked him if he was free for dinner; I didn't know he'd already made plans with a such a handsome pair as you." Trilby blushed bright red, but Wrolen pointedly looked at his watch. Paula turned a coquette's eye on the latter and said, "Maybe we could make it a foursome?"

"Alas," said Trilby, trying to draw her attention from his standoffish client, "we've already dined. Your brother's just meeting us here to pick up some documents." Here he extended a manila envelope to Donald, and waited for Donald to take it.

Donald swallowed his panic, then looked down the street and said, "Say, isn't that Oprah?"

All three of his companions turned their heads and said, "Where?"

He then whipped his left hand out of his pocket, grabbed the envelope from Trilby, stuck it under his arm, and plunged his hand back into hiding. "Oh, wait. It's not her. Sorry."

They turned back disappointedly—all except Wrolen, who continued to scan the street. "Whom exactly were you looking at, Sayer?" he said flatly. "There's not a single black woman anywhere in sight."

Donald grinned nervously. "Must've been a trick of the light."

Paula had her gaze glued to Wrolen's tie. Was that why she was paying him such special attention? Could she discern a millionaire from a single pricey accessory, the way anthropologists could name a dinosaur from one look at a thigh bone? Because it was obvious to even Donald that Paula was making a play for Wrolen, and the only reason anyone would do that was his money. Mitchell had mentioned that the man was worth tens of millions.

"Well, what say we all go out for a drink, then?" said Paula. "Isn't every day I get to meet someone so important to my dear brother." She hugged Donald's arm and smiled broadly.

Trilby seemed charmed by her, but Wrolen still had eyes only for Donald's shoes. "Ordinarily, we'd be delighted," said the senior partner. "But the sad fact is, we've a mission to perform."

"How exciting! What would that be?" She looked genuinely interested.

Now that Trilby had her attention, he seemed loath to lose it. "Well, I don't know if Mitchell has told you any of this—"

"Oh, Mitchell never discusses his work with me."

"As well he shouldn't. But since you're family, and since I'm the one who makes these decisions, I'll let you in on the story here." He sought a corroborating glance from Wrolen, but the millionaire was now staring at Donald's frayed knees, so he simply continued. "Our client, Ben Wrolen, here, is a very successful real estate developer. He's just expanded his plans for the neighborhood by buying almost an entire block around thirty-two hundred Broadway; he intends to build a condominium high-rise. But there are a few holdouts—landlords who refuse to sell their properties. Our job—and this is not for public consumption, mind you—"

Paula made a zipper motion across her lips.

"—our job is to find some way of forcing them to sell up. One particularly obdurate owner rents to a bar, not far from here, where men actually perform as *women*."

Paula made a face like she'd bitten into something bad, and Donald blurted out "Not the Tam-Tam Club!"

His trio of companions looked at him oddly. "Well, yes," said Trilby. "It's in the documents, Mitchell. Surely you've read them."

"I guess Mitchell—I mean I—I guess I didn't read that far—or—uh—"

"You have some familiarity with this Tam-Tam place, then?" asked Wrolen.

"No! No, no. Oh, no, no, no. *Nooo*!" He broke into a howl of laughter.

Trilby looked at Wrolen, and said, as if this might explain his associate's odd behavior, "I believe I mentioned, Ben, that Mitchell himself is gay. But he's a fine young man for all that, and, it goes without saying, not the type who would frequent such a place." He turned back to Paula. "I hope I haven't told tales out of school, Miss Hutsell."

"Paula, please. And no, I'm fully aware of Mitchell's specialness." She hugged Donald's arm again and scrunched up her nose adorably.

"Well, then, Paula—as I was saying, we have a mission. As long as we find ourselves in the neighborhood, we've decided to take a quick tour of some of these establishments—just a preliminary look at them to see if we can spot any flagrant violations of building or fire codes that will help us put pressure on the owners. Of course, Mitchell and one of our other associates, Zoe Briggs—"

"Oh, I've met Zoe," said Paula excitedly.

"So she's said. Well, she and Mitchell will be doing more in-depth title searches and the like, toward the same end."

Paula raised an eyebrow. "Sounds like you're skirting the outer limits of ethical procedure, there, Cyrus."

Trilby reddened and his face fell into a frown. "I suppose you could look at it that way if you so desired."

She reached out and tweaked his sleeve. "My kind of guy." Then, once his face had brightened again, she snapped her fingers and said, "Say, as long as you're going to be playing Hardy Boys, why don't I come with you? We can go to this Tam-Tam place and have a drink *there*, and I'll be the perfect cover for you while you look around. It'll be like killing two birds with one stone!" She released Donald and took Wrolen's arm. "I'll pretend to be your date!"

Wrolen looked at her as though she'd just proposed something horrifically indecent.

"It's certainly no place for a lady," said Trilby, who appeared slightly jealous.

"Sounds like no place for a gentlemen either, so let's be fair about it. I'm a modern girl, and I insist on equal treatment." She giggled. "Besides, it's for a very good cause, isn't it, Mr. Wrolen?"

He opened his mouth as if to reply, then slowly shook his head and gave up.

"So, is it a plan, then?"

Donald said, "Uh—the thing is, see, I have to get back an—"

"Oh, Mitchell!" interrupted Paula. "This is your boss and your client! Learn how to kiss up, or you'll never make partner."

Trilby erupted into a belly laugh that took a full minute to wind down. "Kissing up is *not* what I demand of my associates, Paula," he said, his voice rippling with mirth.

She pretended to be contrite but smiled knowingly as she said, "Of course you don't."

Donald shut his eyes and wondered, Is this how Mitchell feels when he can't get rid of Kitten?

"Very well, then," said Trilby, nodding first at Wrolen and then at Donald. "On to the Tam-Tam Club."

chapter

41

Despite it being a mere ten-minute walk, Mitchell took a cab to the Tam-Tam Club. He'd started out on foot, but the stares—and the pointed evasion of those eyes that *didn't* stare—had unnerved him beyond his ability to continue. And that was only after the first half block. Then he began to think in earnest of the dangers involved: the skinheads, the fag bashers. Still, not wanting to give in to cowardice alone, he told himself that his shoes—low-heeled though they were—were beginning to chafe his feet, and riding would help preserve them.

In the cab, the Pakistani driver eyed him suspiciously in the rearview mirror. Mitchell couldn't understand it; was he really such an unconvincing woman? He had the same delicate bone structure and full lips as Donald, and Donald himself had made him up; why, then, did Donald pass, when Mitchell could not?

Then he thought, It must be the gown. Here he was, on a Friday night in one of the grungier areas of the Lakeview neighborhood, dressed up as though he were on his way to receive a Lifetime Achievement Award at the Oscars. Satisfied that his attire, not his biceps, had betrayed him to curiosity, he sat back and fiddled with his earrings, which kept slipping down his lobes, and feigned obliviousness to the driver's continued scrutiny.

When he arrived at the Tam-Tam, he found himself not knowing what to do next. The place was almost filled, and there was a ravenous energy in the air—like the atmosphere at the Lincoln Park Zoo just before feeding time. One of the girls must be just about to give a show. Amidst the noise and happy confusion, no one appeared to notice him, and he didn't know where to go.

He decided to try having a look down the corridor to the right of the stage, and had squeezed himself past several laughing throngs of queens and party boys, as well as one group of adventuring suburbanites who stared lasers into him as he passed, before he was stopped by a truly enormous drag queen with what appeared to be a fright wig on her head and a cosmetics spill on her face. She took Mitchell by the arm and said, "Well, you did it, didn't you?"

"I beg your pardon?" he said, lightening his voice to sound more feminine.

"I heard Gordy fired you. Can't say I didn't warn you."

"Is Gordy *here*?" he asked, trying to pry his arm from her grip.

The hulking queen shook her head. "Had to step out. But he instructed me to escort you straight to the dressing room to collect your things, and then to escort you right back out again."

With no further ceremony, she started dragging Mitchell across the remainder of the club. Well, he thought, at least I don't have to guess where the dressing room is.

His captor dragged him down an ill-lit corridor, past a pay phone and a coat rack with a couple of ratty chemises and leotards hanging from misshapen wire hangers, to a door bearing a yellowed poster for the Julie Andrews movie "Star!" She swung open the door and rather brusquely helped Mitchell through it.

He turned to ask her when Gordy might be back, but found her heading out the door again, and shutting it behind her. Mitchell sighed, and turned to have a look at his surroundings.

The dressing room—for that's what this must be—looked a lot like Donald's apartment, only much worse. Costumes, shoes, wigs, magazines, and makeup kits were everywhere; every available flat surface was piled high with them. He gazed at it all in awe; it reminded him of a mosque he'd seen in Marrakesh, all swirling colors and textures and patterns.

At the mirrored counter where chairs had been set for the Tam-Tam girls to whip themselves into iconic perfection, he discovered that he was not alone. A leggy black queen was seated there, applying her lipstick with all the concentration of a diamond cutter at work.

He waited for her to turn and greet him; when she didn't, he cleared his throat.

The queen put down her lipstick and smacked her lips in the mirror, then said, without turning, "I see you."

What was *that* supposed to mean? "I see you, too," he said, trying to make a joke of it.

The queen opened a jar of ointment and began rubbing it into her elbows. "Don't you have something to do here besides bother me?"

Mitchell felt a flash of anger. "I suppose I do."

"Then maybe you'd best get your sad ass in G-E-A-R. You don't want to be around when Gordy gets back, Miss Kitt."

Something clicked in Mitchell's head. "You're Regina Upright!"

At last she looked at him, her face a knot of annoyed puzzlement. "I know who I am, you old fat fool."

Mitchell bit his lip. "So what here is mine, anyway? What can I take?"

Regina had returned her attention to her elbows. "I know, Miss Kitt," she said tartly, "that you could not possibly be asking for *my* H-E-L-P."

The weirdness of his surroundings, his protectiveness of Donald, and his uneasy footing in this strange new identity, all

twined together to provoke him into a crazy, exhilarating bold-
ness. "I'm just trying to figure out what belongs to me," he
said, and he strode over to Regina and plucked the wig right
off her head. "This, for instance. Is this by any chance
mine?"

Regina sat for a moment in wide-eyed, bareheaded disbelief, then leaped to her feet. "You lousy *shit*, you give that *back*!"

He dangled it in front of her face, taunting her. "Don't
you mean, G-I-V-E that B-A-C-K?" He laughed. "Well F-U-C-K,
no!"

Regina let loose an animal roar, and lunged for the wig;
he flicked it out of her grasp, so that she went careening clumsily into the wall. He laughed again, harder, almost doubling
over.

"I'LL KILL YOU!" she screamed, and she came flailing at
him like an attacking bird of prey with a really enormous
wingspan.

He felt a kind of delicious terror as he backed away from
her, tossing chairs and props in her path, forcing her to knock
them out of her way. She was positively ferocious; Mitchell wondered what he'd do when she finally caught up with him.

Even so, he couldn't stop himself from provoking her further; his sudden hatred of her was too joyous a drug in his
bloodstream, pumping through him as though powered by pis-
tons. He backed up to the makeup counter, then turned,
grabbed a jar of face powder, and dumped its contents all over
Regina's wig.

Regina stopped short, her eyes wide as tangerines, as she
surveyed the horrific mess.

"Ohhh," said Mitchell with dripping insincerity. "Now
L-O-O-K what I've D-O-N-E." He picked up a flask of nail polish
and poured its magenta contents on top of the powder. "Maybe
this'll help soak it up." He folded the wig in half and started
mashing the powder and polish into a hideous paste.

Regina was shaking with fury. Slowly, she removed one of
her shoes and, brandishing its five-inch heel, she closed in on
Mitchell, silent as a snake. Her rage wasn't just incoherent, it
was mute.

Mitchell dropped the wig and said, "You know, I can already have you thrown in jail for attempted assault. One more step and I swear I'll do it. My brother's an attorney, you know. A damn good one."

She kept coming at him, her lips quivering ferally.

He looked for an avenue of escape; there was none to be had. He'd hemmed himself in, but good. "Okay," he said, pressing into the counter behind him, "I'll pay to replace the wig. Full retail. Swear to God. Put down the shoe, there's a good girl." He silently slipped off his gloves, the better to fight her off, if need be.

She emitted a kind of guttural cry, and suddenly she was on him. He grabbed her wiry wrists, but she was surprisingly strong, and as agile as an acrobat. Despite his valiant attempt to simply hold her at bay, she wrested herself from his grip with one mad twist, then lifted the shoe high, the better to bring its heel smashing down onto him.

He prepared for the worst, and put up his hands to shield his face.

Suddenly she paused, momentarily disarmed by disbelief. "My God, your *nails* . . . you cut off your *nails* . . ."

She stared at Mitchell's hands in sheer incredulity for a heartbeat longer. Then someone knocked on the dressing room door; it sounded like the crack of a rifle.

"Come in!" called Mitchell in dizzy relief. *"Come right on in! Door's open!"*

A burly, balding police officer entered, one hand resting pointedly on his gun. The big drag queen who'd led Mitchell to the dressing room was peering over his shoulder with trembling anticipation.

The cop stared at the obviously violent clinch in which Mitchell and Regina Upright now held themselves static, as though it were some kind of innocuous tableau vivant that held no real interest for him. Then he took a small breath and spoke, in a voice afflicted with an unfortunate pair of speech impediments that together did much to erode his air of authority. "Wondell Davith, aliath Tewenth D'Hiver, aliath Gwegowy St. John, aliath Wegina Upwight?"

Regina's body went slack and her eyes grew big with alarm. "Who wants to know?" she snarled.

The cop looked at the big drag queen behind him, who nodded at Regina.

The cop turned and approached her. "I have a wawwant for your awwetht." He slipped a pair of handcuffs from his jacket pocket. "You have the wight to wemain thiwent. Anything you thay can and wi—"

Without warning, Regina exploded past him and barreled out the door with more speed than should've been possible for someone wearing a single stiletto-heeled shoe.

The cop was after her at once, shouting into a walkie-talkie he seemed to have produced from thin air: *"Thuthpect hath fwed! Thuthpect hath fwed! I am puthuing into pubwic awea! Wepeat: thuthpect hath fwed . . ."*

And then Mitchell was alone in the shambles of the dressing room, blinking in the quiet, trying to figure out what had happened.

There was only one possible explanation: Cora Deene.

He made his way to the pay phone in the hallway, which was empty now. Over the excited hubbub from the bar proper, he dialed Cora's number.

"Deene Detective Agency, Cora Deene speaking. *Joey, be quiet!*"

"Cora, it's Mitchell Sayer. I wanted to ask abo—"

"About the Rondell Davis boy! Of course. I left a message on your home machine not ten minutes ago." She clicked her tongue. "Bad sort, Mitchell. Left quite a trail across three states. A petty thief, but worse than that, an occasional heroin dealer! Did you know that?"

"I suspected it." And he had, once he'd heard about Regina's slanders against Kitten. It was a quirk of human nature, Mitchell knew, that people often accuse others of what they're most guilty of themselves. "Amazing he got away with it for so long."

"Well, that's why he tripped himself up. The criminal m— *Joey, don't make me come up there!*—the criminal mind, Mitchell. After two years of not getting caught, he thought he *couldn't* be.

Got cocky, didn't he; tried to become a TV personality, of all things! As if no one would've thought to check into his background. As a matter of fact, I met another detective over the Internet who was investigating him, too—for that TV station. Once we had the goods on him, I did just as you asked and went straight to the police." She paused. "Now, Mitchell, even though I pooled my resources with that other detective, this was still a lot of work for my Timmy and his laptop. This job will set you back a bit more than the last."

"Worth it," he said. "Just send the bill. And thanks, Cora. You're a gem."

"Oh, you hush!" she said, giggling. "So long, now! *That's it, Joey, I—*"

As he hung up the phone, he was nearly trampled by a trim, attractive, middle-aged Asian man in a Blonde Ambition Tour T-shirt and a vermilion windbreaker, who rounded the corner like a thoroughbred during the Preakness. When he saw Mitchell, he fairly skidded to a halt, then doubled back and grabbed his shoulders.

"Kitten!" he cried. "Thank God I not be too late!" He paused to catch his breath. "Just got back to find everybody leaving bar! Emergency, emergency! Carlotta told me what happened. Bitch Regina! What kind of bad trouble she bringing into Gordy's—" He bit his lip and shook his head. "Never mind that now! You rehired! Get up on stage right now and *start singing!* Anything you want—even sad, mopey stuff Gordy hates. Just *anything* to keep customer from heading out Gordy's door!" He withdrew a nasal inhaler from the windbreaker's pocket and took a quick hit off it. Mitchell now understood all the sniffing over the phone. "You dressed, you ready—what you are still *standing* here for? Get up on stage!"

Mitchell felt the blood rush from his face. "But I can't—I don't—I don't—"

Gordy slapped his forehead. "You don't got piano player? Where *is* that big lazy boy?" He whirled. *"Pierre! PIERRE!"*

An obese young man with a pleasant grin popped his head around the corner. "Right here, Gordy."

"Eavesdropping, huh? Well, I deal with that later! You get

up there and play for Kitten *right now*! Gordy has decreed."
Then, snorting successive hits off the inhaler, he dashed back
to the bar, where he could be heard yelling, *"Everybody stay! Show
about to begin! Lots of entertainment! First-class singing! Oh, boy!"*

Pierre trundled up to Mitchell and hugged him. "Welcome
back, sugar," he said. "Listen, before we go onstage, I want you
to forget what Carlotta told you about me, okay?" He took
Mitchell's hands in his. "When I get upset, sometimes I say
things I don't mean. I love working with you, hon. Honest I
do." Then he smiled brilliantly and said, "So, what'll it be? The
usual repertoire?"

Mitchell was shaking his head, growing ever more anxious.
"I—I don't know." God help me, he thought; the only songs I
know by heart are Christmas carols and German lieder! I don't
know anything that's even *close* to cabaret tunes!

And the voice at the back of his head spoke up louder than
before, coming to his rescue—now that he could see that it *was*
his rescue.

Yes you do, said the voice. *Indeed you do.*

And at that moment Mitchell experienced a little bite-sized
epiphany.

He looked Pierre in the eye and said, "Are you by any
chance familiar with the work of Blossom Dearie?"

chapter

42

A squad car peeled around the corner in full cry, almost knocking Paula off her feet. When she and her escorts had recovered from the shock, they rounded the corner themselves, and found a cluster of excited, chattering patrons milling about the door of the Tam-Tam Club, leaving no doubt as to where the squad car had come from.

"It appears there was some sort of disturbance at our destination," said Wrolen soberly.

Trilby actually rubbed his hands together in anticipation. "You think so?" he asked gleefully. "What do you suppose it was? Nudity? Public sex?" He came close to cackling. "Shutting down this den of iniquity may be easier than we thought, Ben."

Paula grabbed Wrolen's arm for support while she checked the bottom of her shoes. "I could've broken another heel," she said angrily. "I just ruined *one* pair of shoes in an accident, and now some reckless police thug almost makes me do it again."

Donald stood just behind the other three, his eyes as wide as Duncan yo-yos. He could barely take in what they were saying;

he was faint with alarm. A police officer, at the Tam-Tam? Speeding away with his lights flashing? What had happened? Once inside the club, he'd have to break away from his party, get the scoop from someone he knew. One thing was certain: some unfortunate girl had had her act interrupted in a memorable and distressing way. Who would that have been—?

"Oh, my God," he muttered in despair, as he realized that Kitten Kaboodle should have been on stage at this time. His hands flew to his face. "Jesus Harriet Christ in a mudpack! I am *definitely* fucked."

Paula turned and smiled at him. "What, Mitchell?"

He quickly shoved his hands back into his pockets and looked at her blankly. "I forgot something. That's all."

"Something important?"

"A bit."

Trilby turned toward them, aborting their conversation. "Well," he said, "no percentage in waiting. What say we plunge ahead?"

"Why not?" said Donald with a shrill, devil-may-care edge to his voice. After all, it might be interesting to have one last look at the club, in disguise. Because make no mistake, when Gordy saw him again as Kitten, he'd be thrown out on the spot.

By the time they reached the club's entrance, most of the patrons were returning inside. Trilby filed in behind them as though he belonged there; his confidence was rather inspiring.

Donald brought up the rear. He lowered his head so that Carlotta, manning the door, wouldn't recognize him; but Carlotta was looking very distracted herself. Donald saw that she was close to tears.

Inside, the buzz of excitement over the police visit had not yet abated. Donald had never seen the place so emotionally charged; he wondered whether, if he lit a match, the whole club might not just blow up.

Trilby led the way to the bar, holding his shoulders high and his arms close to his sides lest he touch one of the many facsimile glamour girls jammed on both his right and left—big girls, with acres of curled hair, faces like marionettes, and outfits straight from vaudeville. Paula, in her chic, shapeless blouse and trousers and gently waved hair, stood out like an antelope among a pride of lions; their eyes gnawed at her with envy. She pretended to be afraid and leaned into Wrolen, who, surprise, surprise, took her by the arm, as if to protect her. Donald, who knew instinctively that nothing short of a battalion of tanks could begin to intimidate a woman like Paula, admired her instinct for getting what she wanted.

As for his own reception, that was even more surprising; for he found himself utterly ignored. Although many of the girls here, and certainly all the staff, had seen him on occasion as Donald (on those days he arrived in sweats and a baseball cap, and dashed to the dressing room to effect his transformation), no one seemed to recognize him now. It proved what he'd told Mitchell: that in this identity, he was nondescript, a nonentity, an absence on which no eyes could rest. He longed to be rid of himself—to be Kitten again.

But for Mitchell's sake, he couldn't do that yet. He might be angry at his twin for having pushed him into this charade-without-end—at the expense of his career!—but he could scarcely abandon it now. He wanted, above all, to safeguard Mitchell's newly bestowed favor. Having a brother—a real one, not like those hateful siblings he'd inherited when adopted— felt *good*.

He joined his party at the bar. Mickey, the five-foot-five, two-hundred-pound bartender, ambled up to where they were seated and looked right past Donald to Trilby and Wrolen in their power suits. "Hi, fellas," he said in a voice as husky as a corncob. "What's your pleasure? And before you get fresh, I'm talking drink-wise."

Trilby's face went red so quickly, it looked like someone was microwaving it. Thoroughly abashed, he turned to Wrolen and said, hoarsely, "Ben?"

"Scotch, straight," said the dour and unflappable client.

"I'll have the same," said Paula eagerly.

Donald saw that all eyes, unnervingly, had fallen on him. "Brandy Alexander, please," he said. The eyes, to his perplexity, did not immediately depart.

Finally Trilby turned and, refusing to look at the bartender, said out of the corner of his mouth, "Brandy Alexander. And three Scotches."

"You prefer single malt?" asked Mickey. "Or are you the kind who'll take it either way?" He raised his eyebrows, as if this were a terribly provocative question. Donald coughed to cover up a giggle.

Trilby and Wrolen seemed too horrified to answer, but Paula piped up, "I'd like a blend, myself."

Mickey looked her up and down and said, "I bet you would." And he sashayed off to get the drinks.

Donald saw that the lights on the stage were being readied. He checked his watch; nearly time for that bitch Regina to come on and do her derivative, pandering act. Well, at least he wouldn't have to fake being appalled by it to his companions.

Trilby leaned over to him and said, "See if you can determine what happened here to warrant police intervention, will you, Mitchell?" He put a hand on Donald's shoulder. "Ask around; use a little guile. I know you must find this place as repugnant as I do, but you have to admit, you're far better suited to an inquiry of this nature than Ben and I are."

For one heart-seizing moment, Donald thought that Trilby was on to him; then he realized what the attorney had meant. "You mean, because I'm queer?"

He hadn't thought it possible for Trilby to go an even deeper shade of red, but this is exactly what happened. "Well, that's—that's not the term I'd have used, but, yes."

Donald got up and put the envelope of documents on his stool, to mark his place. "See what I can do," he said agreeably, sticking his hands quickly back into his pockets.

He threaded his way through the crowd until he spotted tall, majestic Marina Del Ray waiting by the door to the ladies' room, sipping a sloe gin fizz. Marina was enough of a gossip to have the goods, if anyone did. He made his way over to her and, trusting that she wouldn't recognize him in his Donald identity, he dropped his voice to its lowest register and pretended to be coming on to her. "Hey, baby," he said, in his best TV-movie manner.

Marina batted her pink-speckled eyelashes at him. "Hey, baby, yourself," she said, grinning widely. She had lipstick smeared on one of her front teeth. Donald was dying to tell her so, out of sisterly solidarity, but held back.

"So," he said in a low voice, "you look like you might give a guy a little excitement." Marina blushed and turned her head, and he found he was actually enjoying this butch role-playing.

"I might well do that," she said, stirring her drink coquettishly. "It would all depend on who was asking."

"Well, who is asking depends on how much excitement."

"*Considerable* excitement," she said, and she ran her tongue across her lower lip.

Donald almost laughed aloud; this is exactly how *he'd* always longed to be addressed by a potential suitor, and Marina was lapping it up. Most men, by comparison, were virtually obscene in the way they got right to the point.

The door to the ladies' room opened, and a skinny queen came out, pulling her skintight minidress down around her thighs and sniffing suspiciously, but Marina made no move to claim her place in the loo.

Donald leaned into the wall next to her, careful to keep his fingernails in back of her head where she couldn't see them. She mistook this for an invitation to intimacy and nuzzled up to his arm. "This seems like a pretty exciting place, *period*," he said. "What exactly went on here tonight, anyway?"

"Oh," she said, tossing back her raven black hair, as though this topic were dull and inconsequential, "one of the girls here got arrested, that's all."

"No shit!"

She nodded and took a sip from her drink. "Drugs, or something. Cop cornered her in the dressing room and she tried to make a run for it, but for some weird reason she had only one shoe on. Screwed her up so she only made it as far as the door before wiping out, and the cop's partner was stationed right there, so, you know, she was majorly fucked." She snickered. "Kind of funny, really."

Donald wanted to shriek in disbelief but contented himself

with a low whistle. "Well, *that* much excitement I don't need,"
he said.

She stopped stirring her drink, then coyly turned and said,
"How refreshing to meet a man who knows his limits."

"Few though they may be."

She winked both her eyes at once. The pink sparkles
caught the light dazzlingly. "Listen, doll, could you just hold
that thought a sec while I make a little pilgrimage?"

He nodded. "You seem like a lady worth waiting for."

She pinched him below the ribcage and scooted into the
ladies' room.

Donald sighed and pushed himself away from the wall,
then went back to join Trilby and the others. He hated doing
this; Marina didn't get hit on often—men found her too
intimidating—and ditching her would hurt. But then, she
wasn't really a full-time drag queen. She was really a successful
airline executive named Harold, and in that identity he got hit
on plenty, by the gay sweater-and-loafers crowd. Harold only
resorted to drag occasionally, as a sort of escape from himself.
It's not as though he had a lot of emotional stake in it.

Funny thing, though: Donald liked Marina, but *loathed*
Harold.

When he caught sight of Trilby and Wrolen, sipping their
Scotches while Paula jabbered away at them about something
she apparently found wildly interesting, Donald realized he
couldn't actually go and report what he'd just learned; he might
be *posing* as Mitchell, but if Mitchell's law firm was interested in
closing down the Tam-Tam, he'd have to draw the line at *be-
having* like Mitchell.

At that moment, the rail-thin Tam-Tam emcee, Wesley,
mounted the stage and began adjusting the microphone. Donald knew he had to act fast, before Regina came out and began
her dreadful act. He hurried over to Trilby, grimacing disappointedly as he approached. "What can I say?" he said with a
sigh when he reached his ostensible boss. "They closed ranks
against me. Must be a tight-knit little subculture they have here.
No one's saying boo." Over Trilby's shoulder, he could see an

extremely animated Carlotta through the front window, obviously telling the story to anyone and everyone who passed the bar.

Trilby nodded and said, "Well, thanks for trying. I haven't noticed any other violations or irregularities here, either, so as soon as we've finished our drinks, we might as well go." He handed Donald the brandy Alexander. "And after this experience, I for one, feel like heading home for a long, hot shower."

Donald judged that the bar was dark enough to risk exposing his hands for a second. He swiftly took the drink from Trilby, then turned away from him and sighed in relief. Thanks to him, the Tam-Tam was temporarily safe. He felt a sort of sanctified glow come over him. He'd selflessly protected the club even though his career here was surely over; because, make no mistake, after his no-show tonight, it'd be a million years before Gordy would again allow him anywhere *near* the stage. Kitten Kaboodle would never play the Tam-Tam again.

The lights suddenly doused. "Ladies and gentlemen," said Wesley into the now-live mike; "please give a warm Tam-Tam welcome to the Doyenne of Despair, Miss Kitten Kaboodle!"

Donald dropped his drink; it exploded at his feet and sent shards of glass flying in all directions, like fireworks.

Amidst the applause, the curtain parted, and there in the bright blue spotlight appeared a vision of—himself. His *other* self. Kitten!

He felt suddenly weightless, as though he were dissipating, turning to fog. Kitten was always more real to him than Donald; and there was Kitten, striding up to take the microphone from Wesley. This lesser identity, this Donald identity, couldn't co-exist; it had to go. Yet he looked down at his feet—spattered with brandy and glass—still solid, still here. He hadn't dissipated at all. But he clearly couldn't be Donald. Could he be Mitchell? They were *calling* him Mitchell. He could *hear* them. . . .

"Mitchell?" Paula's voice. "You all right? You cut yourself?"

She put a hand on his shoulder, and it was like an electrical grounding. His disorientation ended in a flash, and when he next looked at the stage, he knew what he was seeing: he was seeing Mitchell. Mitchell as Kitten. He was even wearing the gown Donald had set aside for him.

Of course, what Mitchell was doing at the Tam-Tam Club, assuming Donald's alter ego in Regina's time slot, was so far beyond his ability to speculate that he didn't even try. He just gave himself up to watching him. *Her*.

"Mitchell, I *asked* if you're all *right*." Paula again.

"Fine," he said, testily. "Ssh, now."

"Good evening, everyone," said Mitchell/Kitten. "Um—hello." She looked at her shoes and bit her lip.

Oh, God, thought Donald; she's ruining me.

"I'd like to sing a song for you."

Duh!

"I'm kind of not sure I know the words, but here goes."

Donald groaned and clutched his abdomen.

Paula took him by the shoulders and led him back to the bar, where Trilby was guarding his stool. "I want you to sit down, Mitchell," she said, taking the envelope from the cushion to make room for him. "No backtalk; just do it."

The curtains parted to reveal Pierre, seated at his piano, looking large and shiny and happy. He immediately dropped his meaty hands onto the keyboard and started pounding away. And Donald—Donald didn't recognize the tune. Kitten Kaboodle was about to sing a song that Donald didn't know.

"What's going on?" he said, not realizing he was speaking aloud.

Trilby said, "The show's started, that's what." He made a face. "More than my stomach can bear. I think it's time for us to take our leave."

Donald had his eyes glued to the stage; he quarter-turned and said, "Just sit still a moment, will you?"

He could actually feel Trilby's eyes boring into him; what he couldn't do was care less about it.

Then "Kitten" put her mouth close to the microphone (*too* close—a wave of feedback greeted her first syllable and sent her head snapping back like a trigger) and started singing.

"Gray clouds are gonna clear up," she trilled in a high-octave, almost falsetto voice. *"Put on a happy face."*

Donald's heart sank. There was no song in the world more *un-*Kitten Kaboodlish.

"Brush off the clouds and cheer up/Put on a happy face."

A wolf whistle spiraled up from the audience. The tentative look left Kitten's face; she became more confident—she smiled.

"Take off that gloomy mask of tragedy, it's not your style." With a touch of artificiality even Donald could envy, she turned her head away from the audience while extending the microphone in the opposite direction, then brought both back together again on the beat. The wolf whistles increased. *"You'll look so good, you'll be glad you decided/To smile."*

The audience was with her now, to an extent Donald found difficult—and painful—to acknowledge. Even Pierre was bouncing merrily as he played, a grin on his face making him look like a Cheshire sperm whale.

And as she sang, this ersatz Kitten's voice actually improved, to the point at which Donald was taking mental notes, like, *Vibrato on the first note in the phrase instead of the last; I'll have to try that.*

And as her voice improved, so did her reception, until she had some of the patrons actually clapping along in rhythm. And their goodwill was so strong that when her voice cracked, dropping to an unfriendly lower register as though the note were an egg that she'd accidentally cracked open, the audience laughed and applauded her affectionately; they appreciated this glimpse into the reality behind the glittering female facade.

Soon she was prancing across the stage, making little affected movements with her hands that delighted the crowd and astonished Donald. Until now, Kitten Kaboodle had been known for her Gallic reserve; she was a pillar of rectitude, a temple of strength amidst suffering. She would stand, Piaf-like, clutching the microphone in both hands, exploring every possible shade of agony with her voice, and her voice alone. If an eyebrow arched, it registered as a seismic shock. This traipsing, this cavorting, this teasy burlesque turn Donald was now forced to witness—it was all too distressingly vulgar.

And yet—the audience was eating it up.

He heard a familiar laugh from off to his right; investigating it, he found Gordy—Gordy!—clapping and laughing and enjoying himself like sixty!

Well, this was too much. The crowning indignity. Donald turned to Paula and said, "I'm ready to go now." And he meant it. Let Mitchell be Kitten from now on; Donald would take over as Mitchell. He'd seen enough episodes of "L.A. Law" to fake it. Somehow, a cosmic sneeze had blown everything topsy-turvy; but as it seemed to be better this way, why fight it?

He got to his feet, feeling drunk again.

Trilby was beside him now. "What a spectacle!" he said as he slipped his wallet from his pocket. "Like Gibbon's degenerate Rome. I know you're gay, Mitchell, but certainly you'll agree that this is disgusting. Things can be taken too far." He tossed a five-dollar tip onto the counter contemptuously. "I mean, for God's sake. That's one of *Blossom's* songs!"

Paula and Wrolen were already on their way to the exit, Paula's arm looped securely through the visibly uncomfortable developer's. Donald and Trilby had just begun to follow when Kitten wound up the song with a flourish, hitting a high note and holding it for an impressive interval.

"Decent set of pipes," Donald said in admiration.

Trilby merely clicked his tongue.

And then, above the applause and catcalls, Donald heard something disturbingly familiar. He stopped and turned back to the stage.

Trilby stopped, too. "Something the matter, Mitchell?"

"Just a second, please." He listened harder. The applause was dying down, now, and it was easier to hear.

"*—UCKING FAGGOT! SUCK ME! SUCK MY GODDAMN DICK, YOU FUCKING—*"

Oh, no, thought Donald; back again. The frat-boy heckler from a week or so previous. Apparently Carlotta's tender attempts to dissuade him from returning hadn't been tender enough.

"FUCKING FAG FUCKING AIDS-CARRYING FUCKING TRASH FUCKER FUCKING—"

Donald looked around for Carlotta; he saw that she was still outside, deep in conversation with a departing patron. She was holding her throat, pretending to choke herself.

Shit, he thought; up to me, then.

Kitten had by now heard the heckler, and had transparently become Mitchell again. He stood awkwardly on the stage, staring into the crowd, looking uncertain and nervous and embarrassed, as though he'd suddenly been reminded of who and what he was.

And then he grew angry.

"Oh, yeah?" he shouted. *"Come up here and say that!"*

Donald let out a little peep of alarm; he immediately left Trilby and headed toward the stage.

Trilby called after him. "Mitchell, we're *leaving* now!"

Donald ignored him, and, in desperation, cried out, *"That's not the way to handle him, Mitchell! Ignore him! Just ignore him!"*

Paula and Wrolen rejoined Trilby, clearly exasperated by this delay. Wrolen sighed and said, "Your associate appears to be telling himself to ignore you, Cyrus. This is not quite what I expected of your firm's much-vaunted teamwork."

As he disappeared into the crowd, Donald turned back and flapped his hands at them. "I'll be right back," he snapped, "so you can all just take a pill for a minute."

And as he turned toward the stage again, he overheard Wrolen saying, "Did—did you see his *fingernails?*"

And then he was swallowed up by the frozen mass of Tam-Tam patrons, each held fast by the thrilling confrontation they were now witnessing.

"Just sit on your finger and rotate, buddy," Mitchell snarled at the heckler, who was now visible, a drunken tangle of skewed, stained clothing and matted hair, lurching violently toward the stage. *"Better yet, sit on your mother's!"*

"—FUCKING KILL YOU FUCKING QUEER GODDAMN FUCKER GONNA FUCKING DIE—"

And suddenly the crowd was screaming and yelling and

falling all over itself, and when Donald looked to see why he could just make out that the heckler was wielding a little pocket knife—no bigger than someone's thumb, but in this small space, a nasty, frightening sight indeed.

There was a sudden rush for the doors, and Donald found himself wading against the tide, muttering *"No, no, no,"* all the while.

When he finally broke through and stumbled up to the stage, the heckler was clambering onto it, and Mitchell was kicking off his shoes and balling his fists manfully.

"I *dare* you, you contemptible coward," said Mitchell, his face a lusty red. "Come on, big man! Take on someone with college training in the manly art of fisticuffs!"

Donald scrambled up onto the platform just as the heckler got to his feet and made a mad lunge for Mitchell, who now appeared to see the knife for the first time.

"No, please," Donald shrieked at the attacker; *"he doesn't* know *any better!"*

But it was too late; Mitchell and the heckler were now grappling with each other, the knife still bright and portentous beneath the heckler's white knuckles.

With a mighty heave, Mitchell managed to throw his assailant to the floor. But somewhere in the tussle, his wig had been pulled off.

From across the now emptied bar, Donald heard Paula mutter, *"Mitchell?"*

The heckler rolled back to his feet, his face cinched tight with hate, and said, in a raspy, frighteningly even voice, "I'm gonna cut your dick off."

And he leapt at Mitchell.

Donald found himself literally vaulting into the fray. And in midair, he experienced a moment of such clarity and calm that it almost seemed artificial, like a slo-mo sequence in a bad action movie, and during that moment he thought to himself, with a jovial tang of self-deprecation, *This is a damned silly thing to do.*

And then he took the heckler's knife in the soft area between his shoulder and chest.

"Donald!" cried Mitchell.

He tried to answer, but the wind had been knocked out of him. Instead he lay on the platform and looked at the blood spilling all around him, and wondered, Whose is that?

Then he saw Mitchell haul off and punch the heckler so hard in the jaw that you could actually hear it crack. And the heckler fell off the stage and onto the dance floor and did not get up again. The knife skittered across the bar like a scorpion.

Mitchell shook his hand as though he'd burned it. *"Ow,* God darn it," he said; "that really *hurt."* Then he raced over to Donald, crouched down, and lifted his brother's head into his lap. "Oh, God," he said; "we'll get you to a doctor, hon! Just hold on!"

Donald really needed to speak to him now. He tried to gasp out his words. *"Don't—you dare—"*

Mitchell waited for more, but Donald was temporarily out of breath. "Don't I dare what?" he said, impatient. "Call a doctor? Donald, I have to! Don't worry about the bill. I've got money!"

"Don't—you dare—get blood—on that gown!"

A siren wailed in the distance, growing louder, louder. Trilby, Wrolen, and Paula were still in the doorway, peering inside. Gordy was running in circles on the sidewalk beyond them, crying, *"Everything okay now! Everyone come back! Dollar beer for everybody when they come back! No—free beer! Plus refills, even! Come back now, please!*

A moment later, the sirens reached their highest pitch, then stopped, and another voice drowned out Gordy's. "Twithe in one night we get thent to thith nuthouth. You the owner hewe?"

"Yes, officers! Gordy Trahn at service, officers! Please to tell peoples to come back!"

A slight pause. "Thowwy, not our juwithdiction. Jutht teww us, pweathe, what'th the pwobwem *thith* time?"

As Gordy babbled his answer, Trilby crept up to the stage. "I don't understand a thing that's going on here," he said with iron in his voice. "Which one of you is Mitchell Sayer?" He looked at Donald.

Donald tried to sit up, but pain forced him back into Mitchell's lap. "Sorry—about this," he said, his voice labored. "My name—is really—Donald Sweet."

Trilby knit his brows and grimaced. Then, slowly, he turned his gaze on Mitchell. "Well?" he said humorlessly.

Mitchell looked at him for a long moment, seeming terribly deflated. Then, magically, Donald felt his brother's arms stiffen and his chest swell, and heard him say, "Don't look at me. *My* name is Kitten Kaboodle."

epilogue

Simon posed provocatively in his full-length bedroom mirror, and appraised his appearance with no small amount of pride. He was buffed, tanned, and looking hotter than ever in a black leather choker, a black leather vest, black leather boots, and a black studded belt that snaked through the loops of denim cutoffs so short he could feel the breeze on his balls when he walked.

And then there were the crowning touches: his new tattoos. They'd cost a lot, in both suffering and cash, but they were finally finished, and well worth it. Above his right nipple was the seal of the British monarch and her motto, DIEU ET MON DROIT. Over his left nipple was the ancient slogan of the Royal Order of the Garter, HONI SOIT QUI MAL Y PENSE. On his right shoulder was Her Majesty herself, looking serene and unperturbable, copied from the portrait on the now defunct one-pound note. On his right shoulder, her majesty's logo, a stylized ER with a tiny Roman numeral II tucked in the middle.

He donned a pair of mirrored sunglasses and curled his

upper lip menacingly at his reflection. The expression was suitably wanton; he hoped it might serve him well today. Then, feeling adequately prepared for the Gay Pride parade, he stuffed his keys into his pocket (which did indeed require some stuffing), and went twirling out the door.

The streets around the parade route were thronged with happy gay people and assorted well-wishers; queer energy seemed to be jolting everyone alive. It was as though someone had dropped a Homo Bomb near Diversey and Clark, and its effect was rippling outward for blocks and blocks. Simon was delirious.

He'd arranged to meet Mitchell at the corner of Surf and Broadway. He rubbed and slid his way through the masses of revelers, enjoying the smell of sweat and the press of muscles. The sun was out in full force, and he could feel the heat on his shoulders and on the top of his head. He could happily have died right then and there.

He caught sight of Mitchell standing beneath a lamppost on the east side of the street on which the parade was proceeding, and so he dashed across to join him, darting between an alderman's convertible and a Wisconsin leather bar's teetering float. He grabbed Mitchell by the shoulder, kissed him full on the lips, and said, "Happy Gay Day, sugar! What've I missed?"

Mitchell looked at him in some distress, and Simon realized it wasn't Mitchell at all. The hair was too long, the eyebrows too coiffed—and those fingernails! Plus, Mitchell would scarcely meet him wearing rhinestone earrings and a Jan Brady T-shirt.

Then he noticed the arm in the sling and the deep purple bruise creeping out from the neck of the T-shirt like an oil spill. And he remembered Mitchell's hastily related story about his twin brother's stabbing.

"You must be Donald," Simon said, abashed. "Sorry. I didn't know you were going to be here, and even if I did, I would've thought—you know—you'd be in petticoats, or something."

Despite this prompting, Donald offered no explanation for his appearance out of drag; he merely smiled politely and extended his free hand. "Simon, I take it? Mitchell said you'd be showing up here."

Simon found it difficult to take his eyes off him. The resemblance was positively eerie. "Um—yeah," he said. "*Jesus,* you look like Mitch."

Donald smirked. "*Sometimes* I do."

Simon laughed, then caught Donald eying his nipples. He puffed out his chest and said, "What do you think?" He pivoted on his hip and flexed his shoulder so that the Queen of England appeared to have a mouthful of Meuslix. "Just had 'em done."

Donald's eyes darkened. "Nice," he said dully, barely moving his lips. Then he turned his attention back to the parade. A group of wild-haired lesbians rode by on motorcycles, whooping in glee and raising their fists to the crowd, who whooped right back at them.

Simon shifted onto his left foot and wondered what he'd said to cause Donald to turn cold so suddenly. Then he remembered that Donald had no cause to view him with anything but rancor. He cleared his throat and said, "Listen, Donald, I have to apologize for trying to turn Mitch against you. I'm sure he's told you about it."

Donald looked at him expressionlessly. "Uh-huh."

He shrugged. "Truth is, I don't believe half the shit I told him about drag queens."

"Only half?"

He laughed. "Okay, I don't believe any of it. See, I was just jealous. I thought if Mitch got too close to you, he wouldn't have time for me anymore. I was afraid you were gonna replace me."

Donald rolled his eyes. "You may dress like a thug, but you are one dizzy queen. We're different animals entirely, you and me. One couldn't ever replace the other."

Simon blushed. "I suppose not."

"Never mind." He nudged Simon's arm. "From what I hear, we should *both* of us be jealous of this Kip person Mitchell can't seem to see enough of."

"You said it," said Simon as he cruised a shirtless young Adonis who sauntered past like he was for hire and dared anyone to meet his price. "Still, from what I hear, you're not doin' so bad in the man department, yourself."

Donald said nothing.

Simon stupidly forged ahead. "So where *is* your beau, anyway?"

"If you're referring to Zack Crespin, he's no longer my 'beau.' "

Simon wondered if he'd have any room left over after shoving one of his big black boots into his mouth. "Shit. I'm sorry."

"Don't be. He was sweet to me while it lasted, and that's what counts. Even if he never pretended that I was anything more than the flavor of the month. And he had the decency to call and tell me when it was over, too." He sighed. "Apparently he met some forty-eight-year-old grandmother who's been tattooed from her jawline to her toes, and he went apeshit at the sight of her."

Simon now understood why his own tattoos had found no admirer in Donald. He tried to change the subject. "So, anyway, what's the lowdown on that bitch who was slandering you at your club? Mitchell never did give me the whole scoop. What was her name—Regina?"

Donald's eyes began sparkling again. He turned excitedly to Simon and started spewing forth the details. "That *is* the bitch's name, and as far as I know, she's still in the slammer without a Clinique product to her name. And may I just say, the sooner her skin dries up and flakes off, the better." He brushed an imaginary something off his shoulder, a look of Olympian disdain on his face. "Anyway, last I heard, Mitchell's detective-lady had discovered Regina was using about five different aliases over the past couple of years, and was dealing drugs under every one of them. She also found out that Regina was the heroin and coke pipeline to several prominent gay businessmen, including that Glenn Yardley person at Channel 48— which almost certainly explains how she got the job hosting that late-night movie show so easily. Probably promised Yardley free blow for a couple months if he hired her." He shook his head in comment on the depravity of it. " 'Course, now that Yardley's been booted from the station, the 'Fabu-Flicks' show is on hold. But if their new program manager decides to revive it, he's got *my* résumé waiting on his desk."

"And in the meantime, you've still got the Tam-Tam."

"For as long as there *is* a Tam-Tam," he said with another, heavier sigh. "Mitchell's old law firm is coming down hard on our landlord. Don't know if we'll see out the year. But Mitchell says we should keep hoping, especially now that his sister Paula has her hooks in the developer who wants to raze the block."

A bevy of muscle boys in nurses' outfits marched by, flinging condoms to the crowd. There was a mad scramble for these; people were practically falling at Simon's feet. He craned over them and asked, "What's Paula got to do with it?"

Donald smiled wickedly. "Seems she *loves* having a drag queen for her 'new brother,' as she likes to put it. Gives her something to brag about at chic cocktail parties, I suppose. But the upshot is, she's all for the Tam-Tam staying where it is. Says she can't wait to see my show, once I'm healed. So she's trying to get Wrolen—that's the developer's name—to turn the block into an entertainment complex, and keep the Tam-Tam as one of its venues."

"Think that'll happen?"

Donald leaned close to Simon. "You ever met Paula?"

Simon shook his head. "Never had the pleasure, no."

Donald shut his eyes and slowly shook his head. "Wrolen doesn't stand a chance."

An organization of gay peoples' parents and relatives marched into view, carrying banners that read I LOVE MY QUEER SON and ALL LOVE IS BLESSED BY GOD and ASK ME ABOUT MY GAY GRANDCHILDREN.

Simon excused himself to go buy a beer, and offered to get one for Donald as well. Donald declined, because he was on pain medication, but said he wouldn't mind a bottle of water.

When Simon returned, ten minutes later and somewhat the

worse for wear, he found Donald still alone. "Isn't Mitch here *yet?*" he asked, handing him a bottle of lime-flavored LaCroix. "Don't tell me he's working another Saturday."

"No—for once," said Donald. He took a sip from the bottle, then said, "But, you know, it does take a lot of work to get a private practice going."

"I know, I know." He took a sip of the warm, foamy brew. "Saw his first ad in last week's *OUTlandish.* Pretty impressive. 'Mitchell Sayer, Attorney at Law—Specializing in the Needs of the Gay and Lesbian Community.' " He shook his head. "Never thought I'd see the day when Mitchell Sayer would get radicalized."

Donald said, "You ain't seen nothin' yet," and took another swallow of water.

Simon was perplexed by this remark; but when Donald offered nothing further, he decided not to ask about it. He took another swig of beer and said, "Mitch tells me you and him are planning a trip together."

Donald finished a sip of his own, and wiped his lips with his bandaged wrist. "Yeah. His detective-lady found out who our real parents are, so we're driving up to Michigan to visit the gravesite."

"Cool," said Simon, because he couldn't think of anything else to say.

"And then I'm going on holiday myself," Donald continued excitedly. "Never had one before. But my Aunt Joline has a farm in Scotland, and I have an open invitation, so I'm going to go spend the rest of summer there. Maybe even part of fall."

"What?" Simon cried, pretending to be scandalized. "And leave Chicago without Kitten Kaboodle?"

Donald said, "No, I'd never do that," and took another swallow of water.

Simon was growing annoyed at Donald's inscrutability; he longed for Mitchell to be there, so he could at least count on an occasional straight answer. He checked his wristwatch, then scanned the crowd again. "So, when *is* Mitch meeting us?"

Donald smiled mysteriously. "He's not exactly *meeting* us."

"He's—not?"

Donald shook his head. "He's pretty busy at the moment, helping me out with something I couldn't do myself. Because of my wound." He shrugged the bruised and bandaged shoulder slightly.

"Ah," said Simon, though he didn't understand at all.

"But even though he won't be *joining* us, per se, he will be putting in an app— Oh, hey! There he is now!"

Simon's eyes followed to where Donald was pointing. A huge float was gliding toward them, bearing the crimson logo of the Tam-Tam Club. Beneath the logo hung a banner that read: PRESENTING THE DOYENNE OF DELIGHT, MISS KITTEN KABOODLE.

And atop the float was the lady in question, wearing an enormous feathered headdress and a fringed and beaded bikini, riding a hobby-horse and belting "Half-Breed" into a cordless microphone. Four other drag queens surrounded her, doing a war dance that was so profoundly politically incorrect that it sailed right beyond any possible offense into the egalitarian realm of camp. At the rear of the float, manning a tiny electric keyboard, was an enormous accompanist, his great expanse of skin decorated with so much red warpaint, he looked like something out of Keith Haring's most lurid nightmares.

Simon was speechless. He stared in open-mouthed awe as the brassy, perverse, irresistibly merry apparition approached. When it was directly in front of him, Kitten Kaboodle looked his way, and, with a wink, blew him a kiss.

DUTTON **PLUME**

THE OUTRAGEOUS NOVELS
OF ROBERT RODI

☐ **KEPT BOY.** Dennis Racine has enjoyed a lush life as the pampered "companion" to the fiftyish, filthy rich Chicago theatrical impresario Farleigh Nock. With virtually unlimited access to Farleigh's wallet, pool, and imported cars, he couldn't possibly be better situated. Then Farleigh drops the big one: Dennis must get a job. Unemployable everywhere and in jeopardy of losing his old job, Dennis whisks Farleigh to the Greek isles in this irresistible tale of a slave trying to keep his keeper. (939261—$22.95)

☐ **THE BIRDCAGE.** Now a major motion picture starring Robin Williams! Val and Barbara are about to be wed, but what Barbara's straight-as-arrows parents don't know is that Val's father is a Jewish homosexual who runs a transvestite club and his mother is a middle-aged man who performs cabaret. Don't start ringing the wedding bells just yet . . . (276683—$10.95)

☐ **WHAT THEY DID TO PRINCESS PARAGON.** Brian Parrish, a brash gay cartoonist, is charged with updating the image of Princess Paragon, a creaky and virtuous heroine. His solution: change her hairdo, streamline her Spandex, and haul her out of the closet. "Hilarious . . . wildly funny."—*Lambda Book Report* (271630—$10.95)

☐ **CLOSET CASE.** Ad man Lionel Frank is a hilariously unlikely hero who tries to hide his homosexuality from coworkers and clients. Devoting his days to working among homophobic he-men on accounts, he spends his nights dialing 1-900-BOY-TOYZ. This book mixes bedroom and boardroom farce with the authentic pain of being afraid to be gay—and creates a novel that is both riotously comedic and wonderfully humane. (272114—$11.95)

☐ **FAG HAG.** Brash, outrageous, and hilariously "incorrect" this is a novel that redefines "the war between the sexes", a comedy that takes no prisoners, from and irresistibly irreverent new voice. "A hilarious tale . . . I adored every word."—Quentin Crisp (269407—$11.95)

Prices slightly higher in Canada.

DUTTON ℗ **PLUME**

GAY FICTION

☐ **FATHER OF FRANKENSTEIN by Christopher Bram.** James Whale, the elegant director of such classic horror films as *Frankenstein* and *The Bride of Frankenstein*, was found at his Los Angeles mansion in 1957, dead of unnatural causes. Now the author explores the mystery of Whale's last days in this evocative and suspenseful work of fiction. "A wonderful novel . . . wickedly witty intelligence . . . Monstrously good."—Patrick McGrath

(273374—$10.95)

☐ **TRAITOR TO THE RACE by Darieck Scott.** Charged with the erotic power of the senses and the liberating power of the imagination, this novel introduces a bold new voice in American writing. This stunning debut explores homophobia and self-hatred in the black community through the story of a bi-racial couple's reaction to a brutal murder. It is a breakthrough feat of fiction even in a decade of vanishing taboos

(939121—$20.95)

☐ **SEA OF TRANQUILLITY by Paul Russell.** Blazing a trajectory across more than two decades of American life, from the sky-high optimism of the first moon shots to the dark human landscape of the age of AIDS, this novel tells the story of a splintering nuclear family. A father, a mother, a son, their intimates, and their lovers are all brought to life with immediacy and insight, honesty and compassion. "Breathtaking . . . weaves a web of personal relationships subtly and expertly."—*Kirkus Reviews* (273110—$12.95)

☐ **GLAMOURPUSS by Christian McLaughlin.** This delightful novel is the true confessions of Alex Young, a cute, twentysomething Hollywood actor with a juicy role on a popular daytime soap. When Alex is outed by a national tabloid, chaotic complications ensue, as his career in daytime drama and his relationship with an acerbic pretty-boy starlet are jolted by comic aftershocks. "Utterly hilarious and disarmingly sweet . . . a book with everything."—Robert Rodi, author of *Fag Hag* and *Closet Case* (272653—$10.95)

Prices slightly higher in Canada.

Visa and Mastercard holders can order Plume, Meridian, and Dutton books by calling
1-800-253-6476.
They are also available at your local bookstore. Allow 4-6 weeks for delivery.
This offer is subject to change without notice.